W9-CHR-321

HAZARDS IN
HAMPSHIRE

HAZARDS IN HAMPSHIRE

EMMA DAKIN

W🌐RLDWIDE

TORONTO • NEW YORK • LONDON
AMSTERDAM • PARIS • SYDNEY • HAMBURG
STOCKHOLM • ATHENS • TOKYO • MILAN
MADRID • WARSAW • BUDAPEST • AUCKLAND

If you purchased this book without a cover you should be aware that this book is stolen property. It was reported as "unsold and destroyed" to the publisher, and neither the author nor the publisher has received any payment for this "stripped book."

To Kathy Ackley, who at a chance meeting at Bouchercon inspired this story, and to my family and friends who maintain steady support, an avid interest and the firm belief in my imaginary worlds.

W⊕RLDWIDE™

Recycling programs for this product may not exist in your area.

ISBN-13: 978-1-335-40551-7

Hazards in Hampshire

First published in 2019 by Camel Press, an imprint of Epicenter Press, Inc. This edition published in 2021 with revised text.

Copyright © 2019 by Emma Dakin
Copyright © 2021 by Emma Dakin, revised text edition

All rights reserved. No part of this book may be reproduced or transmitted in any form or by any means, electronic or mechanical, including photocopying, recording or by any information storage and retrieval system, without permission in writing from the publisher.

This is a work of fiction. Names, characters, places and incidents are either the product of the author's imagination or are used fictitiously. Any resemblance to actual persons, living or dead, businesses, companies, events or locales is entirely coincidental.

This edition published by arrangement with Harlequin Books S.A.

For questions and comments about the quality of this book, please contact us at CustomerService@Harlequin.com.

Harlequin Enterprises ULC
22 Adelaide St. West, 40th Floor
Toronto, Ontario M5H 4E3, Canada
www.ReaderService.com

Printed in U.S.A.

ACKNOWLEDGMENTS

My thanks for the many librarians both at home and abroad who willingly search for information for me. My thanks to the British rail system that took me wherever I wanted to go and to the many people I met on the way who talked to me.

ONE

I HAD EXPECTED my hostess at the tea party to be boring.
I hadn't expected her to be dead. When I first glimpsed
her, I wasn't sure if the body *was* my hostess. But she
was the only person in the gazebo and she had asked
me to meet her there. This must be Mrs. Paulson. I
swallowed, tried to steady my breathing and looked for
someone to ask. The street was screened by a trellis of
roses, preventing me from seeing anyone passing by. I
couldn't hear anyone. There was no one to accept the
responsibly of dealing with this except me. Mrs. Paulson wasn't a friend of mine. I didn't even remember
her. She claimed she'd met me at a conference and sent
an invitation to tea which arrived just as I was looking
for an escape from my house.

First thing that morning, I'd tried to fix the sink. I
managed to shut off the water and attempted to loosen
a nut put on by a plumber with sadistic intentions. It
would not budge. I heard the letter box lid clang. Good.
A distraction. I'd give up on the plumbing as an impossible task. I pushed to my feet, cracked my head on the
slanted sink, but managed to stand straight in the tiny
loo and deposit the useless wrench in the sink. Since I
was back in England, it wasn't a wrench, it was a span-
ner. Still useless.

I trailed my hand along the rail as I moved quickly
down the stairs, admiring the warm brown wood some-

one carved many years ago. I smiled. It was all mine. After all my years of traveling, I was surprised to discover I was a nester at heart and passionate about owning a home.

The envelope I fished from the letter box was square, not the usual business style. Inside, I found an invitation to afternoon tea. Today. Afternoon tea? I hadn't been to afternoon tea since I was a child.

"Mrs. Ernest Paulson requests the honour of your presence at her home……" I read the rest of the printed invitation quickly. The date and time, today at two, were written in elegant cursive as was a message on the bottom. "I look forward to pursuing our acquaintance started at the Crimefest in Bristol."

Bristol. I couldn't put a face to her name as there were numerous people who had milled around, chatting and asking questions at the conference. She must have been one of the attendees, living here in my new village. This was a chance to meet someone local. I'd go and leave my plumbing problems behind me.

I walked up her gravel walk, printed invitation with its written gracious message tucked in my rucksack. She lived in an attractive brick two-up-two-down cottage with wisteria rambling over the front porch and yellow roses almost covering the front paned windows. A bee hummed past my ear. It was a beautiful spot, a quintessential English village cottage and garden.

"Take the left-hand path to the gazebo," the instructions had said. "I will serve tea there."

Dutifully, I turned left and approached the charming octagonal gazebo. I could see a table laden with teapot, cups and saucers and a tier of goodies, but no Mrs. Paulson. As I approached the brick steps I saw a foot,

Joseph Siegal shoe, mid-range expensive, then the ankle and finally a woman stretched out on the wooden floor.

"Mrs. Paulson?" I leaned over her. "What's the matter?"

She was silent. A chaffinch twittered nearby and a brambling called its buzzer-like steady note. I could hear a car rumble past on the road. I touched her wrist. No pulse. Every tour guide has to have a first-aid certificate, so I knew how to detect a pulse. I tried at the carotid artery. Again, no pulse. No respirations. Wide open blue eyes, glazed and immobile. Mrs. Paulson was definitely dead. Should I start mouth-to-mouth resuscitation? I hesitated. Could I get her heart working? Should I compress her chest? Those glazed eyes told me not to try. She was dead. I shuddered. *Think, Claire. A* smack above the heart can sometimes re-start it. I'd try it. I punched her hard in the sternum. Her body rolled a little, but there was no response. I struck her chest twice more and could detect no difference. Not even a flutter from her pulse. Whoever Mrs. Paulson had been, she was gone.

I sat back, reached into my rucksack for my cell phone and hit 9-9-9. I was calm. The cell phone was shaking. I gave my cell phone number to the crisp voice on the other end. It asked me to wait. Of course, I'd wait.

I didn't remember her from Bristol. She looked to be about sixty or so, hair still dark and pulled back with a couple of small combs keeping it away from her face. She wore a long vest over a blousy shirt and long pants. Nothing was skewed or disarranged. She hadn't fought off anyone. She didn't look as though she had been hit, shot or shaken. Maybe a heart attack? I worked hard at logically assessing the scene, trying to stem off the shakes that were waiting to rock my body. There was a

scent of roses that was sweet and enduring. Somehow it
was indecent to leave Mrs. Paulson alone, and the ambulance dispatcher expected me to stay. I took a long
deep breath. That was better. I studied the red roses
peeking in through the gazebo supports their canes surrounded by a thick bush. I gazed intently, looking for
a thrush twittering somewhere in that bush. It seemed
an eon before the ambulance arrived. I gave my name,
Claire Barclay, and my new address, The Briars A, to
the young constable who arrived with the ambulance.
I told him what I had done in case there was a bruise
on her sternum that confounded the police surgeon.

"Good of you to try, madam. Not everyone knows
enough to do that." He smiled at me.

"It didn't help." I swallowed. I wished I remembered
more from my First Aid classes.

"Once in a while it does help." He was comforting.

I showed him the invitation I'd received and told him
I couldn't identify her as Mrs. Paulson as I couldn't remember her from the Bristol conference. I hoped I was
making sense. Conference. Bristol. Mystery books. It
might have sounded like gobblygook.

"Not to worry, madam," he said. "I know her."

"Oh, that's good. Is it Mrs. Paulson?"

"Yes, it is. Are you all right?" He was either kind,
or he was worried I was falling apart in front of him.

"Yes, thanks." Mrs. Paulson was a stranger to me but
her death was disturbing. Of course, I knew we all died,
even people I knew and loved. It was cold, blank and
final. I shuddered and the constable glanced my way.

"I'm fine," I reassured him and myself.

When I returned home, I called my sister Deirdre
and told her. She said she'd planned to visit me the next

day, so could I wait and give her all the details then? She was sympathetic but busy.

I made myself a cup of coffee, ate three tarts, paying close attention to the sweetness and the satisfying crunch of the pastry. I finished my coffee, appreciated the beautiful sunshine and the fact that I was alive and returned to my housekeeping. I didn't even *know* Mrs. Paulson. She probably had a heart attack. I did my best to put the experience into perspective as a normal part of life and eventual end of life.

I ignored the upstairs sink and unloaded boxes, to make this place into my home. I needed to think of something cheerful.

Buying a house, particularly this lovely brick and flint house in Hampshire, was not in my life plan. Fate had bumped me off course.

I'd been home in my Seattle flat on a dreary Saturday while the rain drizzled down the windows. The concierge buzzed.

"Yes, Edward?"

"Package for you, Ma'am. Want me to take it up there?" He called the tenants either "ma'am" or "sir." That way he didn't have to remember our names. He had real difficulty in finding the correct verb. If he had enrolled in one of my *Executive English and Etiquette* classes I would have straightened out his choice of *bring, take* and *fetch*. He'd be a challenge to teach because he saw no need to change. The people I taught in my regular job were highly motivated business executives who did not know how to speak. I helped them to get rid of the interjections of "ah," "you know," and "like I mean," and learn a more precise and direct way of talking. Usually, I enjoyed it and my part-time job as a tour guide. I had a tour scheduled in the Hampshire part of England in the fall for Tours of Britain, a Seattle company that employed me on a part-time basis. I'd gone on one of their tours years ago and when their guide had retired, they offered me her place. It was only a few tours a year so I managed to keep my job with *Executive English*. I had to go home to England at least every six months to keep my tax status in my home country, so my employers were willing to allow me to take the time. The tour company then coordinated my time off with their clients. I loved touring, and I loved getting back to see my family—my mum when she was alive, her husband and my sister and her family. I belonged in that circle but had always loved to travel. Settling at home and travelling. It was a contradiction I hadn't resolved. On this rainy Saturday, I was ready for some kind of interruption.

"I'll come for it, Edward." Down four flights of stairs and back up. When I returned, I made coffee and opened the package, just a slim manila envelope. Inside was a letter from a solicitor and my step-father's will. I conjured up Paul in my mind: short, rotund, almost bombastic at times, but kind, very kind, and he had adored my mother. I wish he had come into my life earlier, but I hadn't met him until I was ready to leave Workham, the near-London community where I'd grown up. I had enjoyed coming home to visit with Mum and Paul over the years because they made such a happy home, and it was a relief after Mum' s earlier life with my dad to see her finally blooming. Paul had bought a house not far from Dierdre's in Guildford and Mum was able to see her grandchildren and lead a normal life. Paul and I discovered a shared love of mystery novels. He liked the thrillers where the intrepid detective took on physical dangers to capture the villain. I liked the cozies where intelligent amateurs noticed oddities and connected information about the characters around her. We both loved learning about exotic places. He was always interested in my travels. After twenty-two years together, Mum died unexpectedly. Paul had been bereft. He'd needed Deirdre and me in the days following the funeral. His sons never visited much, at least, I hadn't seen much of them. They came to Mum's funeral, but left soon after. There wasn't much comfort for Paul in that visit. They were both a little older than me and established in their careers—something in banking or some corporate industry. I'd stayed with Paul for a month, and, one night, he told me he had left me something in his will. "You never asked for anything the way everyone else did, and it's only fair. You might need a little security," he'd said.

I know he meant he had helped his sons start their careers and Deirdre get a foothold in law, but *they* needed it and I didn't, and that was fair as well. I was grateful in those days to be relieved of the responsibility of taking care of Mum and Deirdre, but a little legacy at some time would be a help, so I didn't discourage him. He knew how much he had given Deirdre and his sons and he was trying to be fair.

I smoothed the pages, scanned the paragraphs of *howevers* and *wheretofores,* found the figure, blinked and looked again. After death duties and taxes, payment to the solicitor and fees to the government, I would have a huge amount in my bank account. An enormous amount.

This was a life-changing inheritance for me. My

brain froze. I sat in the chair for a long time, absorbing the numbers then wandered around the flat stunned.

I looked down at the letter and then at the large envelope. There was another letter inside. I opened it carefully. Perhaps it was an explanation? Perhaps it was a letter saying it was all a mistake? It was a letter from Paul.

"Dear Claire, I have loved you since your mother first brought you into my life. You were so brave, so determined and so alone, you grabbed my heart. Your mother cautioned me not to put too much pressure on you, to let you fly off on your travels. She said love can be binding and you might feel obliged to stay close, so I never let you know how much you meant to me. You came home often and made your mother and I very happy with your humour, consideration and loving nature. You must know how much your mother brought to my life. I had never met anyone with such a generous nature. You understood that and supported her. I am grateful.

I want you to have my fortune because you will use it to create a wonderful life for yourself. Your mother would have liked me to do this. I have talked it over with Deirdre and she also wants you to have it. She had the advantage of good schools and a stable life as I became her father when she was nine. She would not be happy to share this legacy with you. I took care of Deidre and your mother, which was something I was proud to do.

Do not be tempted to share any of it with my sons. They have had more than their share of my wealth and they are not easy to deal with.

Remember me fondly, and know you have been all I wished for in a daughter.

Love, Paul.

The tears rolled down my cheeks. It was as if he was sitting beside me, talking seriously, smiling at me. I could not grasp all that love pouring out at me. It was overwhelming.

I made myself a cup of coffee and drank it. I stared at the rain running down my windows and waited while emotions chased each other through my mind and body—gratitude, bewilderment, love and some pain as I faced the fact, I'd never see Paul again.

It was some time before I could function and I read the letter again. I had now to consider the legacy and what it meant to me. The total rolled around in my mind as I sorted out brochures for a tour I'd been planning, mindlessly straightened up the contents of my cupboards and dusted pictures. It was the only way I knew to absorb what I had just been given. Organize.

I kept the knowledge of the legacy to myself for a week, turning it over in my brain. It was then that I made some life altering decisions. I'd no idea I was tired of my job until Paul's legacy set me free. I knew I wanted to start my own business "British Mystery Book Tours." I wanted to return home to England, permanently, not just to visit. Now, it was possible. I quit my job and was home in England within the month.

I hadn't realized I wanted to own a house either until I bought this one. On my first night in my new house, I ran from floor to floor, touching the door jambs, running my hands along the window sills, just gazing at it. All mine.

I wondered if Mrs. Paulson had felt this same sense of belonging. Her house was lovely. That gazebo would have been a wonderful place for her to read in the summer. I wished her peace.

TWO

THE NEXT DAY, I tackled the upstairs sink plumbing again. Same problem, same result. I still couldn't get the nut loose so I could fix it. I glared at the sink. It was starting to become a war. I heard my front door creak open.

"Claire, I'm here." My sister's voice floated to the upper floor.

Deirdre. Wonderful. I'd give up on the plumbing as an impossible task. I dusted my hands on my jeans and hurried down the stairs to meet her.

"Are you okay?" She studied me.

"Yes," I said.

"Good." She stared for another long moment and then smiled. She whirled into the small foyer of my terraced house, turning like a dancer in a smooth pirouette. "This place is a find." Her coat flared out and slipped off her shoulders. She stood with it in her hand and a smile on her face, then dropped the coat on a chair.

"Well done, Claire! You couldn't have found a nicer spot."

She definitely brightened my hall. "Yes, I was lucky since I bought it so fast. You helped, so thanks."

She shrugged. "You did all the research online and picked out the houses. All I did was jaunt around with you inspecting them. It's past time you had a change in your life. You're forty-seven and stuck in that teaching job."

"I'm forty-six," I corrected her, "and I liked working for *Executive English* for the most part. I've worked in interesting countries."

"But you've never settled into your own home."

"True. I love owning this." I spread out my arms to encompass my castle, drains and all.

Deirdre shook her head. "It was such a reckless thing for you to do. You only saw three places."

It was something she might have done but an unusual action for me. Deirdre, nine years younger, was determined and decisive. She was spontaneous where I was methodical, generous where I was careful. Even her appearance was at odds with mine. She was short, had unruly dark curls and wore bright colors. I was much taller, with brown hair that, while wavy, stayed in place, and I preferred to wear softer colors. Our careers were different. She was a barrister. I was a teacher. She was used to quick arguments. I was used to explanations. Life was always a bit brighter when Deirdre came into it even in childhood. Although too much of Deirdre exhausted me, the periodic visits were a treat.

"I'd have thought it would take you six months to weigh all the options," she said. I rarely did anything impetuous.

"Changing everything feels a little scary, as if I've been driving a tiny car for thirty years, and now I'm controlling a transport lorry." I was adjusting to my new fortune.

"Uncomfortable and exciting at the same time?" Deirdre queried.

I nodded. "Then there's my new business. One more

tour for Tours of Britain and then my new company British Mystery Book Tours starts." I had a brief moment of fear. What if I failed? I put that idea aside. I could only try. "A new town. And my own house. I've never tried to fix a drain before."

"How's that going?" She cocked her head.

I glanced up the stairs toward the bathroom. "Not well."

She laughed and then the problem didn't seem particularly serious.

"Come on! Let me show you around since I have begun unpacking and getting settled." Deirdre had had two criminal trials back to back and hadn't been able to come to visit "It's looking good now I have some furniture." I ushered Deirdre into my lounge. Boxes lined the walls, but I had managed to clear a comfortable area in front of the small Georgian fireplace. Gas now and responsive to the flick of a switch. The room was inviting. The colours blended. My garnet rug covered the slate floor which was incredible. The walls were now a creamy white after I persistently encouraged the painters to get them finished before I moved in. The two upholstered chairs were a find in an estate sale. I'd re-upholster them at some point, but they were comfortable and seemed to belong to the room as if they had been there for years. I had not shipped much furniture from Seattle over to Hampshire—just a couple of small pieces which I'd picked up in my travels. I'd lived with Deirdre and Michael and the children for a month and travelled back and forth choosing paint, discussing plugs and points with the electrician and washing everything in sight. I was pleased with the homely atmosphere. There was much to do, but I had a good start.

"It's lovely, Claire."

It *was* lovely, though her house in Guildford was twice as big.

I showed Deirdre the small room off the lounge which I'd use for my office. I had the electrician wire it with enough outlets (plug points they call them here) so I could run a couple of computers and a printer. There were two bedrooms upstairs with new beds in each and the wonderful walk-in closet now holding my few clothes from Seattle but providing room for more.

"Let me see that beautiful bathroom again. It looked to have such potential when we viewed the house with the estate agent."

I followed Deirdre into the main bathroom with white fixtures and a truly luxurious tub set under a skylight. The walls were painted a bright white and the mats, towels and Roman blinds a deep green. I planned to put ferns in one corner and some rose-coloured accents in vases, and soaps.

"Have you enjoyed a bath?" She peered at the taps and the spray attachment.

"Several." I grinned at her and waved my hand at the bath salts, soaps and lotions on the shelf. She sniffed the diffuser wafting lilac into the air and sighed.

"Decadent." She gave a last lingering look and headed down the stairs.

"The trouble is," I said as I followed her, "while the fixtures are impressive, the drains are awful. I've been trying to get someone in to repair them. No one answers their phone, and they don't call back when I leave a message. I'd do it myself, but the nuts around the pipes are on so tight I can't turn them." I had stayed in some places, especially in Italy, where a little basic plumbing knowledge was handy. It wasn't hard to do, as long as it was just a matter of changing a washer or replacing a trap, but I couldn't begin if I couldn't get the nut off.

"Don't try. You can make a huge mess. Trust me on this." She'd been a home owner for years. I *should* trust that she knew what she was talking about.

"You live in a village now," she continued. You'll have to go to the pub or the grocery store and let people there know you want a plumber."

"I did let them know at the pub. I've eaten there several times." It was handy, and the owner seemed friendly.

"That will probably do it." She moved across the slate floor of the hall to the new terracotta tiles of the kitchen. I breathed in the smell of furniture polish, window cleaner, a hint of the lilac drifting down the stairs and then a whiff of the drain problem from the upstairs loo. I needed a plumber.

"Now, tell me," she said. "You found a body?" She sat at the kitchen table and leaned forward.

I explained the tea invitation.

"Are you sure it was a natural death?"

Deirdre was a barrister. She believed in mayhem everywhere.

"Looked natural to me." I remembered Mrs. Paulson's foot, her peaceful face and the lack of any violent debris like chairs turned over.

"That's good. You might be asked to sign a statement about what you saw, but that should be the end of it."

"I hope so," I said firmly. It wouldn't be the end of it for anyone who loved the woman. I wished she hadn't died alone but it was over.

She rose and walked over to my cupboards, inspect-

ing the handles then ran her hand over my smooth gran-
ite counter.

"What made you choose Ashton-on-Tinch? Why this
village?" She drifted around my kitchen, pulling open
cupboards, rearranging my spices.

"Stop that," I directed.

"Sorry. Tidying is a compulsion." She sat back down
at the kitchen table and folded her hands. That wouldn't
last.

I answered her question. "Dorothy Simpson wrote
about Hampshire. Kent is close by and there's Elizabeth
Peters, Martha Grimes, Mollie Harwick."

"Mystery writers," she said. We had sent each other
author suggestions for years although Deirdre went for
more procedural mysteries, and I liked the cozies.

"Mystery writers," I agreed.

"There are mystery writers all over the British Isles.
Why didn't you move to Leeds? Frances Brody's characters live there."

"I wanted to be near your kids, my wonderful niece
and nephew," I admitted.

"And me," she insisted.

I watched the light catch the silver bangles on her
ears, pick up the red highlights in her dark hair and
bathe her face. It was so good to be home in England
and so good to have my sister here. I reached out and
hugged her. "And you," I agreed.

She laid her head on my shoulder for a second and
then leaned back and shook her head. "Tea?"

"It's coming. Cookies? I mean biscuits?"

She glanced down at her waist, a little thicker now
than when she was a girl. "Better not," she decided.

The tea was in the pot, and we had settled at the

small circular table by the window when the doorbell rang. Its jangle was startling.

Deirdre's eyebrows shot skyward, and she shook her head "You're going to have to do something about that doorbell."

"Probably." I opened the door to a man about my height dressed in working shirt, jeans and boots.

"Yes?" I said.

"Plumber," he said, curtly.

Deirdre flitted up behind me. "I'm Deirdre, her sister." She indicated me, "Claire," and waited.

"Peter Brown."

"Do you have a card?" I asked. There wasn't a logo on his shirt or any identifying information I could see. Seattle living had made me careful. I read news reports of women who let supposed tradesmen into their houses only to find their house robbed a few days later.

"No." He narrowed his eyes. "Peter Brown. What's your problem?" Direct. Succinct, if a little brusque. At least he didn't lard his speech with "ums," "hums," and "like I knows." I wasn't sure if he was asking about his business card or my plumbing. I chose the plumbing.

"Nothing drains very well. The upstairs loo sink doesn't drain at all, and the water pressure is non-existent," I explained.

Peter bent down and loosened the laces on his shoes, slipped them off and left them by the door.

"I'll look at the top floor first."

I started up the stair. He followed me. Should I get an estimate? It wasn't necessary. Whatever he charged, I could pay it. Even after buying the house, I had money in the bank. I was a woman of substance. It felt a little strange as if fate was going to snatch all that security away. I hoped I'd get used to it.

He set down the awkward case he was carrying, opened it and extracted a long hose.

"Snake," he said.

I glanced at the hose. "Well-named." It was black, long, sinuous and destined for dark places.

"You can leave me to work. Where will I find you?" He was the man in charge.

"Kitchen," I said. His style of speech was contagious.

In the kitchen, I filled the kettle and a pitcher with water. Peter Brown would likely want me to shut off the water at some point, or simply shut it off without letting me know. He did make the request fifteen minutes later. I stood up to turn off the main water supply, but he waved me back.

"Know where it is," he said. He stood without moving for a moment.

"Something else?" I asked.

"The picture on the wall?"

I raised my eyebrows "Yes?"

"The one of all the people at the convention or something." He seemed to be waiting for an explanation.

He must mean the one at the top of the stairs. "The Crimefest Conference in Bristol two years ago." Everyone in attendance got that picture.

"I thought so. Same one on Mrs. Paulson's wall."

"Oh, yes. Poor Mrs. Paulson. She invited me to tea yesterday because she said we'd met at the conference. I wish I could remember her being there."

"You found her dead," he said flatly.

"That's right?" Deirdre decided to answer for me. "Do you know how she died?"

He surprised me as I had expected him to speculate on heart attack, stroke, any number of natural causes.

"Murdered. You know that. You found her. Maybe you know something?"

I froze trying to process what he had said. *Murdered.* My mind couldn't move past that word. She was murdered. My shoulders tightened. *You found her,* Peter said. That was true. *Maybe you know something?* About the murder? He couldn't mean he associated me with murder, could he?

Deirdre leaned forward. "Are you accusing Claire knowing something about the murder?"

Peter snorted. "Just happen she might know something."

Deirdre had a bright, interested, counsel-for-the-accused look in her eye. "Just because Claire found her, you can't assume her involvement in the murder. Be careful what you say."

Now she was intimidating Peter. He hadn't finished fixing my sink. "Back off, Deirdre. Peter's not accusing me of anything. I'm your sister, not a client. You don't have to defend me."

Peter waited for a moment, then said, "Maybe, you could use her."

He returned to his pipes.

THREE

WE SAT IN silence for a moment after Peter left, then Deirdre leaned forward and studied me.

"Murder makes a difference."

Of course, it made a difference, a shocking, outrageous difference. I stared at her. "I didn't murder anyone. I didn't murder her."

"Of course not, but you were first on the scene so you can expect a visit from the constabulary." She drummed her fingers on the table.

"I can't be accused of murder just because I discovered a body. I didn't even know her."

"You had that invitation. You showed it to the constable?" She raised her eyebrows.

"I did."

"Don't throw it away. You may need to show it again." Her barrister's logic was sifting evidence. "I know it's upsetting, Claire, but you should be okay. The constable will come and interview you, take your statement and then perhaps a detective might also ask you to repeat your information. It's unlikely you will be considered a serious suspect." The facts had been evaluated by her calculating brain and the results spewed forth smoothly. I was going to be fine, so she thought.

I nodded, accepting her expertise. She was right. It was only reasonable that the first person on the scene would be interviewed by the police. "It's not just worry about being a suspect that's bothering me. I like it here—and murder? I don't want murder in my village." Murder upset my idea of the village as a place of refuge and relaxation. This village was apparently neither as quiet nor as tranquil as I'd expected.

Dark curls tumbled with the shake of her head. "No place is perfect."

"True enough, but I liked my illusions." I'd gone to a lot of effort to find a village and a house that suited me. I wanted a place where I could run errands for the neighbours when they were sick, join the church choir or have coffee with friends in the middle of the day and make friends. That wouldn't happen if they thought I'd killed someone.

Murder in the village was a little too real. I usually dealt with fictional murder on my book tours, something safely ensconced in fantasy. Deirdre dealt with true mayhem and vice in her job as a barrister. Maybe she found it normal. I don't think the people in Ashton-on-Tinch were going to view murder as normal. They might shun me. I had put a lot of hope and energy into moving from Seattle to this village. I didn't want my notion of village life tainted.

Inheriting a fortune had been a shock—wildly exciting, but disquieting. The first week after I received the solicitor's letter, I drove north of Seattle and west to Whidbey Island, a long narrow island of farms close by the mainland. I headed for Deception Pass State Park. It was late June. The rain had finally stopped and the sun was warm on the windows of my Yaris. I parked in the last slot and joined the tourists scrambling over the trails and spilling onto the bridge between Whidbey and Camno Islands. I had no interest in crossing the bridge or standing among the tourists and gazing at the majesty of the Sound. I headed for a secluded nook beyond the last trail where I could sit cross-legged on the soft mulch below the pines and stare at the Sound.

I wasn't a person who confided in others, perhaps that's why I had few friends. I didn't haul out all my ideas and feelings, hanging them as if on a clothes line so a friend could view them, deem some worthy and others irrelevant. I was someone who did her own sorting. I found my own space like this nook in the rocks. There, I ruminated on my future. The money would make a difference. I had spent my life making decisions that contributed to my security, moving to more interesting jobs and creating my own intellectual and financial life. Friendships took time and propinquity. At least that is what I told myself. I had the kind of life that didn't allow for friendships, except for a few spontaneous meetings of mind and spirit. Elspeth was one of those. We had laughed a lot and talked a lot. She had checked her age at thirty-six, decided she wanted a child, found a compatible man and got pregnant. She married him and followed him to the western edge of Scotland. She was happy. I kept in touch via Facebook but she wasn't here. I was missing Mum and Paul too. I was missing quite a lot, I thought. I would make this move, and then I would make friends.

I watched sunlight scatter diamonds on the Sound far out to the horizon. I heard the summer call of the chickadee somewhere in a bush nearby. I let it all seep into my soul. The money gave me more choices. I didn't have to create financial security, I now had it. I could decide to go home to England and establish myself in a community, make friends, become an active citizen

in one community in my home country instead of a
dilettante all over the world. I decided to fly home.
The money was like the mountain of rock I was sitting
on. Solid, dependable. I could rely on it. I stood and
brushed the pine needles from my jeans. It struck me
as I approached my car that this mountain of rock was
squarely in the middle of an earthquake fault. It could
crumble into the sea at any time. I grinned to myself.
I couldn't even accept the mountain of cash I'd inherited as being real and dependable without being afraid
it would disappear. I wondered how the money would
help me belong or if there was something more I had
to do. I wondered what would it take for me to be part
of community?

I relinquished my brief trip into the past and thought
about being accepted here in the village. People here
might be suspicious of me *because* I was an outsider
with money.

I must have looked worried because Deirdre tried
to reassure me.

"If you run into trouble about this, just call. Michael
or I will certainly help you." She patted my hand. I tried
to smile. It was nice to have barristers in the family,
Deirdre *and* her husband. If I was going to be a suspect
in a murder case, I would have a competent defense
council. Deirdre was a fierce defender of the innocent.
We both were passionate about justice but I was more
often involved in following the lives of fictional characters while Deirdre dealt with the real accused. I suppose
we both suffered from the unfair world of our childhood and were trying to create a world where justice
prevailed. She found justice in the real world, at least
most of the time, and I found it in books.

She hesitated for a moment. "Well, *I* will. But, as you know, Michael's not around much these days." I'd noticed when I stayed with her last month that Michael was often away. She didn't give me a chance to ask more.

"You'll be fine," she said and popped up from her chair. "Let me see your back garden."

We took our tea mugs with us to the back garden where someone had carefully trimmed the small area of grass and weeded the few flowers—bland in various pale shades except for a glorious splash of purple cosmos against the side fence and the daubs of yellow roses along the top of the far stone wall. I needed to plant this garden with a pallet of red, purple and orange. It needed vivacity, passion and exuberance. I'd have to wait until spring to create that scene. I gazed around while I mentally planted scarlet runners by the back gate. The fact that I was almost completely ignorant of gardening wasn't an impediment, and I wanted to learn.

"Enclosed," Deirdre said.

"Yes, the fence and wall are high so they'll give me privacy." No one could peek into my garden unless they were eight feet tall.

"Good." Deirdre seemed satisfied and, instead of going back to the kitchen, put her mug on an overturned pot and headed out to her car.

I had been mentally placing a small table and two comfortable chairs in the corner by the cosmos, imagining myself sitting there talking on the phone, organizing a tour in the comfort of my garden, so I was surprised by her action and turned. "Are you leaving already?"

"No." She spoke over her shoulder as she passed through the door. "I have a present for you in the car.

A house-warming present. Just wait inside." I wondered what she had for me. A planter full of flowers? A kitchen pot?

I wandered back to the kitchen, deposited the mugs on the counter and cocked one ear toward the stairs and Peter the Plumber. I listened for the clanking and swearing which I thought might accompany plumbing. I heard a little clanking but no swearing.

Sunlight flowed into the hall, turning the black slate to blue as Deirdre came through the front door. She was leading a small, cheerful looking puppy, a bundle of white, brown and black. It seemed delighted with itself, wobbling a little, ears flopping.

"What is that?" I knew what it was, but I meant, *what is the puppy doing here?*

"Your present." Deirdre handed me the leash. I was startled but kept hold of the leash and backed into the kitchen. As I sank into a chair, the wriggling swarm of energy jumped onto my lap and licked my face.

"I don't want a dog," I said firmly. I pushed my glasses back up on my nose and tried to sit upright.

"You need a dog," Deirdre said just as firmly. "This is a Cavalier King Charles Spaniel."

The dog snuggled under my arms and gazed up at me. Trust Deirdre to get only the best. I expect he had papers.

"I really don't need to look after a dog. I want to be free to travel. I..." my voice trailed off. "He's adorable." He was about eight pounds, with silky, tri-colored hair—black, brown and white—feathering around his ears and down his tail. He caught my gaze and seemed to be trying to tell me something. I blinked and sat back a little. He nestled in closer and licked my arm. Then he nudged his head under my hand, expecting me to pet him. I complied—and capitulated.

Deirdre, blast her, recognized that and smiled with irritating smugness.

"He's housetrained," she said, "at least most of the time, and registered. I'll give you the papers. They're in my bag." She searched through her oversized bag, fished out the envelope and laid it on the table. "We've had him at home for a week. The kids love him, but we have two dogs already, as you know. He's a sociable sort of guy, easy to love. What are you going to call him?"

The dog squirmed a little in my arms, then settled, his warmth already comforting. "What did you call him?"

"We called him 'Buddy,' but he's too sophisticated for that name. I was going to call him something literary because, hey, he's *your* dog, but I could only think of 'Flush' and that was Elizabeth Browning's dog. Agatha Christie had dogs, didn't she?"

"Yes, always. They were called 'Bingo,' and 'Peter' and even 'George Washington.' At least those are the names I've read about. I don't think I'll pick one of those." I petted the dog. A name was important. "I'll think about it."

I heard Peter coming down the stairs. Even stocking-footed, he thumped on the treads.

"Fixed upstairs. I'll do the kitchen sink."

"Thanks." I stayed where I was. He didn't need a guide to the kitchen sink.

He came over and stared down at the dog in my lap. I held on a little more tightly.

"Nice," he said. "A King Charles?"

I nodded.

"A *Cavalier* King Charles," Deirdre corrected. "They have the cute nose. The plain King Charles has the flat nose."

He reached over and petted the dog's silky coat. It was oddly intimate. The dog, the man and me. Nice. That was the right word. I smiled.

Peter turned to the sink and opened the cupboard door beneath it. I'd have to get up. He'd need help removing everything stashed there. I stood and handed the dog over to Deirdre—I can't keep calling him "dog"—and hurried over to assist Peter.

He grunted his thanks and opened his box of tools. I hauled out the soap boxes, scouring pads and compost basket and returned to my chair. Deirdre gave me the dog. I expect I would put him down soon.

"Tell us about the murder." Deirdre addressed Peter's feet as the rest of him was under the sink.

"Humph. Dead as you saw." He nodded at me. "Lots of other suspects."

I winced. I did not consider myself a suspect.

"Lived by herself." He continued to do things to the pipes, keeping his head in the cupboard, but we could hear him.

"Why do you think it was murder?" Deirdre asked.

"Didn't poison herself."

Poison? How did she get it? In the tea? How close did I come to being poisoned?

"How do you know that?" Deirdre persisted.

He stuck his head out of the cupboard and glared at her for a second or two. "You a barrister?"

Deirdre nodded. "And nosy."

Peter humphed again and went back under the sink, but his voice projected clearly. "Too full of herself.

President of the Mystery Book Society. President of the Women's Institute. Stands to reason. Too important to die."

Obviously, Peter didn't consider suicide possible for Mrs. Paulson.

Deirdre raised her eyebrows but stopped her questions. Murder, thievery and all manner of vice was her life. She probably had a professional interest. Since Peter seemed to be tossing accusations at me, a personal one.

I shouldn't be surprised murder happened here. It occurred everywhere. I wished it didn't, but since Mrs. Paulson was truly dead, I'd have to accept it. I liked to read about murder, but that was as close as I wanted to come to it. Still, I was curious. Maybe I'd find out more at the book club. There were three clubs—one in Ashton-on-Tinch where I lived, one in Basingstoke and one in Winchester. I researched nearby clubs when I was looking for a home. Book clubs are good places for me to advertise, and I'd planned to attend a meeting.

"Which society claimed her as president?" I asked Peter's feet.

The mumble came, but I heard it "Ashton. Bunch of vipers."

Maybe I should avoid the Ashton Mystery Book Club, but if I did, I would never make friends here or be accepted. Joining another town's club would be a social slight, a statement that I thought another club better than the local one. Who knew what went on in the other clubs? At least, the Ashton club sounded lively, and, if Peter was to be believed, deadly. But I doubted it. The idea that the club solved its problems by murder was…well…weird.

"Let's get this little one out to the grass," Deirdre said.

My new dog needed a name. Agatha Christie's dogs had unimaginative names. Odd that, when she was so creative.

"Gulliver," I said.

"What?" Deirdre stopped at the edge of the garden and turned to me.

I put Gulliver down on the grass. "His name is Gulliver."

She looked blank for a moment and then said. "Oh, Simon Brett, the *Fettering Mysteries*. Carol Seddon's dog. That dog was a Lab or something big."

"Too bad. I like the name." It suited him—traditional, elegant, full of charm.

Gulliver, nose to the ground, hurried toward the far wall. He peed at the end of the garden and then energetically scratched the turf with his front paws, allowing one of his back paws to unconvincingly assist.

I smiled. He was a lovely dog. Then it hit me. "Oh, blast. Food dish, blanket, dog bed, leash. I'll need some supplies. Where will I get those?" I'd have to go shopping. I hadn't noticed any pet stores. I hadn't researched that.

"I brought them with me," Deirdre said. "They're in the car."

That was a relief.

She hauled everything into the house, and we snapped the leash on Gulliver's collar.

"I'd better get some kind of license and a tag with my phone number on it." There were likely regulations about dog ownership. There was a village office where I had completed my conveyancing. No doubt they had a dog license department. I frowned a little. Gulliver was going to take some time and attention.

"Done," Peter Brown said as he collected his shoes at the front door.

"Sink in the upstairs loo?" I asked.

"Fixed."

"Invoice?" I asked. I was getting used to his speech rhythm.

"I'll deliver it at the end of the month. Wife does it up."

"Fine. Thanks." We watched his brown back disappear into a small car.

"A quick tour of the village and then I'm off," Deirdre said. "Ballet tonight for Kala and karate for Josh."

Deirdre's kids were thirteen and nine now and their schedules kept her busy. They lived in Guildford southwest and just outside the limits of Greater London, near Heathrow, and not far from me in North American terms, twenty-two miles. In England, anything more than twenty miles is a trip.

We left my house which was on the highest street of the village and walked toward the centre of town. My street meets Bridge Street which slopes down to the river Tinch. The church squats square and imposing in its century-old stone at this T intersection. The rest of the village flows from this point toward the river. I'd chosen the village of Ashton-on-Tinch because it was near Deirdre and close to the cities of Basingstoke and Winchester for convenient shopping. The population of a thousand here supported enough shops to keep me supplied with groceries and sundries and two pubs if I wanted to be congenial. *The Ugly Duck* was a block from my house and small, with room for about twenty. Ashton even had a few specialty shops such as the yarn shop we were approaching.

Deirdre peered into the window. "Lovely stuff. I bet people come from all over to buy here."

The shop was closed, but we could see a group of women and one man sitting around a table, knitting industriously. Teapots sat on the table. I don't think I'd ever join that group. I had a horror of becoming a boring old lady, knitting and sipping tea. Ah, Gulliver. He would need daily walks. He'd get me out. There might be a walking group that hiked the local trails and would allow me to bring my dog. I'd look into it. Maybe I should take up running. Maybe my tour business would be so busy, group knitting would be unlikely. I resisted the notion of slowly slipping into old age before I was fifty.

Gulliver sniffed his way down the street, stopping to mark his progress and leave his scent for the local dogs. He didn't bark when he saw a dog across the street but moved a little closer to my legs.

"Would you like lunch here at the pub?" I asked Deirdre. "I've been eating here quite a lot in the last week. I'm not set up to cook yet." I like to cook occasionally and have recipes and some tools from the countries where I had worked. Every time I'd become frustrated with *Executive English and Etiquette,* I applied for a transfer to another country. I'd lived in Italy, France, Canada and the US. I couldn't cook without my Italian Mezzo Luna knife or my essential Chinois, the French sieve. In Seattle, the Pike Place Market had given me fascinating food and, of course, great coffee. I liked to eat. I just wasn't keen on every-day cooking.

"I have time for that," she said.

We pushed through the doors bringing Gulliver with us. It was lovely to be back in England where dogs could accompany you almost anywhere.

The proprietor called from the bar at the back. "Hi there, Claire. Who's your friend?"

"My sister, Deirdre." I introduced Deirdre to Jack, the owner and waiter. His wife, Annabelle did the cooking.

"Hi, Deirdre." Jack approached us and bent down. "And your other friend?"

"Oh. This is Gulliver." I wasn't prepared for the sense of pride I felt in Gulliver's handsome appearance. I smiled at Jack and realized I was basking in a kind of reflective admiration of my dog.

"How do, Gulliver." Jack turned to me. "Can he have a piece of a sausage?"

"Not today," I said. "I'm not sure what he eats or how his stomach is. Another day, when I figure it out, all right?"

"That's smart. Some of those pedigreed dogs have fussy stomachs." Jack went back to the bar and returned with two menus and a dish of water for Gulliver. Jack seemed particularly friendly today. I usually got a greeting from him, but no conversation. It might be the presence of Deirdre. She was attractive, after all, but I expect it was Gulliver. Having a dog was going to get me into conversations with people in about half the time it would have taken me without a dog. Maybe he would be a help in building community for me. I suspect Deirdre planned it that way to make sure I wasn't lonely. I was a little irked at being manipulated by her, but she was probably right about Gulliver.

"What am I going to do with Gulliver when I'm on tour?" I worried aloud. When I started my own tour next month I wanted to be successful *and* I wanted Gulliver with me. Could I accomplish both?

"This is England. Take him with you."

I considered it and I imagined him accompanying me to the bank, the post office and to meet officials at tour sites. Maybe I could.

We gave our orders, including one for Sauvignon Blanc. When Jack came back with the wine, Gulliver was on my lap. I don't know how that happened exactly. It just seemed natural.

Jack set the wine carefully on napkins in front of us. "I heard you found Mrs. Paulson's body, Claire. Murdered, was she?"

I might as well tell him all I knew. It wasn't much. "I don't know anything more about it than she was dead. I just found her. She looked peaceful. I didn't know she'd been murdered." I shuddered a little. I was glad I hadn't known at the time.

"Tell us more, Jack," Deirdre invited.

He leaned over an empty chair. "Cops can't figure it out. Poisoned. No one believes in suicide."

I nodded.

"Yeah. Right. Peter's fixing your plumbing, isn't he?"

I'd have to get used to the notion that many people here would know my business. With connection to the village people, came their involvement in my life.

"Yes, and he doesn't think she killed herself." I said.

"Naw. Not in a million years. Tough old tarter and thought she was God's gift to the neighbourhood. Mind you, there are some who say the Mystery Book Club might know more about it. She was fighting like Napoleon to keep her position there and lots of them were fed up with her." Jack wiped a bit of moisture from the table as he talked.

"But murder," I said. From my experience with book club tours I couldn't imagine any book club member doing anything so dramatic or violent. After all, they were readers—passively enjoying the action, not instigating it.

"Yeah, well, some of those women, you know, real b…" He stopped. He couldn't find a word that would substitute for bitches. I was distracted for a moment searching my mind for the word—*bullies, barbarians, bodacious broads*? Or maybe he meant *hostile, mean, or nasty mischief makers?* Both Peter and Jack thought the book club was suspect.

A bell rang from the kitchen.

"Your order's up," he said, escaping from his quandary and fetching our fish and chips. I'd missed those in Seattle. They have them, but they just aren't the same as the ones I grew up eating.

We finished up lunch and walked back to my house. Deirdre and I said goodbye. She reached into her car and pulled out a book.

"This is for you," she said. "I know you need a book of instructions for everything."

Training Your New Puppy. I read the title and was pleased. That was thoughtful of her, but she had given me Gulliver. She knew I was going to need some guidance.

"Deirdre," I touched her arm and looked straight at her. "Thanks for Gulliver. You know he's going to mean a lot and…just thanks." I hadn't realized I needed a dog, but she had.

She hugged me, patted my hand, then folded herself into her new BMW, revved it a little and sped away.

She looked happy. I wondered about Michael, her husband.

Gulliver and I ambled to the end of the town past the old Norman church sitting rock solid, covered in lichen and surrounded by the ancient faithful in their tomb-stones. We continued past the elementary school. Children exited the doors, hurried down the steps and onto the street. I saw a school bus and children lined up like ants. A regional school then where children from the surrounding area attended. Would there be school teachers who wanted to socialize? I'd investigate another time. Gulliver understood a tug on the leash, and we headed home and back to my reconstituted plumbing.

Did Jack mean the book club was so acrimonious someone would murder to protect a position in it? Unlikely. They might have another reason to stop an obstreperous member like Mrs. Paulson from meddling. I'd be an outsider and in no danger from any overzealous members, as long as they didn't see me as the prime suspect. I could watch and listen to the club members. Joining the book club would be a business decision. Members of the book club might like to take one of my tours. That was a sensible reason. Was I nosy? I thought about it for a moment and decided I was curious. I was good at drifting into the background and watching others. I liked to observe and speculate. I'd definitely have to join the club, and soon.

The house was quiet. No neighbour occupied the attached house tonight. I opened the kitchen door so Gulliver could do his nightly business. He trotted out happily. The tall fences cast shade restricting my vision to the perimeter of the back-door light. I should get a garden light. Gulliver scooted back inside. He wasn't staying out there in the dark either.

When I reached for a cup on my kitchen counter, I found one of Deirdre's business cards with a note on the back. "I hired a cleaning lady for you. She starts tomorrow at 9 a.m. YOU CAN AFFORD IT!"

I stared at the note. She'd hired a cleaner. She'd presumed I needed one and arranged it. I rarely get angry, but I could feel my temperature rise. I wanted to live near my sister, but I didn't want her to run my life. "You're a pest, Deirdre!"

Gulliver cowered.

"Sorry, Gulliver, pet. It isn't you. Come here." I stroked him until he finally stopped trembling and snuggled under my hand. I also calmed down.

My sister was high-handed. She had to be in her barrister job where she out-maneuvered the legal opposition, but it was spilling over into her personal life. She loved me, but she didn't know how much I was used to taking care of myself.

However, I could afford a cleaner. I truly didn't like window washing and floor scrubbing. What if I didn't like her or she was not a good house cleaner? How would I terminate her working for me? It wouldn't be simple as I might instigate bad feelings towards me in the village. She could be related to half the people here. I would have to accept her, at least for some time and I was imagining a problem even though I had not even met her. I'd cope. I had experience dealing with different kinds of people. I'd manage.

It was very quiet. There was no noise but the occasional hum of the refrigerator. Gulliver sighed and snuggled in my lap. I held him a little closer. There was something about the quiet that was comforting—my house, my dog, my village.

FOUR

THE CLEANER ARRIVED, bouncing on the top step. She was about thirty, slim, athletic, sporting a big diamond ring on her left hand and a shiny wedding band. The street behind her was shining as well. Rain had washed the world last night, and this morning's sunshine sparkled off the drops on the willows lining the street and on the flagstones on my walk. It was going to be a beautiful day.

"Jones," she said. "I'm Rose Jones."

We shook hands and I invited her in. Gulliver peered at her from behind my legs.

Rose squatted down and held out her hand. "Who's this gentleman?"

I introduced her. Gulliver licked her hand, and she petted him. "Lovely dog. He'll give us a fair amount of hair to vacuum, I expect."

I hadn't thought about the fact that every dog should come with a house cleaner. It was funny to think of Gulliver needing a valet. Rose brought in a large amount of supplies and equipment. She straightened and glanced around the hall.

"Are you settled in?" She asked.

I imagined her calculating the amount of dust, dirt and dog hair she would have to clean up. She looked like a dynamic elf about five-foot-four, short, dark, straight hair and huge brown eyes. Energy bubbled from her and bounced around the walls of my entrance. Not something I was used to.

"More or less settled, yes. Let's talk in the kitchen. All right with you?" I said. It was bigger than the hall. Maybe her energy would dissipate a little in a bigger room, I hoped.

"Blimey! This is cool," she said as she viewed the bright light coming through the paned glass, picking up the warm earthy colors of the floor. I had a pot of basil and one of parsley on the deep windowsill ready for the days I did cook. Etruscan pottery from my sojourn in Italy sat on a high shelf beside the stained-glass vase by Sara Cornwell I picked up in Suffolk and a hand-woven Salish basket from the West Coast of America.

"Thanks." I particularly liked my kitchen.

"What matters most to you?" was Rose's first question, once she hung her fleece jacket over a chair and pulled out her tablet.

It wasn't a philosophical question. She didn't want to know my values, religious beliefs or my views on love. She wanted to know what housekeeping priorities I had.

I thought for a moment, "The kitchen, bathrooms and windows."

She typed that into her file and added comments.

"And, of course, vacuuming," she said. "This house will be about a three-hour job once a week. Is that good for you?"

I didn't know if this was going to suit me, but I was willing to try it. I agreed.

"Fine. I'll make good use of the time, no fear." She stood. "Where are your supplies?"

She was organized, sure of herself and she might be

worthwhile. I had a new house and a dog. I didn't know what kind of cleaning I needed but I would find out.

I escorted her to the small closet under the stairs. She examined the cleaning supplies and hummed a little. "I'll use this up but is it okay if I buy the products and bill you for them? I know what works most of the time, I use baking soda and vinegar. It's cheap, effective and not poisonous to the environment."

I glanced at my environmentally hazardous cleaning materials and felt guilty. "Yes, that's fine. It will save me shopping." I mentally squirmed a little, a little ashamed of all the non-environmentally friendly products I'd bought just because I always had. She was right. Time for a change. The environment was important. I realized, I might never touch the vacuum or cleaning supplies again, if this worked out. We exchanged phone numbers. I gave her a spare key. She stated her rates which were fair. I calculated the fee for the morning and made out a cheque.

"Just leave it on the counter. I'll pick it up when I leave." Rose put her tablet on the table and wiped her hands on her jeans. That seemed to be some kind of trigger, a switch in her personality. The efficient, time-sensitive woman disappeared. Her shoulders dropped a little, her hands hung more loosely at her sides. She rocked back on her heels and smiled.

"Well, now, I'll get to work, since I'm on the clock. I'll start upstairs. I'm going to like working here. Such a nice house. Small, convenient."

It suited me and it wouldn't take her long to keep it clean.

She returned to the supplies cupboard and hauled out the vacuum and a plastic caddy into which she put items from the shelves. She moved quickly but talked as she worked as if her constant chatter sustained her like electrical energy. "Have the Stonnings been back to the house since you arrived?"

The other side of the wall of my semi-detached house was occupied only periodically, as the owners lived in London most of the time—or so the estate agent said.

"No, not yet."

"They're a loud bunch. Always partying. You'd think they'd know better, not being so young, you know."

I looked at her hoping for more information. That's all it took.

"About 45, heading up into 50. Middle-aged and not very smart with it."

Middle—aged? That was my age. I *couldn't* be middle-aged yet.

"And her that's the nice vet's sister. They're not a bit alike those two. He's steady. She's flighty. And the noise they make—and drugs! You'll want to buy some ear plugs when they come. I bet the estate agent didn't tell you about that." Did she take some satisfaction in imparting this news. I hoped not.

"No, he didn't." I didn't want to hear any more gossip about the Stonnings. I didn't know Rose well enough to judge if her information was reliable, or if she simply liked to gossip.

"Rowdy crew. You won't like them. Snooty with it."

I'd worry about the noise when it happened. Besides, I might find a little noise and activity comforting, a sign that people were nearby and I wasn't alone.

She paused half-way up the stairs. "Too bad about Mrs. Paulson. Isabel that was, but no one called her by her first name. She liked her dignity. A bit of a know-it-all. Bossed everyone. Not that she didn't do a lot of work for the community, so we'll miss her for that. Did you know her real well?"

I shook my head. "Not at all. I don't ever remember meeting her."

She managed another few steps. "Oh, I thought you might have known her, finding the body and all," she continued. "Have you heard the police are checking into everyone's whereabouts on the day Mrs. Paulson died? That old detective from Alford. Evans. Must be Welsh. Anyway, not from here, is asking questions."

I couldn't resist. "No, I expect they would check pretty thoroughly. The whole town?" Deirdre had warned me the police would be calling.

"Probably you, because you found her, and then members of the Mystery Book Club, people in her church, friends—although she didn't have many friends—but she knew a lot of people. Went to conferences." She slid a sideways look at me. I expect she'd been talking to Peter and knew I had the picture of the Crimefest Conference.

"That Mary Greenwood, a dutiful body, she visited Mrs. Paulson. Gave her vegetables from her garden and the like. The only one who did visit much. Mrs. Paulson didn't have any children. Mary Greenwood might cop something from the will. Maybe everything."

I drew back a little, trying to absorb this stream of gossip and had just turned away when I heard retching from the kitchen. I'd forgotten about Gulliver. I rushed in to find him in distress and vomit on the tile floor.

"Gulliver! What's the matter?" He was hunched over the tile floor, his head low, ears dragging on the tiles.

I grabbed a paper towel, dampened it and crouched

beside him. I wiped his face and his mouth. He gazed at me sorrowfully.

"What's wrong. What's wrong? Did you eat something poisonous?"

Gulliver's eyes were wide. He looked at me intently as if he expected me to know what was wrong and to fix it.

Rose stood at the kitchen door and gave advice. "Mr. Andrews is the closest vet. Do you want to take Gulliver there, or do you think he'll be all right?"

"I don't know enough about dogs to make that decision. I'd better take him to the vet. Where is he?"

"Across the Tinch on River Road. Not far. Take the first right on the other side of the bridge, about two blocks down. There's a big sign *Riverside Animal Hospital*." She gave me the information quickly.

"Thanks." I needed that advice.

"Don't worry about the floor. I'll clean up the mess." She moved toward the sink.

"Thanks," I said again. I grabbed my purse, Gulliver's papers and the car keys, picked up Gulliver and ran to the car.

It took less than six minutes to arrive at the vet's office. There were only two cars parked in the lot. Good. Maybe he'd see Gulliver right away.

The receptionist agreed I could see Mr. Robert Andrews—*Mr.* Andrews here. In Seattle, he would be Dr. Andrews—and took my address, phone number and credit card number.

"I don't think he's an emergency," she said. "Dogs throw up all the time."

I knew she was not a vet, but I took comfort from her

words. She must have seen many dogs. I let out a long breath. By the time I saw Mr. Andrews, I was calmer.

I followed him back to his office and sat with Gulliver on my lap. His office smelled of dog, a spicy, musky scent. He had a computer on his desk and a pre-scription pad. Light filtered in through blinds on high windows and lit the long counter at the side of the room where the overhead glass-fronted cupboards held bot-tles and packages. An examination table, waist high, was behind me at the end of the room. It looked effi-cient and very clean.

The vet was about my age, a little taller than me and kind to Gulliver. "Nice dog. Is he your first dog?"

"Yes. And I panicked when he vomited," I admitted.

"What did he look like at the time?"

I thought back to Gulliver in the kitchen looking up at me. "Sorrowful. Bewildered. Ashamed? Sad," I said.

Mr. Andrews grinned. "Probably surprised. He may never have vomited before."

"What would make him do that?"

"Oh, many things. Most of them pretty harmless. It's a dog's way of getting rid of too much food or the wrong kind of food, or it could be something more serious. Not usually, though. Had you just fed him?"

I thought back to the morning. "Yes. I'd fed him just before the doorbell rang."

Mr. Andrews nodded. "He probably gulped down his food too fast in an effort to get to the door to see who had arrived. He's still young. An older dog would eat first and investigate later. At least, most dogs would."

" Eating too fast will do this?" That hadn't occurred to me. But then, I knew practically nothing about dogs.

"It can. Let me look at him." He petted Gulliver

and then gently ran his hands over him, spending some time examining his abdomen. He took a small flashlight and examined his eyes, mouth and ears and then smiled at me.

"Novice dog owners have to take time to learn about their dog. You'll get used to him. He might do this again. Next time, just wait for an hour or so and see if he improves. You can always call my office for advice. He's fine now. Can you see that?"

I studied Gulliver. That sorrowful look was gone. He was bright-eyed and looking around with interest.

"Yes, I can see that. I have a lot to learn about dogs." I tried not to feel overwhelmed. Even if I was incompetent, Gulliver looked fine.

Mr. Andrews settled into his chair, then leaned back to pull a pamphlet from a rack on the wall.

"Never too late to start," he said and handed me the pamphlet.

I glanced at it "The Elements of Obedience." I shoved it into my purse and brought out Gulliver's papers.

Mr. Andrews glanced at them and pulled out a pair of bifocals. "Gulliver's up-to-date on his vaccines. I'm not much for booster shots, so he should be good for some time."

I don't know why glasses made him endearing, but they did. I've always been charmed by guys in glasses. Maybe, it's empathy, as I wear them myself.

"He'll need brushing every night and at least one vigorous walk a day—two would be better. Make an appointment with me when he is about six months old, and I'll curtail his manhood."

I winced but realized that Gulliver was a pet and not a stud. "Yes, of course."

Deirdre didn't tell me about the brushing or the walking, and I'd forgotten about the routine surgery. Owning a dog was turning out to be a way of life for me. "Are there any trails you'd recommend?" If I was taking Gulliver for walks, I might as well explore the countryside.

He smiled and removed his glasses. I suppressed a sigh.

"I usually take my Labs for a long walk on Sundays. Are you free to join me on some of the trails?"

Was this a date? No, it didn't feel like it. Just neighbourly consideration. His eyes flicked to my left hand. I glanced at his left hand. No rings. Maybe this was a *pre-date*.

"That would be very kind."

"The pleasure's mine." He raised eyebrows and sent me a quick smile. That, Deirdre would say, was flirting.

He escorted me out. "About nine on Sunday?"

"I can't make it at nine. I have to pick up a group of women from Heathrow. I could make it about two." On Sunday, my group was arriving for their week's tour.

"Two it is then," he said.

"Where will I meet you?" I said quickly.

"How about the parking lot at Tinch Bridge? We can walk along the river and then out into the hills." He stood at the door, his eyes warm and interested. I hope I was reading him correctly.

"That sounds wonderful." I smiled back. It would be lovely to get out into the country. And Gulliver would enjoy it. Owning a dog *was* going to make a difference in my social life too.

Rose was still working upstairs when we arrived home.

"Gulliver's fine," I called up to her.

She answered me from the top of the stairs. "That's good. Some dogs puke a lot, but it's best to be sure it isn't something awful. My sister's dog puked like that, and it was dead in an hour."

I didn't want to hear about it. It was time for a walk.

"Gulliver and I will be out for a while. Help yourself to coffee or tea."

"No. No. It's all right. I brought my thermos."

I started toward the front door, but she called me back.

"Oh, and Claire, the water isn't draining very well. You might want to call Peter."

"Again?"

She shrugged and returned to her work.

I escaped out the front door with Gulliver on a lead, my rucksack on my back and made it to the gate before I stopped, took a deep breath and let my shoulders ease down into a more relaxed position. What was the matter with those drains?

Gulliver had recovered. It probably wouldn't be the last time he would scare me like that. I could enjoy the day.

It was a beautiful, late September morning and promised to be a glorious day. It was likely raining in Seattle. I don't know why that should make me feel smug, but it did. So far, Mrs. Paulson aside, this was a good place to be.

A young girl, about seventeen approached me, as she headed for the walkway beside mine, the Stonning's house. She left her small blue Astra parked at the curb. I was in an English village now, not a big city. Ignoring people would be rude here. I nodded.

"Hello," she said as she hesitated at her gate. "Can I pet your dog?"

"Sure."

Gulliver sat while the girl bent down and stroked his head.

"He's beautiful."

Gulliver knew admiration when he got it and held his head up and posed, four feet squared and tail up.

"Yes," I agreed he was. She was beautiful as well, with long blonde hair, big brown eyes and the smooth, clear skin I'd only seen in photoshopped ads. And, she was friendly.

"I'm Claire Barclay. I just moved in." I waved to my front door.

The girl straightened. "I'm Sara Andrews. My aunt and uncle live here." She gestured at her front door. "I clean for them once in a while."

A small truck pulled in behind Sara's Astra. A young man emerged. Ah, an empty house. Boy. Girl. A tryst. None of my business.

"Gulliver and I are off for a walk," I said. "Do you know any good dog trails around here?"

"Sure. Hey, Jay," she called to the young man, perhaps eighteen, tall, thin, but he looked strong.

He frowned.

"This is Jay. This is Claire." Sara made as much of an introduction as she thought necessary. "Do you know if the Riverside Trail is clear?"

"Yeah, it's clear," he said, then ignored me and turned to Sara. "Why didn't you wait for me?"

"I had things to do."

An argument? Fine. I didn't want to hear it. I thanked them both and headed in the direction of the river. From the corner of my eye, I saw Sara stoop and pick a key from under the mat. That was an obvious place to put it. Might as well leave it in the door. Sara Andrews. Perhaps related to the vet Robert Andrews? In a village this small, there must be many connections.

I stopped in at the pub and asked Jack to send my request for plumbing assistance to Peter.

"Drains again?"

"I don't understand it," I complained.

He leaned on the bar. "Probably the willow tree in your front yard. Mrs. Paulson had the village plant willows all along the street. 'A pleasing prospect' she said. Nothing but trouble in the drains since they grew."

I didn't know Mrs. Paulson but I realized I was becoming part of the village and I resented her at this moment. She caused those willows to be planted and, if the willows were causing my drainage problems then I was not pleased with her decisions regarding the village.

I waved at Jack and left. It might be the willows. Peter would diagnose the problem when he made it to my house.

Gulliver and I walked along the riverside. Willows hung over the river. Obviously, no pipes or drains to interfere with here, and ducks and swans paddled close to the shore. Warblers trilled from the trees and bushes. I recognized the squeaky call of the kingfisher and then saw one plummet down to the water, snatch something and dart up to a branch on the other side. I heard chiff-chaffs but couldn't see any. I remembered them as elusive, tiny, green, plump birds, flitting in dark bushes and hard to spot. The sunshine did its magic. Dogs threw up. Willows sought water. I might as well get used to it all. I kept an eye on Gulliver ready to dissuade him from eating anything he found on the ground.

We walked up one side of the river, across the bridge, then along the other side and across the lower bridge, ending up at the pub for lunch. By the time we got home, Rose had departed, and the house was spotless. A flyer lay on my front hall table. Rose must have deposited it there. The Ashton-on-Tinch regular meeting of the Mystery Book Club was set for tonight at 7 p.m.

Later that evening, I changed my clothes twice before the meeting which was unusual for me. There wasn't much danger of choosing anything in my wardrobe that was eye-catching. I don't think I owned any clothes that were flamboyant. My colors were blue, black and pastel with a few warmer corals and pinks. I avoided that hard slate blue color ever since Deirdre labeled an outfit of mine "menopause blue."

I picked out soft grey pants and a warm raspberry sweater, casual but, I hoped, a little dressy. I wore my grey heeled Aquatalia boots. I'm not the fan of Italian purses Deidre is, but I'm passionate about Italian shoes. My silver Northwest native earrings added a little pizazz. It would have to do. I was striving for casual elegance, but probably just managed casual. I peered into the mirror, checking my makeup. Gulliver yipped from the kitchen. I would be down in a moment.

From two feet away, I approved of my look, but I had to get close without my glasses to check that the blush didn't look like clown cheeks, and the eyeshadow wasn't traveling over my nose. The lines around my eyes showed, and I had to admit that forty-six wasn't thirty-five. Ah well.

I wanted to be accepted and make friends. I had

found Mrs. Paulson dead. How would they receive me? I didn't want to stand out—just blend into the crowd.

Gulliver had settled down after his walk and his dinner. I was heading out the back door when I noticed the puddle on the floor.

"Gulliver?"

I turned to him. He had his head between his paws.

He had yipped, and I hadn't responded. I should have taken him out right after he ate. He's a puppy. They can't wait.

"I'm sorry. I'll do better tomorrow." I said to him as if he could understand me.

I grabbed the toweling I kept handy and cleaned the floor. Poor Gulliver had his problems today. The book Deirdre had given me on dogs said I should put Gulliver in a kennel when I left him, so he would get used to it, and my household goods like mats, corners of chairs and shoes wouldn't be destroyed. He cried when I put him in the kennel, so I left him loose in the house. I put my good shoes up high in my closet. I expect he'd climb onto my bed and sleep.

The phone rang just as I was heading out the door. I dropped the toweling in the trash and scrambled to find my cell phone. In my purse. I caught it on the third ring.

"This is the Constabulary of Hampshire calling for Claire Barclay."

"This is she."

A deep male voice continued. "Detective Inspector Mark Evans would appreciate you staying home tomorrow about nine in the morning to receive him. He has some questions to ask you."

I clutched the phone more tightly. "What does this concern?"

"I'm sorry, madam. I am not at liberty to discuss it. Will you be available?"

"Yes, of course."

He was not coming to talk to me about my dog license. It was Mrs. Paulson. It had to be about Mrs. Paulson. Deirdre had warned me a detective might come. It didn't mean I was a suspect.

"Thank you," the voice said.

"You're welcome," I said, automatically and disconnected.

I realized I was still holding the phone. My arm felt rigid and my fingers stiff. It took me three tries to slide the disconnecting bar to the "off" position. There was a justice system that protected the innocent. It was totally irrational to be fearful, but I felt a hollow sensation in my stomach. I wasn't looking forward to tomorrow.

FIVE

I walked up the hill just before seven that evening. The air was still and held the pale, luminous yellow of twilight, blurring the hedges and trees. Constable could have painted this peaceful scene. There were several cars in the parking lot of the church hall, but many attendees may have walked from their nearby homes. Inside, the hall was set up with chairs in rows and a podium at the front. About twenty people were already seated. I slipped into a row of vacant chairs near the back and waited. The room was large, probably built about two hundred years ago with tall ceilings, tall narrow windows and the old upright piano at the side that seems to be mandatory in all church halls. People moved around, visiting with one another and settling into their seats. A large man, dressed in jeans and a green and red rugby shirt lowered himself slowly and heavily onto the chair beside me. A tiny bird-like woman scuttled down the row and perched on my other side.

"Good evening," she said. "Marlene."

I smiled. "Good evening. Claire."

The man stuck out his hand. "William."

If the woman was a wren, William was a very large turtle, with his head set on top of bulky shoulders and a chunky torso.

"Claire." We shook hands. Then we hushed as the

proceedings started. At least these villagers seemed friendly.

The acting president began a report on the current activities of the club. A fancy-dress ball was planned for next week, and the work to produce the event had all been accomplished. She asked for a treasurer's report and then, when it was accepted, launched into a eulogy for Mrs. Paulson.

There was a rustle of movement, then everyone was obediently quiet, except my neighbour.

"Isobel Paulson, our president, died last week," Marlene whispered. "Poison everyone is saying. On Wednesday last. Such an odd way to die." She raised her eyebrows.

I didn't know if I should admit to finding her body. I might as well. Everyone would know soon—if they didn't already.

"I found her," I whispered.

"So I heard," she said. "Must have been a shock."

"Yes, it was. Must be more of a one for those who knew her," I said.

Marlene continued on talking. "Barbara Manning was our past president and she's stepped in to run things. That's her." She surreptitiously pointed to the speaker.

I nodded and turned toward the podium.

"We have all been saddened," the acting president extolled, "by the untimely death of our beloved president."

William beside me snorted. "Interfering old beldame."

I raised my eyebrows. *Who* was an interfering old beldame? Lovely old word. Slightly or even quite insulting.

"Barbara hated Isobel," he whispered. "Mind you, a lot of us found her heavy salt in our porridge." I heard other whispering in front of me but couldn't make out any words.

Barbara Manning went on. "She was a tireless worker, devoted to many causes and a stalwart supporter of this club for many years."

"Well, that much is true," Marlene agreed. Murmurings rose from the members as others made comments *sotto voice*. This was an opinionated group.

Barbara's voice rose, commanding quiet. "She was an enthusiastic and tireless worker for the Mystery Ball, and I hope we can put all our energies into it to make it a resounding success in memory of our dear Mrs. Isobel Paulson." She lowered her head but didn't let the tribute of silence go on for long.

I hadn't heard such a collection of clichés for quite some time, but I suppose people often resort to them when they have to comment on a sad event, particularly when they have awkward facts like murder to avoid. Clichés were a blanket over a mess.

"Thomas, our dear Thomas, is going to continue to look after the library and maintain his position as treasurer. I will step in as acting president until the members hold an election which will be after the ball, as we don't want disruptions so close to the event." She looked around at the audience, but no one objected.

"And what's to say anyone else will get a look-in even then?" William muttered.

The meeting was over and the general rise in volume accompanied by the noise of chairs moving allowed Marlene to speak normally.

"Come on now, love," Marlene said as she stood and

moved toward the centre of the hall. "Let me introduce you to some people. Claire, is it?"

"Yes," I said. "Claire Barclay."

"Ah, here is Thomas." There was genuine affection in her voice and I looked up to see a tall, thin, older man, smiling at Marlene.

"Thomas, this is Claire who is new here."

A singularly sweet smile transformed Thomas' face. "Like mysteries, do you?" he said. "Welcome."

"Love them. I run a mystery tour business, so I bring fans over from America to tour the sites of mysteries."

"Now, fancy that." Marlene said. "Do you go to Agatha Christie country?"

"Sometimes. My next group is going to Wallingford."

"Wonderful museum," Thomas agreed. "It is so well organized and fascinating."

"Claire found Isobel's body," Marlene said with the importance of producing an 'interesting fact', "and she called the police."

"And ambulance," I said.

"Oh dear." Thomas commiserated. "Upsetting."

We moved toward the tea table, and Marlene left us. I smelled the enticing scent of coffee but knew better than to drink any coffee made in an English urn. It would be weak and tasteless. I'd have tea which would also be weak and tasteless but more palatable than coffee. Thomas and I both snagged a cup and a biscuit. I turned to him.

"You are in charge of the library, Thomas?" I said.

"I am. I also manage the library at the school where I teach inquiring as well as reluctant minds. You must come to our house to examine the mystery collection one day."

Thomas seemed to be one of those courtly men, probably about sixty, who learned his manners early and continued to practice them. I've met only a few men who retain those manners. They're out of fashion.

"That's kind of you. I'm very interested in researching Agatha Christie. Do you have anything of hers in your library?"

"A few things. I'm trying to catalogue the collection. It's been put together in a hodgepodge manner as each executive board decides they are interested in one author or another. I'm getting it sorted, but I haven't a lot of time. It's going to a long-term project." He smiled. "Perhaps a retirement project."

I imagined an old, wood paneled library with long tables where I could enjoy a few hours of pleasure among old books and letters.

"I would be thrilled to get my hands on some artifacts and study them. Could I help out?"

"Study what?" A voice from behind me queried.

"Oh, Barbara," Thomas said. "I want you to meet a newcomer, Claire Barclay."

I turned. Barbara was tall, thin and dressed in a dramatic black suit with a stark white collar which emphasized her thinness. She reminded me of a heron, all sharp angles and brittle bones. She smelled of a floral perfume, "Joy", perhaps. More women wore perfume here than did in Seattle, especially older women.

"Claire has a business bringing tourists from America here to study our mystery authors," Thomas informed her.

"What kind of tourists?" She spoke sharply but seemed to have a genuine interest.

"Mostly well-educated women, some of them scholars, but most are mystery fans who want to see the country where the mystery novels they read are set."

"And you guide them around to those places?"

"I do."

She was quiet for a moment as if thinking about my clients. Perhaps she thought they could be temporary members of the club? I was wrong.

"We can't let just anyone into the collection, Thomas." Barbara looked at me and then away. "In any case, she found Isobel's body."

"She had invited me to tea," I said matter-of-factly.

"She would," Barbara said as if both Mrs. Paulson and I had been guilty of poor taste.

Barbara was much like many recalcitrant travel agents I've worked with in the past, determined to make difficulties even when there was no point to the difficulties. They were like rocks in a river. You didn't crash into them. You rippled around them.

"I can understand that," I said.

"I'm sure you can. We do not allow itinerant scholars or shills for business into our library."

Wow, how insulting.

"Now, Barbara. We do allow interested members." Thomas was determined to be civil.

"She isn't a member." Barbara was determined to be obstreperous.

Thomas shrugged. "Well, she will be soon and I will be happy to open the library to her."

Barbara stomped off on what appeared to be Gianvito Rossi boots.

I raised my eyebrows at Thomas. "Is it me?"

"No. No. She is just sensitive right now. It's been a trying week." I imagined Thomas would find excuses for a politician.

"For me as well."

"Of course. You found her body. It must have been." He paused, thoughtfully. "Murder—so difficult."

I agreed with that.

"Ah, Mary, my dear. This is Claire Barclay, and she would like a membership." He turned to me. "Is that right?"

"Absolutely," I said.

Mary, a solid, woman, wearing pants, a long-sleeved shirt and a quilted vest, whipped out a receipt book from her shoulder purse.

"Cash would be fine," she said.

I could see, that while Thomas was the treasurer, Mary did the work. In minutes, I was in possession of a membership card and a receipt.

Marlene invited me to join her for a coffee after the meeting at the Blue Heron Café. It was small with room for about ten people. We collected our coffee and William who sat down heavily beside me.

"What a bulldozer," he said.

"Barbara?" I asked.

"That's right. Frustrated that woman. Should have taken a job of work that paid and kept her busy and out of our hair." He slurped his coffee as if he had to drink quickly and be off.

"There weren't many jobs when she was young," Marlene said. "And she didn't have any special training."

"That's right," William agreed. "All those boys returned from WW II and took their jobs back. They told the women to go home and look pretty, and there they stayed for thirty years. She was born just after the war, but she was young at the wrong time. Not sure she would have taken a job in any case."

"Nothing good enough for her?" Marlene suggested.

"That's right. Anyhow, her old dad wouldn't have let her work. He was an army man. Liked everything the way he liked it."

"Does she ever come for coffee with you?" I asked. Marlene shook her head. "No. No. We're not her class."

"Does class matter so much any more?" I asked. I'd grown up in an apartment over a cheese store in the poorer part of outer London until Paul came into our family. I went to a decent school and had an acceptable accent, but I definitely wasn't from the aristocracy.

"Not as much as it used to." William drained the last of his coffee. "But it still matters to some people."

Marlene leaned closer staring at me intently as if she would be able to see into my bones. "You work?"

Was this an inquiry into my class status?

"I work," I said and then reluctantly admitted, "and I have a bit of an inheritance which helps."

She sat back satisfied. "Thought it might be something like that."

William had waited to hear my answer to Marlene and then left quickly. Marlene and I followed him. I suppose they were nosing out my class status. There was a class system in every country, even in America for all their rhetoric on equality as I found out from living there. The more money you had and the lighter your skin, the higher your class. Here, skin colour wasn't as important to most people, but money was and another almost undefinable quality which everyone recognized but couldn't describe. It had to do with diction, grammar, manners and family. Whatever the criteria Marlene and William used, I hoped I'd been classified as a potential friend.

I walked back to my house to find, as I expected, Gulliver asleep on my bed. I felt restless and driven to some distraction. I left Gulliver, trotted downstairs to my study and awoke my computer. I scrolled down my FaceBook feed looking for diversion and found mayhem, murder, political scandals of various types which were in turn routine, mildly astounding and outrageous. Some gorgeous pictures of eagles rolled into view posted by my friend in Seattle. I checked the time. 10:30. It would be 2:30 pm in Seattle. I might catch her home. I clicked on "live chat", and we texted back and forth for a few minutes. Her kids were due home from school, and she couldn't talk for long. We'd met on a hike on Mt. Rainier and periodically kept in touch. I heard all about the wildlife photos she was capturing, the difficulties she had in getting paid for it and an installment on the saga of her continually inadequate husband. I'd already heard a great deal about him, but since she was still with him, I supposed he only mildly annoyed her. I signed off and felt more satisfied with my life here. I answered two email inquiries for places on an up-coming tour and put the computer back to sleep.

I wandered into the kitchen, poured myself a glass of Chilean Cabernet Sauvignon and took it with me up to my luxurious bath. I spend a long time wallowing in hot water with the sedation of red wine. Gulliver didn't wake as I puttered around the room, putting my clothes away. His eyes flickered open momentarily when I pulled the covers back and slipped in, but he immediately returned to a deep sleep, an enviable talent.

The thoughts I had been avoiding now flooded into my mind. How was I going to deal with the Ashton-on-Tinch Mystery Book Club? Barbara would be difficult, but according to Marlene and William, she was always difficult. Others dealt with her. I could deal with her.

The upcoming tour was my last one with my former tour company. The next one would be the first of my new business. I wouldn't starve if the business failed now but I would feel a profound disappointment. I've wanted my own tour business for years. I loved the planning, the details, the adjustments while on tour and the people. I wanted to make it a viable business I'd manage for years. Barbara's insult reminded me that I might not be successful. I mentally cursed her with some rich and vulgar Anglo-Saxon curses. Why that gave me satisfaction, I don't know, but I dropped into sleep.

SIX

WE BOTH WOKE with a start at the wail of a siren. Fire!
Gulliver whimpered and then howled, as the siren
screamed along the street. His eyes rolled back, and
he looked at me desperately. I grabbed him, held him
close and sniffed the air. No smoke. I ran to the window,
opened it and peered out. Down the street toward the
river, an amber light glowed in the sky. I caught movement, shadows, flowing toward the fire. Now, I could
smell smoke. Gulliver trembled, but his howls ceased. I
put him back on the bed and grabbed my jeans, a hoodie
and a jacket. I carried Gulliver downstairs with me and
let him out for a nervous pee. I shoved my feet into my
wellies, left Gulliver in the house and joined the men
and women hurrying down the street.

By the time I got to the fire site, there was a crowd
of people, sifting into groups, their pale faces here and
there illuminated by the headlight of the fire trucks. I
spotted William leaning on a wall.

"Whose house is it, William?" I asked him.

"Hello there, Claire Barclay. Well, it's Thomas and
Mary's house. It was her old great uncle Harry Sand-
ers house that she inherited. Nice old place. Be a shame
if the fire damages it." He turned to survey the smoke
and fire.

I saw Marlene fluttering past carrying a basket. She
was heading for a stone wall. I followed her and saw her

add her contribution to a collection on the flat surface of the wall. There were thermoses full of coffee and tea, buns, biscuits, pasties and pies. It was a feast. It looked incongruous, somehow, a pile of offerings heaped onto the stones while dark-clothed villagers and officially-garbed firefighters hustled around it.

The house looked to be intact. The amber firelight I'd first glimpsed had disappeared, no doubt doused by the first responders. Firefighters padded through the front door, looking like aliens in their bulky black suits with reflective stripes and bright yellow helmets pulled low over their faces. Some of the helmets had a visor that reflected the lights from the fire engines and dehumanized them even more. They moved quickly and purposefully but without panic. Although smoke drifted around us, I saw no more flames. Marlene pressed a cup of tea on Thomas who had just moved toward us.

"My dear," Marlene said. "What a sorry event. Here, have a cuppa."

Thomas seemed bemused.

"What started it?" William asked coming up behind him.

"Hello, William." Thomas indicated the food on the wall. "Help yourself."

"I'll do that, anon. What started it?" he repeated.

"I have no idea. I had smoke alarms installed just last year, and while it is a nuisance to keep batteries in them, and they sometimes sound irritating alarms when there is no fire, I'm very glad of them tonight."

"Caught the fire early then?" William asked.

"Yes. The alarm set Gracie off, and she howled."

"Smart dog," William said.

I thought of Gulliver. It must be a common reaction. The siren probably hurt their ears.

Thomas sipped his tea. "And the firefighters were here smartly."

We all watched the firefighters roll up hoses and confer with each other.

"Where did it start?" William persisted.

"In the library."

"Oh no," I said involuntarily.

Thomas shook his head. "Yes, the worst place indeed, but I don't think there is much harm done. Everything was behind glass or in cabinets. Only a rug and a table were damaged. A small fire, really. The problem was the chimney. The soot caught fire and shot all those flames into the air. The walls upstairs in the bedrooms that the chimney services will have some damage."

"You have the insurance?" Marlene asked.

"Indeed. Although I worry that the insurance people will think I started it myself."

"Why would they?" I asked.

"It was deliberately set. A window to the library was broken."

"That's a cock-up. You're telling me?" William said.

"I am." Thomas turned to stare at his house.

"Arson, was it? Nasty that." William shook his head.

Thomas agreed. "The insurance company might think I started it and broke the window myself to make it look like an intruder did it." Thomas was obviously less oblivious to deviousness than I'd first thought. All those teenagers he taught might demand a realistic view of people.

"Shocking idea." Marlene's little body quivered with

indignation. "You whose family has been here for centuries." She glanced sideways at me and then quickly away.

She'd been friendly and now was she setting me in the 'stranger' category? Would I, as a newcomer be a suspect? Was I more likely than a long-term resident? It made me uneasy. Gulliver wasn't going to be much of a witness to my whereabouts if D. I. Mark Evans came around asking me where I was tonight.

"Not that you'd be guilty of any such thing, Claire, my dear, so don't you think it," she added hastily.

"Thank you." I did appreciate her saying that to me. In trying to reassure Thomas, she neglected to see the insult to me until she'd uttered it.

She turned back to Thomas. "What a criminal idea. Nonsense too. With Mary inheriting all the money from Mrs. Paulson, you could pay for improvements to your house yourself. The very idea they would suspect you. Let Mary deal with them."

"Good idea," Thomas agreed.

I imagined Mary dealt with most of the difficult things in their lives.

With the fire out and the firefighters packing up, the crowd gravitated to the food-laden wall. I moved away and watched Mary and Thomas host what seemed like an impromptu party.

Robert Andrews, Gulliver's vet, joined me in watching the crowd.

"Odd fire," he said.

"Yes?"

"Thomas is a careful sort. I can't think why a fire would start in his house…and in the library."

"A murder and a fire. Not your usual village events." Certainly not what I was used to. Mayhem and vice had been common place in Seattle, but here I was more involved.

He shook his head. "Everyone's a little nervous."

"Is that why so many people are here?"

He watched the crowd slowly moving away and back toward their homes. "Perhaps. Although some people like to come out to see if they can help or just to watch."

"Which one are you?"

He shrugged. "I usually sleep through once I know where the fire is. Most often, Sarah, my daughter, wakes me if she thinks a dog is in danger, but she's away tonight. Mary has a dog. I came to check her out."

"Sorry. How is the dog?"

"Good. Mary picked her up and brought her outside. She's nervous, but fine. Not Mary, Gracie. I'm not sure Mary has nerves."

We stayed for another half-hour, watching the dark shapes of the villagers slide away from the wall-cum-banquet table and head up the hill. Some wore reflective clothing, so we could see stripes and circles bobbing in the darkness for some distance.

No one offered any more reasonable suggestions about what started the fire than "Must have been kids." And "Maybe a homeless person looking for shelter and left a cigarette burning." Neither of those explanations was at all satisfying. The fire occurred without cause, apparently. I drifted back home and back to bed.

I should check to see if I had a smoke alarm, and if so, did it need new batteries?

I woke very early. A wren twittered occasionally, as reluctant as I was to start the day. Anxiety over the coming police interview wiggled in my brain, carving pathways between the reassuring logic of my frontal cortex which said "There's nothing to be afraid of. The police are only checking" to the irrational welling of emotion from my lower brain which said "Wrongful convictions can happen." I peered out the window at the dark street. A streetlamp near the crossroads cast a pale light on a circle of pavement. Gulliver dropped off the bed and padded to the door. I flicked on the bedside lamp. He cocked his head and waited.

"I agree, Gulliver. We might as well get up."

He turned his head and gazed at the door.

He wouldn't be able to wait. I threw on my woolly dressing gown and padded barefoot down the stairs to the kitchen door. Gulliver darted out and disappeared into the dark of the garden. I waited a few minutes and then called. He dashed through the door and sat on the mat, waiting for attention, eyes bright.

"Food," I responded. I was getting to understand him. I picked a dog treat from the top of the fridge and gave it to him. I would get dressed and ready for the day and then feed him.

I took some pains over my clothes. I was aiming for respectable with neat jeans, tidy shirt and vest.

I threw on my jacket and headed down the front walk with Gulliver. Whatever was scheduled for the day, he needed his walk. I met Sarah Andrews coming from the Stonning's house. It was early for her to be cleaning. I glanced up the street and saw a car pulling away from the curb. Jay. Not cleaning.

She hesitated. "Hi."

I waved. "None of my business," I said and kept walking.

She called after me. "Thanks."

I don't know how much Robert Andrews knew about

his daughter's meetings with her boyfriend, but it was not up to me to tell him.

The Detective Inspector arrived just as I was finishing my breakfast and still sipping my first cup of coffee. He wasn't a tall man, but stocky and filled the front doorway. Gulliver rolled on his back, inviting pets and attention. The Detective Inspector complied.

"Lovely dog. King Charles?"

"Cavalier King Charles," I said with a newly acquired pride of pedigree in my voice. I wasn't planning on becoming one of those "my dog is better than your dog" people, was I? "Come in."

He smiled. "I'm Mark Evans, Detective Inspector from the Criminal Investigations Department of the Hampshire Constabulary. And you, I take it are Claire Barclay."

I agreed I was.

"I'd like to talk to you."

"Kitchen?"

He followed me, and I set a mug of coffee in front of him. He settled into the chair and took a sip of coffee. He looked up quickly. "Fabulous coffee."

I grinned "The best there is in Seattle."

"It's a treat. Thanks."

I relaxed a little.

He pulled out an old-fashioned notebook of the spiral end variety as well an e-tablet. He created magic with his fingers on the tablet and called up a program. "I'd like to record this. Is that okay?"

"This will be short. I don't know anything." I said.

"Perhaps not," he said. "I'm checking into everyone who knew Mrs. Paulson."

"I didn't know her."

"But you were going to tea with her?" He raised his eyebrow.

I told him about the invitation, discovering her body, my feeble efforts at resuscitation and subsequent call to the police and ambulance. He asked the same questions the constable had. Did I notice anything? See anything?

"I noticed she had an old-fashion three-tier plate of sandwiches, the kind with the crusts cut off."

He nodded.

"And petit-fours and seed cake. She'd set it up like a very formal tea, the kind you get at weddings and wakes."

"Anything else?" His dark eyes studied me.

"Nothing had been disturbed that I could see. That's why I thought she'd had a heart attack. I take it she didn't?"

"No, she didn't. Tell me about the picture."

For a moment, I didn't know what he meant. "Oh, the picture on my landing upstairs?" How did he know about that? I wondered.

"Where was it taken?"

"At the Crimefest Conference in Bristol two years ago." I explained that I'd been a speaker at the conference, and that I worked for a mystery writers' tour company, Tours of Britain, and brought my customers to mystery writing conferences and sites of the novels all over Britain. He nodded and seemed interested as his fingers flew over the tiny keyboard.

He sat back and then reached for his coffee. "I like a good mystery myself. The puzzle ones. You know, the ones where you start with a body and then search through the clues."

"Doesn't that seem like work to you?" After all, he did that in his job.

"It's not the same. In the novel, everything works out neatly. In life, it's messy and doesn't always work out."

I thought about what he said. "So you get the satisfaction of the completion of a case without the frustration of unresolved messes?"

"Something like that. I'll need to see the picture." He was polite about it, but that was a more of a demand than a request.

"Enjoy your coffee. I'll fetch it."

The picture was easy to detach from the wall, and I laid it before him on the table.

He snapped a photo of it with his tablet.

"Which one is Mrs. Paulson?" he asked.

"I'm not sure. I don't remember her from the conference. I was the speaker, so she remembered me, but she was one of sixty in the audience. I saw her in the gazebo, but then she was dead and dead people......" my voice trailed off.

"What?" he said a little impatiently.

"I'm not sure I'd recognize her in this picture."

He looked at me as if to question what I said.

"A dead face is...." I tried to describe her dead face. Blank? Slack? Unreal?

I studied the picture. "Going by what I saw of her only yesterday, she might be one of two of these ladies. This one or that one," I pointed at the picture with my forefinger. "Why do you want to know?"

"Collaboration that she was at the conference, and therefore her invitation to you was reasonable."

"You could probably get the Bristol Conference organizers to rout out her registration form. She had to pay to attend," I informed him.

"Good idea," he said.

Had he probably already done that? I was curious now. "Which one is she?"

He pointed. She was shorter than the people she was standing beside. Her head was tilted a little and her eyes looked bright and inquisitive. I was imagining that part but I shook my head. "It's not fair." I said.

"What?"

"Well, life, I guess. She didn't do anything so dreadfully bad, did she? I mean she wasn't starving orphans, putting kids in cages, procuring or dealing drugs. Or was she so bad that someone would murder her?"

He raised his eyebrows. "Not that we know of."

"She shouldn't have died. Well, of course she shouldn't have died. That's a simplistic statement. Still, no one, not even someone dealing drugs, deserves to be murdered."

"I feel like that often," he said.

"Oh." I looked at him. He had dark, thick hair and the stocky build of a rugby player. He'd be a determined adversary and I wanted him on my side.

"I'm not really a suspect, am I?" I asked.

"Everyone is a suspect until I know better. You found the body. That puts you on my radar." He continued. "Now, you say you had never met Mrs. Paulson, yet you have her picture on your wall?"

"Along with the picture of the other fifty-nine people standing with her." I liked the photo of that mystery tour. It felt like it belonged in England so I brought it with me when I moved here. "That doesn't mean I know her."

He grunted. "You moved here the week she died. She invited you to tea. Naturally, I want to know if there is any connection. Did you talk to her after you arrived?" His voice was brusque, and he spoke rapidly.

"No."

"Think hard. Any number of people will have noticed your activities last week."

"I didn't meet her. Her invitation was a surprise to me." People usually believed what I said, so I was beginning to feel I had to defend myself.

He continued. "I want you to remember where you were and who you met last week."

"All week?" I had a good memory, but I knew it wasn't infallible. "I couldn't possibly remember everything."

"Do the best you can. Write it down, and I will come back for it and go over it with you."

Gulliver chose that moment to stand on his hind legs, put his paws on my leg and whine.

I switched my attention to Gulliver. "I have to take the dog out."

"That's fine. You do that. You can go about your business. But don't leave the area without letting me know." He handed me his card with his email and telephone information.

I picked up Gulliver's leash and my jacket and walked the Detective Inspector to the door. My initial impression of D.I. Mark Evans was that he was attractive and had a lively mind. He was investigating me with regards to a murder and I felt as if he was examining me like a detective. It was unnerving. I was a new person in the village and even though the British legal system is fair, it sometimes makes mistakes and the innocent are accused. It even *felt* unfair to be considered a suspect—although I knew that was an unreasonable reaction.

Gulliver and I had a brisk walk around the village. I packed the rental car with water, a sandwich, some dog food and a thermos of coffee. I emailed Mark Evans and told him I was driving out of town for the day, checking on sites my tour customers might find interesting. I promised to be back by evening and left my cell phone number. He couldn't complain that I hadn't let him know my plans.

Gulliver and I headed for East Hampshire and the settings for Carola Dunn's books.

I had a good map of Southeast and Southwest England and the GPS that came with the rental car. I hoped they didn't have a clause in there prohibiting pets in the car. I hadn't read the contract to find out because Gulliver was coming whatever it said. I would turn this car in and rent a van for the upcoming tour, and then, I would buy my own.

I was looking for a town, something a little larger than a village, where Carola Dunn's Daisy Dalrymple might have searched for stately homes to write about while she fell over bodies. I had a tour scheduled for next month and had it tentatively organized, but I wanted to research another in Hampshire and Kent.

I arrived in Grayshott about two and found the local park where Gulliver could trot around and relieve himself. I also found some picnic tables and ate my sandwich, ignoring the fresh wind that reminded me October wasn't far off. The hot coffee was wonderful.

I took notes on the dates the Grayshott Stagers held their theatrical performances and was delighted to find the show scheduled for three months from now was set in the 1920s. That would tie in nicely with the Daisy Dalrymple connection. I stopped at a couple of B & Bs and inspected them. There was only one that was big enough to take a group of six which made choice easy. I made a tentative booking. I stopped at a car park to check out the heathland and woodland walking trails. Gulliver flew from the car and dove onto the path.

"Hey, wait!" I grabbed the trailing leash just in time to prevent an escape.

He jerked to a stop and danced back to me.

His energetic attitude was infectious, and I looked forward to the walk. This area was billed as "East Hampshire Area of Outstanding Natural Beauty", and I could see why. Miles of farmland, woods and hedges surrounded us. At a hilltop, I had a far vista and saw the farms laid out in rectangles with the peculiar and fascinating patterns that appeared in geometrical designs in the fields. They must have ancient significance. I'd have to do some research so I could answer questions. There was one section of the walk that took us through a forest of huge trees, sureiy a hundred years old or more. This should delight the travelers. It was spiritually restoring, mystically empowering, and physically relaxing. At least, it would be for most people. It provided solace for me and I felt better.

I drove home about six and met Peter just leaving my house. The drains.

"What did you find?" Gulliver and I stopped on the walk and faced Peter and any bad news he was about to deliver.

He pushed his ball cap back on his head and stared up at the sky. Finally, he turned back to me.

"Thirty years ago, Isobel Paulson twisted the ear of the Council and had willow trees planted along this street."

We both contemplated the tall trees with their thin yellow branches, drooping over the pavement.

I waited.

Peter looked down the street and then along the edge of my yard. I followed the direction of his gaze. Everything looked normal to me.

"And?" I said.

"Willow likes water."

He seemed to think that was all the explanation I needed.

"And why is that a problem?"

"They sneak their roots into the drains to get that water."

I imagined roots twisting and driving into drain pipes. "And plug them?"

Peter grunted.

I eyed the edge of my yard. "Do you think my drains are slow in emptying because the drains to the street are plugged with tree roots?"

He nodded.

"Now what?"

"Bobcat."

I shook my head. As far as I knew, a bobcat was a lynx, and I didn't think there were any in Hampshire, much less Britain.

"Bobcat?" I asked.

"Machine. Digger."

"Oh."

"Small one."

"You are going to have to get a machine to open up the drains, cut out the roots and replace the drains?"

"Right."

That was going to be expensive. Then I remembered I had money to cover the expense. "Go ahead."

"Soon," he said and left.

A machine in the yard would make a mess, but even without great explanations from Peter I understood it had to be done. I wondered how many people living on this street would have to do what I was going to do get the drains to work. Isobel would have had a lot to answer for from the villagers—if she had not been murdered.

SEVEN

I HELD UP my sign "Tours of Britain" and waved it at the oncoming blank-faced stream of passengers disembarking at Heathrow. It was shortly after eleven on Sunday morning and the drive to the airport had been easy. Millions of drivers slept in on Sunday mornings. I had let the D.I. Mark Evans know of my plans again. On arrival, I'd exchanged my rental car for a shiny silver van that seated nine. I'd try this van out on this tour, and, if I liked it, might buy a similar one.

The airport was busy, as always. I was used to the security guards with their bullet proof vests, radios, phones and what seemed to be small parcels attached by clips to their vests and antennae poking up behind their shoulders. The checkered black and white bands on their caps should mean police, but they might mean a separate division of security guards. They held lethal automatic weapons that were capable of mowing down the oncoming crowd in seconds. Four guards stood impassively, their eyes constantly moving, a reminder that violence might strike at any moment. A fifth was standing at a coffee kiosk. I might as well ignore them. They were part of the scene.

I had pictures of each of the four women I was meeting, gleaned from their Facebook pages. Marybelle, Faith, Aurora and Katherine were members of a Book Club in San Francisco. Average age? Sixty-six. If they were well off, they might demand additions to the tour. If they weren't, they might look to economize and cut out some planned diversions. I'd find out soon. I assumed they were friends and probably would be willing to compromise and cooperate on this tour. I'd find that out as well.

The ten-hour British Airways flight is tedious for most people, unless they fly first class and they are first to exit the plane. My group were at the head of the line.

"Claire," the leading lady grabbed my arm.

"Marybelle?"

"Yes, I am. Smart of you to figure that out." She smiled.

I herded the women to the side of the flow of traffic. They started to introduce themselves their voices bubbling up and interrupting each other.

I held up my hand. "Wait. First. What do you need right now?"

"A restroom," they said together and laughed.

I swept my hand to the right, pointing them the way. "I'll stay with your luggage."

They piled the luggage around me and fluttered off—scarves, sweaters and shoulder bags floating around them. Aurora, I thought it was Aurora, even had one of those foam-filled cushions still encircling her neck.

They returned at a calmer pace, talking among themselves and looking around the airport. Aurora had removed the cushion.

"Would you like to have a drink? Something to eat? Or load into my van?" I asked them.

"Into the van." A tall woman with short salt and pepper grey hair answered for the group. "Katherine Aitkens," she said and reached out to shake my hand. Her grip was firm, and I was impressed with the strength of it.

"A pleasure to meet you," I said.

"Lovely to be here."

"I'm Aurora." The shorter woman waved her hand in front of her plump face, as if trying to get some fresh air. If Katherine looked as though she lifted weights and ran a few miles every day, Aurora looked as though her hobbies were crossword puzzles and reading. I noticed her ankles were a little puffed. I hoped she was healthy.

I pushed forward the two porter's carts I'd nabbed earlier, escorted the women to the carousel and picked off their luggage. The women helped me load the luggage onto the cart. This was a good sign. Some tourists stood while I did the work and that usually predicted a difficult trip. These women thought it was normal to assist.

"I'm Faith MacDowell," another tall woman said.

"I'm Marybelle Jones," the woman beside her said. "I just retired from teaching fifth graders in June, and I can't tell you how thrilled I am to be on vacation in September."

"Playing hooky, are you?" I smiled at her and balanced a particularly large floppy bag on top of the cart. I saw knitting needles sticking out.

She beamed. "It feels that way."

"I couldn't stand retirement," Faith said. "I just had to get my hand in and sell the occasional house or condo." She brushed her hands together after having stacked two pieces of luggage neatly on the cart.

"But we do nothing that interferes with traveling," Katherine said.

"Of course not," Marybelle agreed.

"I am so looking forward to this." Aurora flapped her arms as if trying to fly.

The others laughed.

"This way, then." I moved them toward the door. I had a special permit for short parking in the tour bus section which was close by. It cost a yearly fee, but Tours of Britain had paid for it and secured parking until the end of the year. It was so handy I'd renew it in my own company name.

The van was a Ford Transit, high off the ground with huge windows, nine seats and was very comfortable. I was used to driving vans, and this vehicle was fairly easy with a six-speed automatic transmission. The only down side was its rear wheel drive. Our English roads were not steep, and we weren't going to be driving in snow. We should be safe.

"Would you like to stop in a small village for tea, coffee or wine? It isn't far," I asked the group.

I saw Katherine turn and check with the women behind her. They must have nodded because she said, "Sure. Oh, look how flat everything is."

We had risen up on the motorway and had a quick view of the surrounding area. I remember thinking the same thing when I returned from Seattle where mountains rise around the city. The majestic Mount Rainier and the Cascades on one side and the mountains of the Olympic Peninsula on the other. England was a green and flat land compared to Westcoast America.

I pulled into the Bakehouse in Basingstoke.

"Did I read that sign, correctly?" Katherine said. "Is this street called 'The Street'?"

"It is," I said.

"Why?" she asked.

"It was probably the one and only street for a long time and so got the name of 'The Street," but I'm just guessing here." I had to admit I didn't know.

"That's the name of the main street of Plummergen in the Miss Seeton series," Marybelle said. "It might be a common street name."

I led the way into the restaurant. Asters bloomed in tidy pots around the entrance. The door was open on this mild day, and the scent of basil and tomatoes met us.

"It's a pub," Aurora said as we entered.

"We eat in pubs, here," I informed the group.

"I feel wicked," Aurora said. "Going into a pub in the daytime."

"Live it up, Aurora," Faith said. "I'll have wine."

They settled at a round table, and the waitress moved toward us. She was a large-framed woman who moved with confidence. "Yes?" she said and smiled.

Faith returned the smile. "Why is the street called 'The Street'?"

"It always has been," the waitress said.

"But…" Faith began.

"Are you from America?" The waitress rolled her question over Faith, stopping her inquiries.

Four heads nodded. "Do you have some strange names there as well?"

"We do," Marybelle said. "What about Death Valley?"

"Riverbank. We have a city called Riverbank in California."

"There were some different ones in Washington State," I offered. "Puyallup for one."

The women came up with a few more.

I smiled at the waitress above their heads. She had managed that very well. Loreen, her tag said.

"Would you like the breakfast or the lunch?" she asked.

They ordered drinks and their meals and sat back looking around them. The weather was cooperating, the sun flooded through the huge windows and the women absorbed the relaxed atmosphere.

Loreen came with the drinks. Coffee for me and Aurora, wine for Katherine and Faith and fizzy drink for Marybelle. Katherine frowned with disapproval at Marybelle's choice.

"Soda pop?" she said.

Marybelle grinned at her. "Button up, Katherine. I'm not going to spend five days with you criticizing my eating habits. I promise to make sure you have lots of time for long walks if you leave my food choices alone."

Katherine threw up her hands. "All right. All right. Sorry."

Loreen came with the food, and everyone gave it their full attention. There were no gluten free, dairy free vegans or fish allergies on this trip, so my restaurant choices would be easy. Although Katherine had checked "No red meat" on the questionnaire I'd sent out, that wouldn't difficult. I'd just have to remember to have another choice available for her.

When they were on their second drink, everyone chose coffee. It was time to pass out a package to each of them which included the dates, times, destinations and points of interest around the sites. Where there were options, I explained them. I had found that doing this after a meal was the best way to have everyone's attention about the tour.

"You will see that there are a few spots where you can make choices. I would like you to decide those tonight, if you would, and let me know so I can make arrangements. We should have good weather for the whole trip. As far as I know, no museums have closed their doors and no restaurants have shut down."

They smiled. It would be frustrating for tourists as well as for me to look forward to something that never materialized. In the past, museums had decided to shut for renovations or cleaning, and my carefully planned tour had to be reconfigured.

"I love murder mysteries set in England. Too bad you can't arrange a suspicious death for us to solve."

I contemplated her in silence for a moment but decided to share what had happened in the village I lived in and where they would be staying. "As a matter of fact...."

"No!" Marybelle leaned forward. "Do tell."

I told them. After a few perfunctory expressions of sympathy, they were avid for details.

"I'm sorry," I told them as we headed out to the van. "I really don't know much more." I was fascinated by Mrs. Paulson's death and was curious about who had done it. It was as if a mystery novel I had read was like my life. But I didn't know these women well enough to discuss it with them. Perhaps later.

"Well, we don't expect you to," Katherine said. "Still, it's interesting to speculate."

"How long before we get to our accommodation?" Marybelle asked.

"About half-an-hour. We aren't far."

"What is the name of the town?" she asked.

"Ashton-on-Tinch. It's where I live now."

"Really? Do we get to see your house?"

"Certainly, and my dog."

"Love to meet your dog," Faith said, whipped out her wallet and extracted pictures of a dachshund.

"This is my beauty. His name is Edgar."

The rest passed around pictures of their pets.

"My cat."

"My boy, Charles."

We admired one another's pets and then returned to our conversation about the events coming up on the tour. I'd checked with them online, and they had approved the itinerary. I was always surprised, though, how many times someone approved the itinerary prior to coming and then arrived with a fistful of papers, advertising places and events that were not included and asked for an adjustment. That could be maddening. These women had ideas about things they wanted to see in the cities and towns we were scheduled to visit, but no side trips or long detours to see something they had failed to mention. They did have some ideas of their own, though.

"I'd like to take in as many wool shops as I can," Aurora said. "I like ones where they feature local wool."

"I'd like to compare California wines with what's available here. I know you only have a tiny wine industry in England, but you get French wines and I'd like to see some variety on the menus," Katherine said. Her request would be easy. Most places had good wine.

"Some history for me," Marybelle said.

"But mostly, I want to see the sites and settings for the mystery novels. I'm looking forward to that," Faith said.

So far, so good.

I pulled into the B & B near the river and at the

far end of the Ashton-on-Tinch just where it meets the farmlands.

"The Badgerhouse," I said. "Operated by Carol and Jason Badger."

"That's cute," Marybelle said.

"Shouldn't it be Bader Sett?" Katherine asked.

The others groaned.

The welcoming hosts were on hand to pick up luggage, so I asked the quartet whether they wanted to rest, go for a walk with me and Gulliver or just be left on their own to putter around the village before we met at the pub for supper.

Aurora opted to sleep. Marybelle decided to check out the shops. Faith planned to walk around the village to see how it was organized. She liked to look at construction and city design and how they tapped into water and what they did with their sewage. She could educate me on those aspects of village life. I should get her advice about my drains.

Katherine found her room and freshened up then came back to my house and met Gulliver.

"Gorgeous." She rubbed his belly and fondled his ears. Gulliver was ecstatic.

We headed down my street to the river and along the riverside walk to the end of the village. I would be bringing Katherine with me on my walk with Robert Andrews. I hoped he would not mind. We were only three minutes late for my meeting with him.

Katherine squatted down, easily I noted. She'd given me her business card this morning, and I realized she owned several fitness centres. She must use her own equipment, because she moved like a woman half her age. It wasn't easy to reconcile her fluid movements with the birthdate on her passport. I should take note. She petted Gulliver's silky fur.

"Hey, Robert," I called.

"Over here."

I heard his voice beyond the thicket at the edge of the car park.

We started up the trail. Robert stood on a small rise overlooking farmlands. I introduced him to Katherine. He stooped to pet Gulliver.

"Where are your dogs?" I surveyed the small patches of thickets with long narrow, golden leaves and the deep green boxwood with scarlet berries. I saw some hawthorn and hazel in the hedgerows.

"Just making a nuisance of themselves at the edge of the field there."

He pointed and I saw two specks plunge into a drainage ditch, then emerge and shake themselves. Beyond the dogs were hedgerows bisecting the pale fields, but closer to us lay a wood with trails disappearing into it. It seemed to encircle the pond except for the clear area at the furthest point where the dogs were. I caught the fresh scent of water, grass and a whiff of something sweet like clover.

Robert whistled.

The dogs stood completely still, their heads turned toward us. Robert changed his whistle and the two dogs bounded toward us as if released from springs. They were up the rise and swirling around us in what seemed like seconds. Gulliver, young and inexperienced, glued himself to my leg and then carefully sat back and let the Labradors sniff him from end to end. Once they'd completed their survey, he got to his feet and tentatively investigated the closest one.

"What are their names?" Katherine asked.

"Muggs is the chocolate Lab and Jetty the black. Do you have dogs?"

"A poodle."

"Lovely animals," Robert said politely. "Standard?"

Katherine's blue eyes sparkled. "Yes, and Charles has such a personality."

"Dignity too," Robert said. "'Charles', not 'Charlie'."

"That's right."

"Where are we walking today, Robert?" I scanned the trail ahead. I hadn't been here before.

"How much time do you have?"

"About an hour."

"Okay. We'll take the B route. It circles the duck pond. My guys will love that and it isn't too far for Gulliver." He glanced over at Katherine, correctly assessing that distance would be no problem for her.

Katherine walked ahead with Robert, asking him about the countryside and the trails around Ashton. I heard him explain the rights-of-way that allow the public to walk all over Britain on walking trails. Local councils are required by law to maintain these paths and post them.

"You mean anyone can walk over a farmer's field?"

"If it's posted as a walking trail," Robert assured her.

I imagine that would interest her as a fitness guru. Muggs and Jetty tore up and down the trails, expending more energy than I thought dogs could possess.

Gulliver trotted happily by my side. I could see the wisdom of choosing a breed carefully so a 'one-sedate-walk-a-day' person doesn't pick a 'six-hours-a day-at-a-gallop' dog.

We strode up a hill on the easy trail and then down

into a small valley where we followed the edge of the pond. Muggs and Jetty were in heaven, wading at the shore, barking at ducks and investigating everything. We found a park bench by the water. Katherine pulled a bottle of water from her rucksack and drank.

"This is a good place for you to let Gulliver off leash for a few minutes," Robert told me. "Here in this big cleared spot."

I viewed the graveled area. There was a thicket behind us and the pond in front.

"You can see him, and he can do a little investigating on his own. Do you have any treats?"

I nodded. I kept some in my jacket pocket. I unclipped the leash and Gulliver just sat beside me for a few moments. Then he got up and walked over to Katherine.

"Hello, sweetie." She petted him.

He moved on to Robert who also petted him. Then he trotted down to the pond and drank. We all watched him as if he was the most fascinating creature ever created.

When I was sure he wasn't going to bolt away from me, I remembered I was a tour guide. "This area," I said to Katherine, "could be in a scene from a novel."

Katherine looked interested. "Like *Suspicious Death*?"

"Yes, Dorothy Simpson. She set her Inspector Thanet into the Kent countryside, but it looks similar. We will see those areas later on in the tour. Carola Dunn set her mysteries in Hampshire."

"Inspector Thanet? Isn't that a TV show?" Robert seemed interested.

"It was a book first," Katherine said firmly.

Robert picked up on her disdain of film when a book was available and let his questions drop.

Gulliver was cautious about his investigations. He walked along the edge of the water and finally turned back toward me.

"Now, call him," Robert said quietly.

"Gulliver, come," I said.

Gulliver raised his head and stopped. Waited.

"Gulliver, come."

"Don't repeat commands," Robert said. "Just say things like 'That's good boy' if he moves your way."

Gulliver did start my way.

"That's a good dog," I said. "You're going to make it. Doing fine." And he walked right up to me.

"Now, the treat," Robert said.

I offered Gulliver a small square of liver. He gobbed it up and sniffed my hand for more.

"That's enough," Robert said. "He should earn his treats."

"Wow. That was amazing." I couldn't believe Gulliver had done so well. We might make a good team.

"Just do what you did there. Reinforce the behavior you want, and soon he'll come on command."

"Nice," Katherine said. "Can I walk him back?"

"Sure." I handed the leash to her, and she started on the last section of the trail.

Robert and I walked behind.

"It's lovely here, Robert. Thanks for inviting me." I felt the afternoon sun on my back, the warmth relaxing my muscles.

"I'd like to do some longer hikes with you. Want to?"

"Yes." Then doubt hit me. "How long?"

He laughed. "Not more than five miles."

"I can do five miles."

We walked in quiet appreciation of the beauty around

us. The air was still warm without the crisp tang of
the morning. A sparrow chirped from a thicket. Many
fields away, a cow complained about something in a
long, low call. After a few minutes, Robert said, "I'd
like to ask advice."

Oh. Oh. I was good on travel, the English language
and mystery writers. I didn't have vast knowledge about
much else.

EIGHT

KATHERINE WAS ABOUT twenty yards ahead of us, conducting a one-sided conversation with Gulliver. Robert and I had dropped back. I hoped whatever he wanted to ask me wouldn't be personal. I hardly knew him.

"What about?" I ventured tentatively.

"My daughter."

That was a surprise. "Oh, hey, Robert. I know next to nothing about raising kids, particularly late adolescents."

"No. No. It has nothing to do with raising her, although I never know what I'm doing there. It's about her ambitions. She wants to be a writer."

I glanced at him quickly. Did he want her to be a writer? He looked a little morose as if he'd just pronounced bad news. She didn't want to be a rock star. She didn't want to run off the Africa or sell drugs in London. Was this so bad? I shook my head. "I'm not a writer. I wouldn't know how to advise her."

"You taught English. You run tours about writers."

"That's a long way from *being* a writer. I like words. I like the beauty of language. That doesn't make me a writer." I said.

Robert made his objections clear. "I don't want her to be an artist of any kind. She can't make a living that way."

"Hmm." I thought about his attitude for a moment. I found I did have an opinion and it differed from his.

"I taught students English. I didn't teach them how to write, so I don't know much about the life of a writer. I study writers for my tours, and it seems to me many of them make quite a bit of money. The new world of film, TV and online productions needs writers, so it might not be the impecunious vocation you imagine. When Agatha Christie's daughter died in 2004, she had an estate of 600 million pounds—from the proceeds of Christie's writing."

Tour guides have snippets of knowledge about many things. It sometimes surprised me what esoteric facts I remembered—little tangential oddments of information that I was certain were correct.

"That's what she tells me. Writers can make money," Robert said, "but there's only one Agatha Christie, and I remember all those art and literature students at university who had no idea how they were going to pay their bills. Most of them either got low-paying jobs at petrol stations or periodic contracts with school boards teaching English. I'd like her to have some way of paying her own bills and some security in a job."

I refrained from holding forth about the brilliance of Agatha Christie and the pioneering work she'd done in mystery writing. I just commented, "Security looks very dull to a young woman."

After all, I had left my home and gone abroad as soon as I could because I wanted adventure through travel. Pensions, reliable employment and predictable benefits didn't rate high. I took the first job that gave me a chance to get away from home and allowed me to travel. I had minimum credentials, but I improved my qualifications over the years until my pay was as good as a university graduate's. It had been a satisfying work life. I wouldn't criticize any young person's choice.

"Would you talk to her?"

"I'd be happy to spend time with her, but I'm not going to give her advice." I said. "I am not sure that she would welcome someone who didn't know her telling her what to do. In any case, Robert, I don't know what she should do."

He was quiet for a moment and then shrugged. "Oh, well, she'll do what she wants anyway." I wondered though why he was asking me to get involved with his daughter.

"What did you do when you were eighteen?" I was curious.

He gazed at the pond. His shoulders shook and he reached out and gave me a quick hug.

"I shipped on as crew on a sailing boat in the Caribbean, got tangled up with an older woman and had a wonderful time." He squeezed my arm and released me. "I'll try to back off the criticism with Sarah since I'm not a great example of the sane and steady choice."

"Good."

He turned to me quickly. "Don't tell Sarah."

I promised.

He smiled, looked around, checked on the dogs and called to Katherine. "Don't let Gulliver eat those berries." His voice was sharp. Katherine pulled Gulliver away from a low hanging bough.

"They're yew berries," Robert said as we approached.

I examined the tree with some curiosity. The berries were red and succulent looking. I remember my mother telling me not to eat them. As I watched a small brown wren flew into the tree and nipped one off the branch.

"The birds eat them. Wouldn't that indicate that humans could as well?" I asked.

"The red part is not poisonous. It's the seed inside that's toxic. The seed passes right through birds. It might pass through dogs too, if they don't chew it, but don't take the chance and keep the dogs away. The needles are poisonous too, but dogs aren't likely to eat them."

Katherine and I agreed we would keep Gulliver away from them.

We moved toward the car park and joined the path along the river. Muggs and Jetty were following sedately now. Robert leashed them as we neared his clinic. We waved goodbye and headed up the small rise and onto the first street of the village, parallel to the river and downhill from the main street. Elegant houses lined this street—Victorian and some Georgian. I saw one with a thatched roof. That must be expensive to maintain. Flowers were profuse even this late in the season, spilling over stone walls and giving the street an air of elegance and gentility. It was a storybook picture of an English village, but there are still many places where fantasy matched the reality. This street was one.

Katherine almost whispered, "This is delightful."

"Lovely, isn't it?" I agreed.

The sunlight picked up the coral of a climbing rose and we stopped to admire it.

"I wonder what it's called," Katherine said.

A voice wafted up from the other side of the wall.

"It's called 'Ophelia.' It's a David Austin." A head followed the voice, and Thomas Greenwood popped up from his garden.

"Hello, Thomas," I said.

He looked at Katherine and then me. "Oh hello, Claire."

"This is my visitor from America, Katherine Aitkens. We're admiring your roses."

"Do come in." Thomas walked along on his side of the wall, and we walked along on our side until we came to a gate. He opened it for us, and we entered his beautiful garden.

"Oh my," Katherine said.

"Gorgeous," I agreed. There were roses everywhere. "Thomas, I had no idea," I said.

"Yes, it's spectacular, isn't it? You should see it in June. Mary and I have been working hard on it. We have some wonderful roses, a truly elegant French one over here. Claire, I'd like you to enjoy 'Bienvenue' from Millard in France." He stood back as if he had just introduced me to a friend. I stepped forward and smelled the rose.

"Beautiful. So fragrant."

"It's over its prime right now—they all are—but it still gives a many-petaled show and a heady fragrance."

We duly admired the pink rose, pinker in the centre and lighter pink on the outside. I'd never seen so many petals in one rose. It was as if someone had gathered up all the rose petals around and crowded them into one bloom.

"You must enjoy it here, Thomas." I gazed at the house, stone upon stone up three stories.

"Yes, we had thought we would have to work another ten years before we could retire and pay attention to the gardens, but we think we might be able to stop working in a year or two." He looked around with satisfaction.

I suppose Mrs. Paulson's legacy would make that

possible. I hadn't given one thought to legacies before I acquired one. I hadn't thought about the passing of goods and a life-style from one generation to the next. My own dad left nothing. He had been a teacher when he and my mother married, but he had lost that job and many others until he only worked occasionally, filling in for people on holidays at the local grocery store. My mother had acquired very little. I hadn't expected to inherit anything. I hadn't expected to have to consider *leaving* a legacy. I'd have to think about it now. I blinked and brought Thomas's face into focus.

"No ill effects from the fire?" I asked.

"Still renovating, I'm afraid."

"Will I be able to get into the library?"

He brightened. "The library is fine. We were lucky the chimney took most of the smoke and fire, so there was little damage to the library. Yes. Do come."

He started toward the house.

We followed him. I was aware of Katherine taking in the wainscoting in the hall, the lovely wall sconces and the hardwood floor, probably two hundred years old or more. The library lived up to the Victorian décor. The ceilings were at least twelve feet high and the wainscoting a lustrous dark wood. The lead-panelled casement windows allowed a diffuse, soft light that bathed the room in the gentile ambience of Victorian times.

"We won't stay, Thomas, as the other ladies are waiting, but thank you for showing my guest your home."

"Yes," Katherine added her voice. "Thank you. It's beautiful."

Thomas beamed. "The mystery book club artifacts are there." He pointed to the other end of the library.

I almost salivated I was so eager to riff through the

books on the shelves and dig into the filing cabinet. I metaphorically hauled myself by my hair and turned to the door.

"I'll come another day."

"I like having the collection in the house, but Mary says we may not be able to keep it. I know Isobel Paulson wanted it in her house, and now Barbara is making noises that *she* wants it."

Rivalry about housing the collection? Could that be a motive for murder? Would that be something D.I. Mark Evans would want to know? I would have to get in touch with him.

"Do come again and bring the others," he said.

"I will if we have time, but you'll see them at the ball."

We followed Thomas back down the hall to the garden where Thomas escorted down the walk.

Katherine admired the roses again.

"You have quite a lovely rose in your own garden, you know, Claire." He stopped at the gate.

"I do?" There could be any number of rare and beautiful plants in my garden and I wouldn't know. The Kew staff could have stocked it with exquisite specimens. A collector could have imported rarities and they'd be invisible to me. I might pull up some priceless plant in total ignorance of its importance to botany.

"Yes, you have a Climbing Lady Hillingdon."

I heard Katherine laugh. Thomas turned to her politely.

"Oh, it's just such an English name." Katherine said.

"Yes," Thomas agreed. "It is an English rose. Bright yellow, golden even. It's like sunshine on the wall. You must look for it and appreciate it."

"I'll do that." Roses seemed to be his passion. I'd met people with more peculiar obsessions. One of my students at *Executive English* in Seattle collected beetles and went on at great length about the power of beetles to control the environment.

Katherine waited until we were almost at my house before she allowed herself a more indulgent laugh.

"Honestly, Claire. You couldn't have arranged a more English experience."

"Thomas does seem a bit of a stereotype of a charming English teacher doesn't he. But he is genuine and kind."

"I agree," she said. "It was the rose that I couldn't believe. Climbing Lady Hillingdon. I can almost see her in her yellow crinolines climbing up a wall."

"Climbing Lady Hillingdon," I repeated. "I must look for it."

We joined the others at the pub for dinner. Gulliver stayed home, sleeping off his excitement of the day.

Jack was serving plates of the pub's special, Beef and Badger pie and chips. Marybelle sniffed appreciatively. "Badger?

"Not really," I said. "Beef."

"I'll have some of that."

"It comes with horseradish mash," I advised.

"What is horseradish mash?"

"Mashed potatoes and…"

"Horseradish," Marybelle said. "I'll definitely have some of that."

Katherine checked the menu. "Seafood salad. Looks good."

Faith chose a burger and Aurora fish and chips. I added my order of scampi and chips to Jack's list and

a to-be-shared plate of nachos to keep us going until
our meals arrived.

"Annabelle is working hard tonight," I said to Jack
as I handed him the menus.

"Got that girl of Robert Andrews working with us.
Sarah. She's a good worker."

Did Sarah need another job? Was she supporting Jay?
After talking with her father on the walk, I was curious
about her. Was she just a hard-working "girl" as Jack
said? Robert might not know what she was up to. I saw
her delivering meals at the tables near the snug end of
the pub. She might be an incredibly hard worker, much
more diligent than her father expected.

Jack was quick with the drinks and nachos and eager
to please the visiting Americans. I thought he was good
at his job and interested in people and he saw my clients as the first installment of potential years of business from my tour company.

In any case, he gave me the nachos without charg-
ing for them and I thanked him as we left. The ladies
were tired but happy with their first day. They knew
their way around the town now, and I parted with them
at the end of my street. They had another two blocks
to walk to their B & B but assured me they would not
get lost. I arranged to pick them up at 8:30 after their
breakfast for their second day of the tour.

It was a soft night. Twilight settled slowly over
the village. I looked forward to getting to know these
women with their decided opinions and interests. I always learned something on these tours, and this group
was going to prod me into working hard for them, finding out information and opening up opportunities. I had
picked the right job. I breathed in a sigh of satisfaction,

then checked my cell phone. A text from D.I. Evans with instructions. He will be around in the morning to talk to me. "Be home."

I texted back. "Can't be home. Have a tour. Will be in Wallingford at ten a.m. Meet me in the George Café."

His text was short and I hoped that he was not telling me what to do. That was the problem these days with emails and texts, it was hard to figure out what people where really trying to say and what mood they were imparting. I hoped that D.I. Evans would understand that I was a woman with a business to run and responsible to the people who hired me. Tomorrow morning would tell me a lot about his character.

NINE

WE DESCENDED ON the Wallingford Museum on Monday morning promptly at nine a.m. The woman at the gift shop where they sold the tickets told me, with smug satisfaction, that the museum was closed on Mondays.

I said patiently. "I have a letter here telling me that the museum will open for my tour—my private tour." I laid the letter on her glass counter.

"I don't know anything about it," she snapped and shoved the paper back to me.

She looked like the hundreds of volunteers all over Britain: sixty-years-old with glasses and the attitude that customers were a nuisance. She drew back as if she had given me her last word and I and my entourage should scuttle away.

"I would like to see," I turned the letter toward me and glanced at it. "Mrs. Hancock."

Her eyes slid toward a closed door. "I wouldn't want to disturb her."

"I think you'll want to do that," I said. "My complaint to your board will show that she did not fulfill on her promise." I read the woman's name tag. "Louise." I wrote her name down at the bottom of the letter.

Louise watched me, her arms still folded, but her shoulders hunched now.

I stayed calm. "Please let Mrs. Hancock know I'm here."

Louise rolled her eyes. It was not attractive on a teen-ager, and it was worse on an older woman. But she slid away toward the office door.

Mrs. Hancock emerged in response to Louise's knock. She was small, about five-feet tall and a little older than me.

"You must be Claire Barclay." She came toward me, her hand outstretched and a welcoming smile on her face.

"Yes, I am. These are my visitors from America." I gestured to the group.

"I'm happy to meet you." She increased the watt-age of her smile.

I introduced the group individually, and Mrs. Hancock turned toward her office. "Just let me get my keys. I'm so glad to be the one to show you the museum."

We waited for a moment while she fetched the keys. The American women glanced at each other and then as one turned and glared at Louise. She fluttered her eyelashes rapidly at them and backed away. I repressed a laugh. Truly, my ladies were intimidating, but Louise had asked for it.

"This way, please." Mrs. Hancock ushered us toward the stairs. "I understand you are most interested in the Agatha Christie exhibit."

"We are," Aurora said, "but after we have seen it, and if you have time, I'd like to see more. This looks most interesting." She adjusted her swaying skirts, holding them away from the display cabinets and peered at the small vignettes of early life in Wallingford,

"This town was established in the ninth century," Faith said. "Or so I read."

"That's right. We still have Saxon ramparts at the edge of town. You must see them," Mrs. Hancock said.

I made a mental note to point out the ramparts when we were leaving town.

"The town is on the River Thames?" Faith inquired.

"Yes, that's right."

"The same river that runs through London?" Marybelle checked with me. The ladies on the tour had done their research about what they were seeing. Wonderful.

"That's right."

Mrs. Hancock opened a door and presented a large room. It might have been a lounge or even a ballroom when Flint House, the museum, was a private residence. She escorted us to a glass-topped, mahogany cabinet displaying some artifacts.

"Here are some of the letters Agatha wrote. She was very involved in the theater in Cholsey where she lived at Winterbrook. That's only three miles away. She promoted the local theater at the Corn Exchange here. If you stay this evening there is a film, 'Agatha' that is fictional account of those lost days in 1926 when she disappeared."

Aurora seemed to light from within. "Oh." She turned to me. "Can we stay?"

Katherine intervened. "Of course not, Aurora. That would throw everything off." Katherine's trim figure was a straight as a ruler. She and Aurora were a contrast in styles.

"Starring Vanessa Redgrave," Mrs. Hancock added.

Aurora squealed.

"Agatha hated that film," Marybelle said. "It was more a fantasy than an explanation."

"Maybe we could rent the film sometime?" Faith said. "Let's pick up the information on it."

"A compromise," Aurora agreed.

Mrs. Hancock moved forward to show us letters the townspeople had written about Christie. We spent an interesting forty minutes examining the exhibits. The ladies were engrossed. Mrs. Hancock was pleasant and accommodating. I viewed my tourists with the satisfaction of a nursery school teacher when the class was quiet and productive. I reminded myself they were independent adults and this feeling might be a delusion. They were capable of giving me challenges. Perhaps not this morning. I had to get to my meeting the D.I. Evans.

"I'll meet you at the George," I said. "It's on this street, High Street, toward the river." I handed them a map with the restaurant marked on it. "You'll like this restaurant, especially you, Katherine. They have vegetarian options that are excellent. Just come when you're ready."

I had prepaid the tour of the Wallingford Museum, so the women only had to enjoy it. I left the museum without saying goodbye to the obstreperous Louise and hurried down the street.

The George was a comfortable pub where the women could indulge gastronomically. I'd promised D.I. Evans I'd meet him at ten. I hurried across the courtyard and into the pub at 10:05. He was seated at a small table at the back.

"You're late," he said as I sat down.

"Yes, I agreed and nodded at the waiter. He arrived and took my order for cappuccino. I was five minutes late.

I hadn't had time to get nervous this morning, but I

was approaching that state now. "What do you want?"
I asked, I was pretty blunt.

He had his notebook and his tablet beside him. He'd
been studying it before I arrived.

"First of all, I don't appreciate having to chase you
all over the country to get some simple answers." He
frowned at me.

I smiled at the waiter who put my order in front of
me.

"I don't suppose you do." I was careful to keep my
tone professional. I had years of experience with cranky
tourists and irritating officials like Louise. D.I. Evans
could complain. I gave myself a mental shake. I'd better cooperate.

"I don't suppose my irritation is a big concern for
you," he said that almost philosophically.

"I have a tour going right now. I'm busy with work."
That sounded curt. I didn't mean to be so short with
him. What was the matter with me? *Be reasonable,
Claire. He's a police officer. He has a job to do.*

"What do you need to know?" I responded in a softer
voice.

"Do you have the list of where you were last week?"

I fished in my rucksack and handed it over to him.
He nodded his thanks.

"Okay. Okay. I understand that you are working.
But I need to have some details about your activities
last Wednesday."

I put my coffee down carefully. "Does this mean you
suspect me?" I was concerned that I was being questioned and not sure what that meant.

"No, it doesn't. It means I need proof of your innocence. Not quite the same thing. Give me proof. Where were you?"

I went through my day minute by minute, including my fight with the bathroom taps. He nodded again and wrote down everything I said.

"She didn't have a heart attack," I stated. I already knew that, I was just convincing myself.

"No."

"So? What did she die of?"

"Poison."

Peter was right.

"Fast-acting? Slow-acting? I am thinking of all of the mysteries I had read," I said to him and I realized it was true.

"No idea. Only got a preliminary diagnosis. No one is sure what she died of. They're going to get details for me."

I thought about why the kind of poison was important for me to know. He might have been reading my mind because he elaborated.

"I don't think you could have given her a slow-acting one—at least it is unlikely—possible, but not probable."

"Why?"

"You didn't get the invitation until the first post."

"Right!" I remembered the gazebo and the tea set out on the table. "If I had given her something on the tea table, my fingerprints would be on the china, and I didn't touch anything on the table."

He nodded. "Those bits of evidence are important for proof of your innocence."

I watched him, sipping his coffee, considering the possibility that I was a killer, or that I was *not* a killer.

"Thanks for that. Does anything else clear me?"

He nodded again. "No motive."

I let out a deep breath. "Good."

We drank our coffee in silence for a moment.

Now that I knew I wasn't sitting high on his suspect list, I was curious. "What do you know about the murder? What do you need to know?"

He rolled his shoulders. "It should be straightforward. We think she took some kind of drug, maybe Fentanyl, something quick. Fentanyl overdoses are really Fentanyl poisonings. Poisoning fits. Could have been an accident. No real indication of suicide. Really odd that a woman like her would get her hands on an illegal drug, but it often surprises me who's using it. I'm not convinced she ingested Fentanyl, but it's a possibility."

"The murderer couldn't have given her the poisoned tea, left her and expected her to die a few hours later then."

"It's possible, if it was murder. Or laced something with a drug earlier in the day and had no idea when she'd take it. But there isn't any evidence that she had been ill, so it looks like she died soon after the poison was administered. Not cyanide. That's easy to tell."

"I suppose you'll have more indications of what she took when the toxicology report comes in. It makes sense to know who visited her and when."

"I know who visited her. At least I think I know. Thomas Greenwood, Mary Greenwood, Mrs. Taylor, Sarah Andrews, perhaps Barbara Manning, and, if none of them murdered her, one more person."

"Somebody should have seen something." Mrs. Paulson's house was in the village where everyone could see who was visiting whom.

"You'd think. But most people work these days and

aren't home, or if they're home they have the TV on and aren't looking outside. The other complicating factor is the easy access to her back garden. It's not overlooked and anyone can come from the footpath behind the house. Likely, it was someone she knew." He finished his coffee, and the waiter swanned by to refill it.

"True," I agreed. "As I understand it, she knew most of the villagers."

He closed his notepad with a snap and reached for his newly replenished cup. "So tell me, Claire, what's it like running tours? Do you do it in other places than Britain?"

Business over. Social chit chat begun. He called me "Claire." I'd call him "Mark."

"No, I just run them here in Britain."

"Have you been part of any other mystery book clubs?" He seemed interested, head cocked a little, hands relaxed on his coffee cup.

"Yes, I joined one in Seattle and in Luca, Italy, when I lived there."

"No kidding? What was it like in Lucca?" His voice sharpened. He was truly interested.

I told him about living in Italy. "I loved it there, so much beauty, so much music." Lucca was the home of Puccini, and I could hear snatches of opera almost any day when I walked in the streets there. The huge plane and chestnut trees spread over the city, especially in the centre square and the extensive promenade on top of the city walls—all had been a joy. It had been a luscious experience.

He talked about his travels to Corfu, about the beaches, the food and the casual friendliness or the people. Then he asked about mystery book clubs.

"What do you know about their libraries? Do they have artifacts and books the way the local one has?"

"Some do. They specialize in different authors. There are Edgar Allan Poe societies. They try to collect materials from Poe's work. There are Arthur Conan Doyle societies. There are lots of Sherlock Holmes artifacts around." I'd done some research on mystery societies, as not all my clients were cozy mystery fans.

"Would there be much of value in our local collection?" We were back to the business of murder.

I thought about it. "You never know, Mark. That's what's intriguing about libraries. There might be something special in that collection." I shrugged. "And maybe nothing. Was the fire in the library connected to the murder?"

He shot a quick look at me. "Not sure. Not much damage there."

"Maybe it was an attempt to get rid of something. A clue? Fingerprints?"

He nodded, a thoughtful frown on his face. Then he looked up and smiled.

I blinked. That smile transformed him. His brown eyes widened, and he appeared more open, more attentive. I felt the pull of chemistry, a kind of warm, sparkling awareness. Ahh. That was unexpected.

He leaned toward me. "Are you attending the Mystery Book Ball this week? It's a costume ball."

"Yes, I'm bringing my ladies. They're looking forward to it. Are you going?"

"Wouldn't miss it."

A detective at a mystery book club ball. It was a little farcical. "Mark, are you going as Sherlock Holmes?" I teased him a little.

"Wait and see." His eyes lit.

At that point, I spotted Faith entering the courtyard. I picked up my mug, left my empty plate and moved toward a bigger table. "Come and join us, Mark," I called back to him. "My ladies have never met a British detective before and will be thrilled."

He raised his eyebrows but joined me at a table for six. I introduced him, and it was true. The ladies were thrilled.

"My heavens. Such a pleasure," Marybelle said. "Now what is your rank?"

"Detective Inspector."

"Do you know what that would equate to in the US?"

He shook his head. "I've no idea. I imagine they have different names for different jurisdictions." He smiled at her.

The waiter was quick to attend us and pass out the menus.

"Want to join us for lunch?" I asked Mark.

"Sure." He checked the prices and shot a glance at me.

"I will buy as I invited you."

"No thank you, department rules," he said.

I also wondered if he was old-fashioned about paying for a woman's meal. "The food's good, I hear," I said to the table at large.

"It looks wonderful." Katherine was happy because there were many veggie and healthy food choices. Aurora was happy, because, in addition to healthy food, there were fries. Mark ordered a burger. When the food arrived and everyone had given it reverent attention, Faith led off with questions for Mark.

"We could have used a detective in the museum," Faith said.

Mark raised his head, suddenly still. "What happened?"

"Nothing," Marybelle said. "I expect Faith is thinking that you might be able to shed some light on Agatha's disappearance."

Mark glanced over at me for help.

"For ten days in 1926 Agatha Christie disappeared, and there was a nation-wide hunt for her." I gave him the gist of the mystery. "Her husband, Archibald Christie, wanted a divorce and her mother had just died. The poor woman probably wanted a rest."

"She abandoned her car and didn't tell anyone where she was staying. Her books were selling pretty well by then, so she was a kind of celebrity." Trust Aurora to have the details of the story.

"A banjo player at *The Old Swan* in Harrogate recognized her and told the police, so dear Archie came and collected her," Faith said.

"Like a misplaced parcel." Marybelle obviously saw Archie Christie as the villain, as did most Christie fans.

"She's signed into the hotel as Mrs. Teresa Neele. Neele was the surname of her husband's mistress." Katherine put out more facts. Either the women had read about this before they arrived, or they had paid avid attention to Mrs. Hancock in the museum.

'She never said, not a word, about why she was there. Not a word for the rest of her life. People thought she'd had amnesia." Aurora waved a French fry in Mark's direction.

"Detective Inspector, that's what we know. What do you think is the answer to her mysterious ten days?"

Katherine summarized and made the demand. "Why did she go to Harrogateand did she have company?"

Mark shook his head and smiled. "I haven't a single explanation for it."

"No?" Katherine said. "Well, no one else does either."

Most of the ladies attended to their meals, but Katherine continued to ask Mark questions.

"How are you coming on the local murder?"

"Steadily," Mark said.

"Any clues?" Marybelle said.

"A few." Mark was pleasant, but uninformative.

Aurora offered her solution. "Possibly she had a long-lost daughter who resented being put up for adoption and came to kill off the mother who abandoned her."

"Maybe," Faith said, "but I'd opt for someone she was blackmailing. Maybe a councillor in the town, and he had enough." She offered her theory and returned her attention to her meal.

"Or she refused to let anyone in the mystery book club look at the accounts," Marybelle said. "Lots of murders are motivated by money. The three main motivations are greed, revenge and jealousy."

"Or she was blackmailing the vicar," Faith said, "and he decided he was fed up and offed her."

I had trouble holding back my chuckles. Mark looked mesmerized.

"Or," Aurora said, "she had a secret lover who was frustrated after years of being held away."

The other three women regarded her doubtfully. Mark's head had been swiveling while he tried to follow the solutions offered by the women.

"Anyway, "Aurora said. "Someone has a secret."

I have never seen a man eat a burger so fast. Mark

stood, deposited some pounds at my plate and bounced a little on his feet.

"Thanks for the pleasant lunch. Sorry, I have to leave. Ladies, nice to have met you all."

I risked a quick glance at him. He looked preoccupied. I waved as he headed for the door. He nodded and scooted out.

"That was nice," Faith said. "A real detective. Thanks, Claire."

I accepted the thanks, as if I had magically produced him for their entertainment.

We took our time over lunch and then headed out of town. I pointed out the Saxon ramparts, drove the three miles to Cholsey and stopped in front of Winterbrook, the home of Agatha Christie and her second husband Max Mallowan, the archeologist. It was a beautiful, solid-looking, Queen Anne brick house. It was still a private residence, so we couldn't visit, but I pulled over so they could dismount and take pictures of the lovely entrance.

We arrived at Deirdre's house about 1:30. I took Gulliver inside and left him there. Josh and Kala were at school, but Michael was home and received Gulliver. Their black Labs, Troy and Sparta, pounced on Gulliver. Michael squatted down and protected my little one, holding back his own dogs with his body, but Gulliver did the right thing and rolled over on his back offering his belly—a submissive posture according to the dog book. Michael laughed and petted all the dogs.

"Hello, little fellow. Coming to stay with us again?" There was genuine affection in his voice.

"Just for the day," I said. "I'll pick him up tonight. The ladies are shopping."

Michael gathered Gulliver into his arms and stood. "So I hear." He smiled. "Gulliver is welcome here."

I thought Gulliver would be fine. He was well acquainted with Deirdre's dogs, and Michael would watch him.

When I returned to the van, Deirdre had introduced herself and was chatting with the women. She liked helping me with a tour occasionally. She said it introduced her to normal people who didn't have a criminal past.

"Is everyone up for shopping?" she asked the group.

"Where? For what?" they asked.

"You're all going to the costume ball this week, correct?" Deirdre had settled into a middle seat.

"Right. We were wondering what we were going to do about costumes." Marybelle said.

"Claire thought you might be. Would you consider going as characters from Rhys Bowen's Spyness series? It's set in the early 1930s. The vintage costumes for that era are stunning." Deirdre had done some research as I had, and we hoped the women would be interested.

"Oh, right," Faith agreed. "Drop waists and fascinators and long dangly beads."

"Strapped shoes. Shawls. Long elegant cigarette holders." Aurora must have been watching *Miss Fisher* on TV.

"What do you think, ladies? You can put together your own costumes, or we can hit the vintage shops. What's your pleasure?" I threw the choice over my shoulder.

I hoped they would agree to shop, because Deirdre was eager to conduct this part of the tour and she knew the places to go.

A glance passed between them.

"Much easier and time-efficient to go to one shop and choose a costume, than try to put one together," Katherine pronounced. "Let's head to the vintage shops."

As we approached the shopping area, I thanked Deirdre for keeping Gulliver.

"Nice that Michael was home to look after him," I said. It reassured me that Gulliver wouldn't chew up any of her expensive Italian purses.

"Nice that Michael was home, period," Deirdre said.

"Oh," Aurora chirped. "Is your husband away a lot? Is he having an affair?"

Deirdre's eyes widened. "I… I don't think so. Maybe." I caught the horrified look she shot at me in the rear-view mirror. I concentrated on driving.

"I had an affair once," Aurora said with complacency.

"Really?" I glanced at her well-groomed but unmistakably older face. Who knew whom would have an affair?

"I remember that," Marybelle said. "What a wild time that was."

"It was good for my marriage," Aurora told us. "My husband stopped taking me for granted and started treating like the queen I am. Of course, you have to be almost desperate to take the chance that he won't dump you, or that you might find the affair more supportive than the marriage, but it worked for me."

"Good to know," Deirdre said faintly.

"You might consider having one, Deirdre," she said matter-of-factly.

"I don't think I have time," Deirdre said and then was quiet. It usually takes quite a lot to suppress Deirdre and

I thought Aurora was more than Deirdre expected. The ladies, tactfully, let the subject drop and asked Deirdre how she liked living close to London.

Deirdre had called ahead to three shops in Guildford, so we didn't have to go into London city and Guildford is famous for its upscale shops.

The first establishment looked fabulous. It was basically an elegant second-hand clothing shop, specializing in vintage clothes that the ladies could rent for the evening.

Two clerks plus Deirdre and I ran for gowns and accessories. The women tried on their costumes and came out and modeled for us, even when the dresses were ridiculous.

"Look at all these feathers," Aurora said." I look like Big Bird. I even waddle like Big Bird." The gown was a brilliant yellow with feathers surrounding her shoulders in a cape. She was right. She did look like Big Bird.

Faith patted her on the shoulder. "There'll be something for you."

I searched for another gown that would give her more dignity and found a claret, velvet calf-length gown with a low waist and slim sleeves.

Deirdre was better at finding accessories and soon had Aurora looking like visiting royalty.

"Who shall I be?" Aurora asked.

"How about Queen Mary?" I suggested, "wife of Georgiana's cousin, the king."

"She wasn't a very kind person." She'd read her Rhys Bowen mysteries.

"She had impeccable taste in clothes," I said, "and fabulous jewelry."

"True." She gave a satisfied wave to herself in the mirror and turned back to fitting room.

The other ladies found outfits that had them oohing and ahhing over beads, sequins and intricate patterns.

"Now you." Deirdre came at me with an armful of dresses.

"Me?" I slid a glance at my group who were waiting in line to pay the rental on their clothes. They might not want to wait.

"You bet," Katherine said. "You don't want to disgrace us by wearing something unsuitable, do you?"

I raised my eyebrow at Katherine whose wardrobe so far seemed to consist of yoga pants and athletic shirts.

Deirdre shoved me in the fitting room and soon all five women were handing me clothes and accessories. I didn't even make the decision. They all agreed that that green velvet would be best. The matching cloche hat and cream-colored slippers made the outfit. Deirdre added a clutch purse.

"Gorgeous," Marybelle said.

I was stunned at the reflection in the mirror. The woman in the mirror looked to be ten years younger than me and was much brighter and exciting than I thought I was. What was it about clothes? I felt beautiful.

"You'll take it," Deirdre said firmly.

"I'll take it," I agreed.

"You can be Georgiana," Marybelle said from the Royal Spyness Series.

"She didn't wear glasses," I protested.

"She should have," Faith said. "Then maybe she would have seen Darcy's worth more clearly."

I laughed. These women were so much fun that I hoped they would rebook my tour again.

We loaded everything into the van and deposited Deirdre back at her home with profuse thanks for her help. I picked up Gulliver who acted as if I'd been gone for months and headed back to Ashton-on-Tinch.

"You're doing very well," Katherine said. "A mystery ball, a real live detective and a murder."

There was a sudden silence.

"Perhaps that wasn't in good taste," Katherine said. "A murder is tragic, not entertainment for us. Sorry I said that."

Marybelle said almost without a thought, "Murder is intriguing. Why would anyone act in such a brutal way?"

"Greed," Katherine said. "Usually, there is money involved."

I thought of Thomas and Mary. Money flowed from Mrs. Paulson to Mary. I didn't think Thomas would kill, but would Mary? She was the determined one of the couple. But Thomas was no fool. If he didn't participate in the murder, could he have colluded?

"Passion," Aurora said. "A lot of murders are committed in a frenzy of hate, religious mania, righteous conviction or thwarted love."

I mentally ran through Mark's list of suspects. I didn't know them well enough to diagnose passion, but I might be able to find a motive if I thought about it enough.

"Fear is a huge motivation," Faith said. All the women read mysteries. They sounded like they were experts in solving crimes. "Who is afraid their secret will be discovered?"

"Everyone has secrets," Aurora agreed.

I thought about Sarah Andrews and her tryst with Jay at the Stoning house. It wasn't much of a secret— perhaps from her father—but surely others had noticed. Not much got past Peter or Rose. Barbara Manning had lived in the village her whole life. There couldn't be much that she and the other sharp-eyed gossips had missed.

I was driving the back roads and needed to concentrate on the blind corners created by the tall hedgerows. Anyone could be coming toward me and not necessarily on their own side of the road. I murmured something encouraging to the speculating ladies as my mind turned to Mrs. Paulson. Mark thought the solving of the murder should be straightforward, involving the list of suspects he'd named. The back-garden access complicated his investigations. Anyone in Ashton could be a murderer.

TEN

We stopped at The Sun Inn just outside Bentworth Village. I had to drive down narrow lanes, praying no cars were coming my way, but it was worth it as the inn was lovely. It had been a sixteenth century free house and looked it. Ivy climbed the plaster walls, chimneys with their double pots squatted on a slate roof and late roses spread a scarlet path along the stone walls. An aura of tradition and permanence enveloped it.

The menu was above average pub food, including a healthy-food section for Katherine. We hustled in, bringing Gulliver with us. The women settled around the table. Aurora rocked a little as she adjusted her weight on the chair. Gulliver lay beneath my chair, and the waiter set down a bowl of water for him. The women marveled at the pub owner's tolerance of dogs.

"In our country," Aurora said, "we're obsessed with protecting everyone from germs."

"Now they tell us that this obsession has caused asthma in kids," Marybelle complained. "And dirt is now good for them."

"I heard a family pet, as long as it's been there for the child's first two years, protects the child from immune diseases," Katherine said, sounding sure of her facts." They get germs from the dogs and crawl around with it and pick up dirt from the floor."

"The conclusion," Faith said, "dogs are good."

Pet owners all, they beamed at one another, approving the British policy of pets in pubs.

We had a convivial evening and I dropped them off at their B & B about nine. I imagined them writing in their journals about their experiences of the day. They'd have different views and so interpret their experiences differently.

I had just fed Gulliver and let him into the garden and back in for the night when my computer pinged an incoming call. It was Deirdre. I clicked on the video chat where I could see her in her study at her home, books behind her and what looked like a football on a chair.

"Thanks, for your help today, Deirdre. That went well. The ladies were happy."

"Those women are special." She shook her head. "Amazing."

I agreed. "I've been lucky with them. I hope my next group is as congenial and enjoyable." I'm not a pessimist, just a realist and an experienced tour guide. There was usually one person on each tour who thought they deserved special treatment and that I should devote myself to them exclusively. Not this time.

Deirdre cleared her throat and changed the subject. "I called to talk about your finances."

"What prompted that?"

"Those women. They impressed me. They are all well off and can afford the take these trips. I want you to be in their position at their age. I've been thinking about all that money you inherited."

"Yes?" I waited.

"I think you should put some of it into an annuity."

I relaxed. I had hoped she wasn't going to ask me for some. I'd give it to her, but I would also worry that she wasn't managing well and would wonder why. She was usually a wizard with money. She didn't want any of it. She just wanted to help me. Deirdre was clever. I might learn something.

"Mum!" I heard a yell from somewhere outside her study.

"In my office," Deirdre yelled in reply.

My nephew, Josh, age thirteen, came into view. "Have you seen my football?"

Deirdre waved toward the computer. "Say hello to your auntie."

Josh leaned closer to the screen and waved. "Hiya, Auntie. How's the mutt?"

"Doing good. How's it going, Josh?"

"Good." He turned back to his mother. "Where's my football?"

She silently indicated the chair.

"Oh, thanks." He lumbered off with the white and black ball in his hands.

"Where were we?" she asked.

"You were suggesting I buy an annuity."

"It's a good idea. You're young enough to get good value from it, and you don't have any kids who would feel cheated if you, perchance, died early. Stashing quite a bit of your inheritance would protect it from a too generous impulse on your part".

"Like what?" I didn't think I was spontaneous or reckless.

"Like sharing with my kids when they are older. You aren't obliged to do so, and I would prefer they didn't think you could."

I hadn't considered that I would give money to my niece and nephew if they asked. Hmm.

"And," Deidre continued. "I know you. You still feel a little guilty because you got the money and those tight-assed sons of Paul's didn't. You never know, you might feel guilty enough to share with them. Paul wouldn't like that, and *I* would be furious." Nice to have that razer sharp mind working on my behalf, but I didn't anticipate much trouble.

"Thanks, Deirdre, but Paul gave me the money."

"True, and I want you to keep it."

She did. She really did. I appreciated her fierce determination to protect me from myself, even if she treated me as if I couldn't manage without her. At times, I realized I did want her help.

"Neither of Paul's sons has approached me yet. I don't think they're going to be a problem." I couldn't see the stiff James and the withdrawn Harold finding the nerve to ask me for money. They lived in London and had rarely visited my mum and Paul when I'd been around. From what my mum had told me about them, they'd been cold to her. Paul's first wife had been an emotionally distant woman, so Mum said, so perhaps that explained the sons.

"They will be annoying," Deirdre said grimly. She frowned. "I heard from someone who knows them that they've been complaining about the will and making noises about it being unfair."

"Well, I can see their point."

"See! Stop that," she said fiercely. "They had lots of financial support from Paul. So did I. We are *not* entitled to any more. No guilt. Got that?" She sounded stern. I remembered Paul's letter to me. He definitely didn't want me to give his sons anything. I missed him and caught my breath. He had been so good to my mum and to Deirdre and I had found such a warm and loving relationship with him. Stepfathers should all be like Paul. I missed my mum. Waves of sorrow washed over me. It happened like that. Something would make me think of them and I'd grieve a little. I brought myself back to the conversation. Deirdre was trying to help.

"You can't just command me not to feel guilty."

"Go to a psychologist then and straighten out your feelings, but don't give them any money."

I laughed.

"No. Come on, Claire. Get to the bank and buy an annuity. I'll email you about three choices and outline the advantages and disadvantages of them all."

"Thanks, Deirdre. I'll do that." It would be smart to at least read the material. "I would feel more comfortable if some of this amazing fortune was protected." Money was a responsibility. I understood it was my responsibility. I didn't think I'd spend into poverty, but I might stash my money in low-yield accounts, simply because I didn't pay enough attention to it. Deirdre had made a very good point.

"You know," Deidre said. "I am so glad you have it."

"Me too. I can rent my vintage costume, buy a new van, pay all my bills and afford dog food."

It was her turn to laugh. "Tell me, how's Gulliver?"

We talked dogs for a while and then said goodbye.

I printed out the material she sent by email, took it to bed with me and studied it.

In the morning, the ladies were up early and ready to leave by eight. We were heading for the haunts of Martha Grimes, Heron Carvic and Elizabeth Peters and the town where Arthur Conan Doyle lived and worked.

"Dorothy Simpson set her novels in Kent, didn't she?" Marybelle asked.

"Yes, her Inspector Thanet series took place in the imaginary village of Sturrenden," I said.

"I've always liked her writing, even if it is pretty old now." Marybelle said.

"I think she wrote in the 1980s," I said.

"That's right," Katherine had more facts about writers in her head than I did.

We were traveling through East Hampshire toward Sussex and Kent. I had picked out the town of Crowborough in East Sussex as a place big enough to give them choice of activities. We could stay overnight and journey on to Kent and then back to Ashton in time for the mystery ball on Thursday. Tonight, we were booked into the Fairstowe B & B on the edge of Ashdown forest at the outskirts of Crowborough. The town bordered the Weld, the beautiful rolling hills where early Britons hid from the invading Saxons who around 900 AD, ravaged without mercy. It appeared peaceful now. Fields fell away from us with hedgerows neatly bisecting the green in dark lines.

"Lots of walking trails here?" Katherine asked, as I pulled the van into the Fairstowe gravel parking lot.

"Lots," I agreed. "The B & B proprietors will have a map for you, so you can explore the nearby forest. There's a park in the middle of town of Crowborough as well. They have reforested an old quarry and, apparently, the bird life is astounding."

"Any yarn shops?" Aurora asked as she helped pull the luggage from the back of the van.

"One, The Woolcraft. I hope it will have what you

want." I'd researched it last night when I realized Aurora was a knitter.

"It will be a pleasure to look, in any case," Aurora said.

I took Gulliver out for a quick pee on the lawn and then returned him to his crate. He seemed happy enough to curl up and sleep there.

The women had unloaded the luggage and brought it into the foyer of the B & B. It was a two-storey Edwardian country house, really a small hotel. We allotted the rooms. I took the single room in the coach house because Gulliver was allowed there. Faith and Katherine took the twin room in the same Coach House and Marybelle and Aurora took a single room each in the main house.

"Aurora snores," Katherine said. "She gets her own room as much as possible."

Aurora shrugged. "What can I say? It's out of my control."

Katherine frowned as if she doubted that, but before she could comment further, the proprietor Trish handed out the keys and explained the amenities.

"There is a heated pool, but outdoors, I'm afraid," she apologized.

Marybelle brightened. "I'd like that."

"We are next to the Ashdown Forest, so there are miles of trails."

"Good for me," Katherine said.

"Winnie-the-Pooh's Hundred Acre Wood is part of it," I added.

"Aww." Marybelle said. "Let us know if you meet Eeyore."

"Yarn shops?" Aurora asked.

Trish smiled. "One in town and a smaller one close by. They have local wool and do a spinning demonstration. Would you like to book into that?"

I hadn't heard about that place. It sounded perfect for Aurora. She nodded.

"I'd like to just walk around town," Faith said.

"Studying the sewage system," Marybelle intoned, as if the sewage system of Crowborough was of great importance.

"I can't help it. I'm interested," Faith protested.

Good. There was something for everyone at this stop. I had been going to ask her about my drains, but decided that Peter had it in hand and I didn't need to become any more intimate with my drains than I already was.

"Come to my room when you're settled," I said. I had a suite, so there should be room for all of us to gather.

They arrived in about forty minutes, and I laid out the plans for the afternoon and evening.

"This is the town where Sir Arthur Conan Doyle lived," I said. "I know he isn't one of our authors, but he was a contemporary of Agatha Christie's. When she disappeared, he took one of her gloves to a psychic and asked for a reading."

"What did the psych say?" Aurora wanted to know.

I grinned. "That she was dead."

"Obviously got that one wrong." Aurora snorted.

"I thought you might like a guided tour of his hometown and see some of the landmarks where Conan Doyle set his stories. Interested?"

They were.

"I've scheduled that with the local guide at six tonight. We could do the tour and have a supper afterwards."

"Suits me. Does that mean we can wander around this afternoon?" Faith checked the times on her itinerary.

"If you like," I agreed.

"I'm for the pool," Marybelle said. "And a snooze."

"I'm for the forest," Katherine said, predictably.

"If you can drive me to the yarn shop, I could be there for a couple of hours. Maybe I could get a private spinning demonstration." Aurora bundled her itinerary into her large bag.

"Why don't I drop you off at the yarn shop and take Faith into town?" I offered.

So that's what we did. Faith, Gulliver and I ended up in the centre of town. It was picturesque and quintessentially English. Three-storey town houses crowded along the main street with bay windows overhanging the pavement. We stopped for a snack to fortify us for our town tour. The Café Baskerville offered us coffee in an ambience of wood and glass, 1930s style. The décor was so period-correct we expected to see Sir Arthur in his double-breasted suit and watch fob stroll in any moment.

I planned to walk around the town with Faith, staring at eaves and drains, but that changed when a man in the coffee shop overheard us talking and introduced himself. He was a local councilman and as enthusiastic about drains as Faith. He offered to take her to the town hall, just down the street to look at the drainage system blue prints. Faith's eyes lit as if she had been offered a bouquet of orchids.

"Lovely," she breathed.

I caught the eye of the waiter. I walked over with my

bill and, while I was paying, asked him if the man really was a councilman.

"Sure. Walter Nevil, local greengrocer and councilman." The waiter, twenty something and thin, raised his eyebrows.

"Reliable then?" I asked.

"Yeah. Yeah. Not a white slaver. Your friend will be fine."

I smiled at him. "Thanks." I passed him a five-pound tip. I hadn't lost a tourist yet and didn't want to.

I arranged to pick Faith up in an hour. Gulliver and I returned to the van and drove to the Crowborough Country Park, a sixteen-acre park built around an old quarry. Gulliver jumped from his crate and bounced beside me. He was getting used to the crate. It helped that I threw a liver treat into it before he had to enter. I clipped on his leash, and we started down the first trail I saw. It really was beautiful, but a kind of sedate beauty. Katherine would enjoy the wilder woods of Ashdown Forest more than this. I liked it, though. Gulliver was delighted. He pranced at the end of his leash, barking at crows that swooped too close and cavorting with anything that moved—grasses, swaying branches and children who approached him. He created a diversion wherever he went, so I was entertained as we walked. In spite of having to always consider his comfort, spending time with Gulliver relaxed me.

After the best part of an hour, we returned to the van, and I toweled off the mud and moisture he'd picked up by a pond before I lifted him back into his crate. Faith was waiting for me on the curb in the city centre, clutching a roll of papers.

"He made me copies." She waved them at me.

"Very exciting for you." I bet she'd frame them and put them on her wall at her home.

"Well, it is. Some of the basic drainage system has been here since Roman times."

"Those Romans, they built to last."

She laughed. "You know how it is in America. We think anything built in the nineteenth century is old. Here they are still using systems built 2000 years ago."

It was impressive, and I was content that she was pleased.

We had to rout Aurora from a yarn bin. She was head first in the huge oak barrel, pulling out skeins of wool, then straightening and comparing them to a few she had laid out on a chair.

The proprietor was a young woman, wearing an unusual jacket composed of magenta, yellow and green wool. On her, it looked stunning. Her hair, short and spiked, was also magenta, blonde and green.

"She's having a good time," the young woman said to us.

"I can see that," Faith nodded. "Has she bought anything?"

The clerk gestured to three full bags standing on the counter.

"A bit."

"Aurora, stop," Faith said. "You won't be able to carry all that on the plane."

Aurora stood beside her bin, grinning. "I'm so happy Like a pig in sh…ooops. Really happy. She's going to mail all that."

The young woman shrugged her shoulders and smiled. "Of course."

Of course. Aurora probably dropped five hundred pounds for the wool.

"I just need to get something to knit on this trip. Aha!" She pulled out a skein of wool in variegated shades of green and turquoise.

"That's lovely," Faith said. She felt the wool. "It's so soft."

"I'll make you a scarf," Aurora declared.

"Will you? Thanks." Faith smiled.

We waited while Aurora selected needles to go with the wool and paid for the lot. The proprietor put the last purchase in a separate bag and gave Aurora a form to fill out for mailing.

"Do you have your VAT number?" she asked.

Aurora nodded and handed her a plastic card. These women traveled a lot and were well aware of the savings to be had if they registered their exemption from the Value Added Tax.

Back at the van, I waited while they settled into their seats and then took them on a small tour of the Weald, the high ridge—well, high by English standards—where they could see the beautiful landscape for miles. It is much more wooded than some of the other areas we had seen, and Faith and Aurora appreciated the green fields, the clusters of trees and the overall magnificence of it all. We stopped occasionally so they could take pictures and Gulliver could bounce around us. We arrived back at the Fairstowe B & B in time to change into warmer clothes for our guided historic town walk of Crowborough.

I fed Gulliver and loaded him into the car. He could take the tour with us. We met our tour guide at Sir Arthur Conon Doyle's statue in the centre of town.

"It's a two-mile, one-hour walk," Bruce, the middle-aged man dressed in Conon Doyle's signature double-breasted suit, said. "Are you up for it?"

The three women looked at Aurora.

"Oh, for heaven's sake. I can do two miles. Really, just because I don't *choose* to walk much doesn't mean I can't."

"All right then," Bruce said. "Follow me."

I moved up beside Aurora. "If you find it difficult just let me know. I can go back and get the van."

"I'll be fine," she said curtly.

I stepped back, a little affronted. I had to offer. How else could I have tried to help? I mentally tried out a few different approaches. If you want to skip this, I can find a nice coffee shop? Let me know, and I'll drive you back to the B & B. None of them would have elicited a different answer. They all implied she was unfit.

Our guide took us to Sir Arthur's favourite eateries and to the parameters of the town as it was in Conon Doyle's day. The tour lacked any real sites of interest, but the stories of Sir Arthur were fascinating, and I thought the women enjoyed them. Aurora didn't seem to need any extra rest stops.

"I'll take you to his house," I said, once I had them in the van. We drove up to the Beacon Hill area where I pulled into the driveway of Wildesham Manor, Conon Doyle's former home. It was now a residential home for the elderly.

"Not a bad place to end up," Marybelle said. "Look at those gables—five of them. Very graceful. Those windows! They form a wall at each end."

It was a beautiful house, and I recalled what I'd read

about it when it was the private residence of the Conan Doyle's.

"That long front part used to be one room, a billiard room, the entire length of the house. They rolled the rugs back and had a ball there occasionally."

"Really?" Even by American standards this was a huge house.

"Imagine," Katherine said," being able to buy this house on the proceeds of your mystery writing. Hard to do nowadays."

"Maybe J.K. Rowling," Marybelle offered.

"Or Stephen King," Faith said.

"Very few even successful authors could do that today." Katherine continued her thought.

"You have to trade something like oil today to get a house of this style and elegance." Faith agreed. "Not words."

"Still," Aurora said, "there's something romantic about a time when a person's imagination could produce enough to buy this place."

They took some pictures, but the light was fast fading, and we returned to our B & B.

I established Gulliver in his crate in my room. He could be comfortable there but still restrained from gnawing on my suitcase or ripping up Trish's lovely cushions—not that he had done that yet, but he could. I told Trish I had left him in my room, but in the crate.

"If he howls, is it okay for me to bring him into my area of the house?" she asked.

"Would you?"

"Certainly. Why don't you take this baby monitor and set it up in your room? I'll put the receiver in my office. If he howls, I'll hear him and bring him here. Just turn it off when you come home."

"Thanks so much." That was a relief. I wouldn't worry about him.

We met at the van, ready to find a good spot for dinner. Katherine and Marybelle said they were starving after their exercise of the afternoon.

"Don't underestimate the energy it takes to buy wool," Aurora said. "I also worked up an appetite."

"I'm hungry as well," Faith agreed.

I offered them two choices for dinner—The Crow and Gate where they would get upscale food and lots of choice, or a Thai restaurant. Crowborough seemed to have many Thai and Chinese restaurants.

"Let's keep with the English food," Marybelle said. "We can get Thai at home."

"Thai will give me more options," Katherine said. "I'm always accommodating to the rest of you."

"True," Marybelle said. "Keep it up. There are more of us."

Katherine gave up.

At the Crow and Gate, we were given a table in a corner which gave us some privacy. The women retrieved their reading half-glasses from their bags and perused their menus with intense concentration. They were determined to get every bit of pleasure from this trip. The smells were tantalizing: garlic, basil and a spice I couldn't name, perhaps cumin.

"You can get a seafood risotto here, Katherine, and Moroccan-style couscous salad," Faith pointed out.

" I can get lamb," Aurora said with enthusiasm, "and slow-cooked ham hock with malt whisky, marmalade glaze, spring onion mash, honey-roasted carrots and a white wine cream and pea sauce. Oh, my." She fanned herself with the menu. She read the menu as if it was poetry.

The others peered at their menus, giving them serious study. They took their time. I ordered two bottles of wine. They settled on their choices of entre and side dishes and happily worked their way through a substantial meal.

Aurora gave up at the dessert stage, but she read out the menu, marveling at the selection.

"What's 'Eton Mess'?"

"Basically, strawberries, meringue and cream," I told her.

"Bakewell Slice?"

"It's a cake made of shortbread crust, raspberries and almonds." I'd eaten a lot of those when I was a teenager.

Each woman with the exception of Aurora ordered a different dessert. Everyone had a spoon, and we all had a taste of each.

By the time the waiter served the coffee, decaffeinated for all, the women were relaxed and content.

"We go back to Ashton tomorrow?" Marybelle inquired.

"Yes. We'll drive through the Kent countryside for a short distance. I've picked out a spot where I think Heron Carvic might have set his Miss Seeton mysteries."

"I love his writing. It's such a spoof on mysteries. You almost have to be an avid mystery fan to get his irony." Marybelle had probably analyzed books for their structure when she taught high school.

"We should give a little thought to our own mystery," Faith said.

"The murder in Ashton, you mean?" Aurora asked.

"Right. I don't think our Detective Inspector Evans was impressed with our theories."

"Not much," Aurora agreed.

"Who are the suspects, Claire?"

I listed them. "Thomas Greenwood, Barbara Manning, Mary Greenwood, Mrs. Taylor, because she also visited Mrs. Paulson that day, Sarah Andrews and, really, anyone who managed to enter the house by the back garden."

Marybelle, ever the teacher, hauled paper and pens from her bag and spread them out on the table.

"Now," she said. "Let's talk about this under the categories of person, motivation and opportunity."

The woman agreed.

"Let's start with the girl, Sarah." She turned to me. "What do you know about her?"

I told them she was the daughter of the veterinarian, working part time in her dad's clinic, as a house cleaner for her aunt and occasionally as a server in the pub. I didn't tell them about her boyfriend, Jay, the way she was using her aunt's house or her ambitions.

"Any motivation?"

"None that I know of," I said.

"What would she be doing at Mrs. Paulson's house?"

I shook my head. "I don't know."

"Something to find out." Marybelle wrote that beside Sarah's name.

"Now, Mrs. Taylor. Why was she there?"

"Her daughter cleans for me and she did tell me that her mother disagreed with the way Mrs. Paulson was running the WI. Maybe she dropped by to tell her so."

"WI. Writers' Institute? Wayfarer's Institution?" Katherine asked.

"Women's Institute. It's a benevolent society," I said.

"Of course. It features in some of the mystery stories." Katherine nodded as if storing away the information.

"How likely is she to poison Mrs. Paulson?" Marybelle held her pen poised above the paper, ready to record information.

"I don't know her, but from what Rose tells me, not very likely. She is a forceful, straightforward character. Poison would be too devious for her." I was guessing here.

Marybelle wrote that down.

"Now, Mary and Thomas Greenwood. Motivation?"

"They wanted to keep the mystery club library in their house?" I said that with a question in my voice because it didn't seem a very strong motivation." Mary inherits from Mrs. Paulson."

"A lot?" Katherine asked.

"I don't know. Maybe."

"And Barbara Manning?"

"She wanted the library in her house, but I don't see how poisoning Mrs. Paulson would get it there."

There was a long silence and all the women turned to look at me. The silence lengthened, and I realized they were studying me as a suspect.

"Me?"

"Well," Marybelle said. "You found the body."

"I didn't even know her," I protested. "That was my first glimpse of her, or rather it was the first time I knew who she was. She was one of many at the Bristol conference."

"What did the detective say about you as a suspect?" Aurora asked.

"He said I had no motive."

"Did you?" Katherine asked.

"No," I said firmly.

"Well," Marybelle said as she stacked her papers together and returned them to her bag. "That's a muddle. Maybe we'd better not hire ourselves out to the Constabulary of Hampshire just yet."

I was relieved they had stopped questioning me as a possible killer. They had such active imaginations, I expect they could create a motive that fit me. I didn't want to think about it.

They continued to talk about the murder and speculate on who could have done it and how the killer had gotten away with it. This mulling over of suspects and motivations hadn't helped in any way to solve the case, but it enlivened the after-dinner conversation and the women were happy. I was content as long as I was not the subject.

I regarded them with some affection. Who would have thought that such a respectable pleasant group of women would spend time reading mysteries and thoroughly enjoy involving themselves in the details of the local murder? Marybelle looked like the sixty-four-year-old or so retired professional she was with her slightly plump figure, conservatively encased in a blazer and trim pants, with reading glasses slipping further down her nose. She was discussing Sarah Andrews.

"Young people," she said, "have motivations that can be obscure and eccentric. You'd be surprised what they think and feel. What you see on the surface is often not what is going on inside." She had a vast knowledge of the psyche of the young.

Katherine with her athletic build, high energy and almost compulsive attention to her diet and exercise also looked as though murder only swam into her ken with the occasional news story. She wasn't a coroner, a forensic scientist or a police officer. What could she know of murder except what she read about it? Perhaps her reading was immensely informative. I didn't know her past. Perhaps she had special knowledge?

Aurora was the most unlikely mystery fan. I realized that her vague and agreeable manner masked a sharp intelligence. Her indolence seemed so ingrained that it was hard to see her making an effort to do anything but knit. Still, she liked the puzzle of the mystery.

Faith liked to have all her crime arranged systematically, so she could figure it out.

No one observing us at our table would imagine the spirited discussion going on was all about murder.

ELEVEN

I WAS UP early and took Gulliver for a quick stroll around the Fairstowe property. It was set on the top of a hill with sloping meadows wherever I turned. The air was cool and crisp. The sun lit the trees in the copse at the edge of the meadow, creating dappled patterns on the nearby ground and the trails below. Rolling hills stretched in vistas to the edge of the forest of the Weald. Gulliver found a frog sunning on a rock and was fascinated, making quick forays, darting close for a sniff then bouncing back in case that strange moving creature bit. He gave up on the frog and galloped around me on the trail, throwing up his head and prancing as if he were on springs.

When we returned to the B & B, I toweled much of the dirt and damp from his hair, brushed it so it wouldn't mat, fed him and left him curled up on the bed. By then, the ladies were in the breakfast room tying into the "full English breakfast" of eggs, bacon, blood pudding and yeast breads—except Katherine who had eggs and toast.

"Coffee's great," Marybelle said. She was dressed today in a purple and turquoise tunic top and leggings. She had her itinerary beside her plate, her glasses perched on the end of her nose and her gaze intent on the agenda.

"Cranbrook?" she said. "Why do we want to see Cranbrook?"

Katherine smiled a good morning. She had a small teapot in front of her with an herbal tea.

I helped myself to a full plate except for the blood pudding which I don't like. One of the perks of a tour guide was the fabulous meals. Walking Gulliver had given me an appetite. I wondered if the calories I burned off in the walk were enough to compensate for the meal I was about to consume, and then decided I didn't much care.

"We're going to Cranbrook because it's a village that looks to be a prototype of Plummergen, Miss Seeton's home."

"I adore Miss Seeton," Aurora said. "Such a stumbling, bumbling heroine."

"A spoof, surely." Katherine said.

"Oh, I agree." Marybelle slathered apricot jam on her home-made toast. "But painted, as she might say herself, with a delicate hand."

"She romps through quite a number of books." I liked Miss Seeton as well.

"About twelve, I think." Faith pulled her draped sleeves away from the honey pot. She had one of those soft, flowing tunics which I never wear because there is so much material and I'm never sure where it all is at any given moment.

"I think there are about twenty," I said, "but I'll google it later for you."

"They weren't all written by the same hand, were they?" Aurora asked. It was the first time I'd seen Aurora in jeans. She was impressive in stretch fabric with a long T-shirt over the jeans. The outfit worked well. She had incredible confidence, and I admired her for it.

"No. The first were written by Heron Carvic. Then

Roy Peter Martin wrote some as Hampton Charles." I flipped my mind back on the topic.

"I wonder why two authors." Aurora said.

"Maybe Heron Carvic died and the publisher wanted to keep the series going," Marybelle offered.

"Then Sarah J. Mason wrote quite a few as Hamilton Crane." I'd done my homework for this tour, but I'd already known that.

"Now, that's intriguing," Katherine said.

Trish swept in from the kitchen with a fresh pot of coffee. "One of the Miss Seeton books mentioned our Ashford Forest."

"Which one?" Marybelle looked interested and held up her cup for a refill.

"*Miss Seeton Plants Suspicion*. The Nuts, Eric and Bunny, wander into the forest looking for beechnuts."

"I bet they find a body," Katherine said.

"They do."

"The authors, or at least one of them, must know this country well." Faith gazed out the bay window at the meadow and the woods beyond.

I left them to their last cup of coffee and returned to my room.

I checked online while I waited for the ladies to pack. Miss Seeton seemed to be the heroine of twenty-two books. Heron Carvic wrote the first five, stopped writing and then died. Roy Peter Martin, writing as Hampton Charles, wrote three more and then Sarah J. Mason wrote another fourteen.

While I had a moment, I checked online into Agatha Christie's correspondence. I know there were some letters at the museum in Wallingford, but there must be more. Surely, she wrote letters to her sister, Lady

Margaret (Madge) Watts. I didn't understand why they wouldn't be saved somewhere, collected by someone, perhaps a relative. Those two sisters were close and Agatha stayed at her sister's palatial home when she wrote *After the Funeral* and the short story *The Adventure of the Christmas Pudding*. Her sister's house was the basis for Chimneys, a country house and seat of the fictional Marquesses of Caterham, in *The Secret of Chimneys* and *The Seven Dials Mystery,* so why wasn't there correspondence between them? Wouldn't her sister have been interested in the novels that featured her house?

Nan Watts, her sister-in-law, was a close friend. Wouldn't Agatha have written to her? Most of the intrigue and controversy around Agatha's 1926 disappearance has been teased out and resolved into a reasonable explanation, but it took about sixty years to do it. Christie had woven such a creative story around her missing days which seemed to be motivated by a spiteful desire to upset her husband. Not that I blamed her. He was spending that weekend with this mistress. She hadn't expected a horde of journalists and interested and concerned public citizens to search for her. Her husband lied to the journalists several times, as did others, including Agatha. Journalists check facts, and they didn't believe Agatha, but they couldn't disprove her story.

Many years later, participants in her disappearance began to offer the truth, and slowly a more credible explanation arose. She staged a dramatic disappearance to upset her husband and holed up in the Harrogate Hydro hotel because she couldn't deal with the publicity. Then she refused to discuss it thereafter. There was always the chance that more happened than had yet been discovered, or more people were involved than we presently knew.

I certainly wanted to check through the Ashton-on-Tinch Mystery Books Club's library. Thomas seemed willing, although Barbara didn't approve. Even if the correspondence was minor or dealt with only mundane issues or domestic problems, there would be some scholarly value to them and monetary value as well. If I did find them, the local club would own them, but I definitely wanted to read them. I was avid to read them—if they existed. It would be a good story for mystery tours who visited the area. My mind immediately came up with all kinds of ideas.

Gulliver whined, and I realized I was in danger of being the last one at the van. That's the trouble with online investigation. You can get lost in the ether of the Internet.

I thanked Trish whole heartedly as everyone had been very happy with their accommodations and meals. She gave me a list of prices for the next year and hoped I'd return with another tour.

We motored on to Cranbrook. I was relieved that Gulliver slept when the van was moving. This was going to make it easy to take him along on tours. I've heard some dogs get car sick. I was lucky. He simply slept. The high road along the Weald gave a view of the woods and meadows. The weather cooperated with bright fall sunshine, lighting the countryside and bringing forth oohs and aahs as we saw vista after vista.

We were in Cranbrook before noon where the woman decanted from the van and assessed the main street.

"It's bigger than Plummergen," Aurora said.

"Yes, but it has a flavour of the place," I said.

"Sure does," Faith said. "Look at those old shops with living quarters above. They've probably been here for a hundred years."

"The town began in the thirteenth century, although these buildings aren't that old. Many of them are probably built in the eighteenth century, though the church St. Dunstan's was built in 1425."

There was silence from the women. Were they disappointed in this town? They didn't have many days on this tour, and I didn't want them to feel I had wasted their time.

I was getting a little nervous when Aurora spoke, "I can't get over the age of these places. It blows my mind. In San Francisco, we think the earthquake of 1906 was a long time ago. My mind just won't accept 1425."

"So old," Faith agreed. "This place does have the look of Plummergen," Faith said. "Look at that lovely little house there." She waved her hand at a charming white, painted, rendered house with a red roof and pale orange late roses blooming on the stone wall in front. "The Battling Brolly could sashay down this street and fit right in."

I pointed at a building about a block away. "The post office looks like my vision of the local post office in Plummergen with a little bit of everything for sale."

"It sure does," Aurora said. "You almost expect the Nuts, Blaine and Nuttel, to come bustling out to have a look at us." The two characters from the Miss Seeton series were notoriously, obsessively nosy. If my group could imagine them here, they would probably be happy with the town.

I relaxed a little. I had been afraid it wouldn't match their view of the fictional town of Plummergen, and if what a tourist sees doesn't match what they expect, they are usually disappointed.

I explained. "It's much bigger than Miss Seeton's Plummergen, but it *is* in Kent and on the Weald, and it's surrounded by farms. If you can image just the centre portion of the town as Miss Seeton's village, you might see her poking her brolly into trouble."

They nodded and continued to gaze around at the town.

"She had a collection of umbrellas," Katherine said.

"Including the gold-handled one." Marybelle said. "The Battling Brolly, they called it."

"That's what they called Miss Seeton not the umbrella," Katherine said.

"I stand corrected," Marybelle bowed to her.

"How much time do we have?" Faith asked.

"We have a half-hour here. I'm sorry it's not longer, but we need to be back in Ashton-on-Tinch for the ball tonight."

"This is a wonderful trip, Claire. Maybe we can do a longer one some time?" Faith turned to me and smiled. Good. They were happy.

"I'm certainly willing. You people are a treat."

I wasn't always so lucky. Next time, I might get two or three who required special treatment and a rein on my temper.

"Are we having lunch someplace else?" Aurora asked. "I'm not hungry yet."

"Yes, we'll stop in about two hours for lunch. Closer to home."

"Good." And then she was off. Shops beckoned.

I took Gulliver for a walk around the cricket grounds. We met a man with a young Labrador. Gulliver hung back, but finally was persuaded to touch noses and stand for a sniffing investigation.

The ladies were waiting when I returned. The group was punctual. I kept waiting for something untoward to happen such as a quarrel between two of them, a demand I couldn't fulfill, or a crisis from home—but so far all was serene. They kept their cell phones off. They must have had a few rules they agreed upon before they left home. It's maddening to plan a great tour and have one or two people constantly on their cell phones. I've had nasty thoughts of snatching phones and pitching them out the van window. I know these women had cell phones. They just didn't use them in the van.

I took them along the high road along the Weald, so they could get at least some impression of this part of Kent and then back into West Sussex where we stopped for a late lunch at the Norah's Ark pub. There's a vintage shop below the pub and the ladies had their meal and a browse through the shop—without Katherine. She was averse to shopping and joined me and Gulliver for a short walk.

"Look at the apples on that tree." Katherine pointed to the red apples hanging low on the other side of a stone wall.

"Beautiful," I agreed. They were Cox apples. One of my favourites.

The walk, like so many in this countryside, was peaceful and pastoral. Willow bushes, yellow after a frost, lined a small stream in the field beyond the orchard. We walked into a copse where oak trees climbed their gnarled and awkward way into the sky, the leaves, for the most part, still green but turning orange in patches.

Katherine stopped. "What is that?"

I listened. It wasn't at all a musical sound, more like keys jingling in someone's hand.

"A corn bunting. A small bird, not impressive to look at, but a determined talker."

"And that?"

I heard a warbler but didn't see it. We listened to the "chit chit rattle rattle chit chit rattle rattle." Again, not really a song.

"A warbler. A sedge warbler. A small plump little thing. See?"

I pointed it out to Katherine.

"Yes, I see." She sounded excited. "So many different birds are singing around us."

"This one will be leaving us soon for its winter home."

"Are there other warblers?"

"Lots. And they sound different. The garden warbler is the opera singer of the family. He sings a real song, musical and melodic. Lovely to hear. And his cousin the marsh warbler sounds like an incessant complainer, clatter, clatter, clatter. No music in it at all."

"How do you know so much about them?"

"My dad taught me." I thought back to those few lovely days with my father. The few sober days when he took me on walks and taught me to listen to the singing bushes.

"There are some birds in San Francisco," she said. "Seagulls, pigeons, sparrows." She surveyed the area. "Not like this."

"Seward Park Audubon Centre on Lake Washington near Seattle was quite wonderful," I said. "Is there nothing like that in San Francisco?"

Katherine was silent for a moment. "There's the Baylands Nature Preserve. So, yes, there are birds, but they aren't as accessible. I can't just go out onto my street and see them."

I agreed with her. It felt as though the woods were alive around us. I was glad England had preserved so many areas where wildlife could live. It's different from the forestland out of the Seattle area where bear, deer and cougars prowl and birds were numerous, but distant, not close by unless you hiked into those forests in the mountains. Here, it was just off a highway, or, just on the other side of a car park, birds thrived.

My cell phone chimed as I walked back to the van. I checked the message. From Mark. "Investigation inching along. Save me dance tonight."

I smiled and texted back. "Will do. Looking forward to it."

As I was putting Gulliver in the van, my cell phoned chimed again. I wondered what Mark had to say now? But it was Robert. Same message. "Will I see you at the ball tonight?" I texted back. "Yes, I'm coming with my ladies."

"Save me a dance."

"Okay." Then I turned the sound off. If the ladies weren't accepting phone calls, then I wouldn't. Shouldn't anyway when I was driving.

I ought to let Deirdre know two men were intent on dancing with me. She was always looking for opportunities for me to meet men. She was much more eager than I was to find the perfect someone for me. I wasn't so keen. I had spent ten years of my life, from my mid-twenties to my mid-thirties, with the wrong partner. We hadn't married so disentanglement was fairly easy, but not painless. Pleasant company? Fine. Permanent commitment? Not likely.

I heard a ping and then Aurora say. "Oh. Oh. It's John. I'd better answer it."

The other three women snapped to attention.

"Better pull over when you can," Katherine said. "This is important, and we don't want her to lose the call in a dip where the signal disappears."

This was the first time anyone had either taken a call or made one in the van. At the top of the next rise, I pulled over into a layby and turned off the engine.

Aurora was listening intently. I was surprised to see Marybelle with her notebook in hand and pen at the ready. Katherine had pulled out her cell phone. They were acting like a team who understood a problem and were preparing to deal with it.

"Yes. Yes. John. You can go to The Anchors. I'll call them and give them my VISA." There was silence. "You are doing the best thing for the moment, I agree. Certainly. Tell me where you are and Michael will come and pick you up." She nodded at Katherine.

Katherine hit a number on her cell phone and waited. She kept her voice low but obviously connected with the correct person. "Michael. This is Katherine. Great holiday, but your brother is in trouble again." There was silence. "Thanks, Michael. Your mom's on the phone with him. I'll give you the address of where he is right now."

Aurora listened and then repeated the address aloud, and Katherine relayed it to Michael. Aurora was in her sixties. These sons couldn't be teenagers. More likely men in their forties.

Katherine spoke in low tones on her cell. "Please text your mom when you have him at the care home, would you?" She smiled. "You too."

Aurora was still talking to John. "Michael is on his way. I know. I know. You're doing the best you can. It's tough getting off methadone. Really tough and you can use a week or two to get your brain chemistry balanced." She listened for a moment.

"Don't go there, John. It isn't a lack of character. When your enzymes are balanced you are a totally moral, honest citizen, so you are doing the right thing getting yourself into the care home until those enzymes settle down."

I watched the women, leaning forward, listening intently. Marybelle was making notes, including, I expected, the address Aurora had given Katherine. She also noted the times of the call. Faith was patting Aurora's shoulder.

Aurora continued to listen. Then said, "I love you too, my dear. Text me when you get to The Anchors and before they take your phone away." She chuckled. "Yes. Yes. I think you are doing very well. I'm glad you called. That's what families are for."

The tension in the van rose when Aurora slid the disconnecting bar across her phone.

"Where is he?" Faith said.

"At the Salvation Army Centre downtown."

"How long will it take Michael to get there?" Marybelle asked.

Katherine answered. "About fifteen minutes."

"John will wait for him," Aurora said. "He wants to get to The Anchors. They'll keep him, if I pay."

She punched in another number. "Hello, June. It's

Aurora Kasiak. Just fine, thank you. John will be coming in. Michael is bringing him. You *do* have a room for him?"

There was a collective breath-holding in the van. I imagined the difficulty in trying to arrange an alternative spot for this son if his usual refuge was full. Aurora wanted him in a safe house. Out on the street, even at the Salvation Army Centre, it would be tempting for him to go off the treatment regime and back onto street drugs. Fentanyl, that dangerous, deadly street drug, was easily available and no doubt a constant worry to those who loved addicts.

"Oh, good." She said.

An audible release of tension sifted through the van.

"Here is my VISA number." She rattled it off, including the expiring date and the odd number at the back of the card. "As long as he needs to stay, but it will probably be only a couple of weeks. He is coming off methadone."

She was quiet. "Yes. It's rough, but he's doing very well. Just needs a little help right now. Thanks."

We sat quietly, letting the silence of the countryside sift in through the open windows. Aurora heaved a huge sigh. "Thanks, everyone."

"He *is* getting better," Katherine said, firmly. "Last year he had a drug problem. This year he has a problem with his medication. Not the same thing."

"True," Aurora said.

I glanced in the rear-view mirror. Tears trickled down Aurora's face. She reached into her purse, fished out a tissue and wiped her face. "Thanks again, my dears."

These women were all well aware of Aurora's son and his problems of recovering from addiction. Methadone was prescribed to help addicts get off street drugs. At least it was in Seattle and probably in San Francisco as well. The trouble was, methadone is an opiate and getting off the cure can be as bad as getting off the original street drugs.

"Michael will get him to safety," Marybelle said. "He's reliable."

No one mentioned his father.

"John's come a long way," Faith said. "He'll be fine."

"He knows to call you when he needs help." Katherine said. "He's doing the best he can."

"Yes, thanks everyone. It's all right now, Claire. You can drive on. And thanks."

I started the car and a subdued group continued on to Ashton-on-Tinch. Just before town, Aurora's cell phone pinged.

"A text," she announced. "From Michael. John is in The Anchors."

"Great. Now we can get back to our holiday," Faith pronounced.

"Absolutely," Aurora promised.

We were home in Ashton-on-Tinch by four. The tension had dissolved and the ladies were looking forward to a short rest and a light snack provided by the Badgers, then dressing for the ball. I promised to be back for them about seven.

When I parked in front of my house, I saw Peter's small car and then Peter in my front yard.

"What's the diagnosis?" I asked.

He took his time answering. "Got to dig up the front garden. Got a digger coming tomorrow."

I wish it didn't have to happen. I wasn't looking forward to having my garden a mess, and my beautiful lit-tle house marred by dirt and noisy machinery.

"I suppose it has to be done." I was resigned.

Peter nodded.

"Okay." I looked around me for a moment, enjoying the last look at my tidy garden.

"You figure out who killed Mrs. Paulson yet?" he asked.

"Why would I figure it out?"

"You're in tight with the detective, aren't you?"

I shook my head. "I wouldn't say so." Being on a first name basis didn't constitute "being tight."

"Isobel Paulson probably found out stolen jewelry that came from…" he nodded his head in the direction of the other half of my house.

"Mrs. Stonning? Has she lost some jewelry?"

"Yeah. Bet that niece of hers took some jewelry and sold it to the Greenwoods."

"What?' That was bizarre. "How do you know any-thing is lost? Where did you get this?" Accusing people of theft, especially without any evidence was wrong. I hated that.

Peter raised his head like a horse when it's startled. Maybe I was transgressing on some village protocol by questioning him. Maybe everyone simply believed everything he said. Or maybe no one believed any-thing he said.

"Rose knows something. She says the Greenwoods started the fire to cover up the theft. Her mother says Sarah sent for her passport. She is going to run."

"Oh, for heaven's sake. Peter. That's really far-fetched." I suppose I was now offending him mightily. If it stopped him from spreading scurrilous stories, I'd take the risk. But I suspect nothing short of a bolt of lightning cracking his forehead would stop him or Rose from gossiping.

He shrugged. "You'd be surprised what goes on in the village."

I'd been surprised at Aurora's family troubles. I was constantly surprised at the heights and depths of experiences of others. A village would be full of unexpected life stories.

I tugged on Gulliver's leash. Maybe I would be astonished by what went on in the village, but Peter's particular story was unjustified and unsubstantiated. I would not pay heed to what he said about others.

TWELVE

SOME DAYS ARE full of small details. I settled Gulliver and then drove to the bank. I hoped my business with the accounts manager wouldn't take much time. I needed to be home in time to dress in my finery for the ball, and I didn't want to be late in picking up the ladies. Punctual as they were, they would expect me on time.

The account manager's name was Judith Taylor, one of the many Taylors in this village and probably related to Rose and her mother. She was about thirty, slim, dressed in a muted blue suit with a printed shirt under it. She wore flat shoes, Alexander Wang's, expensive and comfortable. I had a pair—stylish, but practical. I had always indulged in shoes even when I had very little money. I loved shoes and buying them was one of my indulgences.

I took a seat on a chair on the other side of her desk in her private office. I had put my money in this bank and the amount would make me a very attractive customer. It felt odd, as I had never been in a private office in a bank as part of my banking experience. I didn't feel as if I quite belonged in her private office. I took a breath and went directly to business.

"I'm looking for an annuity. I have three possibilities here." I handed her the printed description of Deirdre's picks. "I'm leaning toward this one," I pointed, "but what's your advice?"

She took the papers and read them, concentrating for a few minutes. I remained silent.

"They are all good choices," she said, looking up at me. "The one you have chosen is probably a little better than the other two. You are single?"

I nodded. Annuities were a problem if you wanted to pass your assets down a generation. One type of annuity allowed me to take out the money on a regular monthly basis when I reached pensionable age, but if I died, a year later, my heirs would not get any money. Another allowed me to have a joint beneficiary. I could name Deirdre, so, if I died, she would get the pension. That plan paid me less but seemed to at least have a safeguard on the money. The basic principles of annuities were that I gave the insurance company a lump sum of money. They kept it, invested it and promised me a guaranteed, regular amount of payment for a term, perhaps fifteen years or my life-time. The payment was guaranteed 100% on the first 2000 pounds paid out monthly and only 85% guaranteed on anything over that amount. There were a lot of details and Ms Taylor took the time to make sure I understood them all.

Once I decided where to put the money, I couldn't get it back. That was the drawback. I had large amount of money and the advantage of the annuity was that, once I signed the papers and put the money in an annuity, I wouldn't have to think about it again. I would also be investing a good chunk of my money, not all of it.

I disciplined my mind to focus on what Ms Taylor was saying. It was important to make the decision correctly. I listened, thought about it and decided on the plan that allowed Deirdre to inherit.

"Good. Fine. Would you like me to buy this for you?" She tapped her finger on the annuity I'd indicated.

"Yes, please." I told her how much I wanted to put into it.

She showed me how much I could expect to receive and when.

I waited while she printed out some forms which set out what I had agreed to. I signed and within an hour I had transferred a sum of money from my accounts to the annuity. It's amazing how easy it was.

For most of the time, I forgot about how much money I had. I made decisions the way I always had when I lived on a salary and I'd remember I could afford more. It was good to have at least some of the money safely tucked away.

I pulled into my driveway and saw a dark, late-model car parked across the street. As I shut the van door, a man got out of the car and started toward me. I recognized him as he moved closer.

"James," I said. "How nice to see you." Now that was a socially ingrained lie. It was not "nice" to see him. I suppose he was my step-brother, but we both ignored the relationships. I'd loved his dad who was a loving step-father to me, but I hardly knew James. I checked my watch. It was now 5:30.

"I have a tour in town, James, and haven't much time, but I can give you a cup of coffee and half-an-hour." Keep a "civil tongue in your head" my mother told me regardless of who you were talking to. "It costs nothing to be civil". That was another of her bromides. While I understand how polite behaviour helps keep society running smoothly, I sometimes think a cracking good insult would clear the air.

"Really? You're working?" His eyebrows raised as to raise a question of doubt.

"Yes, I'm working," I said.

"I suppose you need some kind of hobby."

Oh, James, I thought as I filled the coffee carafe. *You are such a patronizing louse.* There was a certain comfort in knowing that the opinion I had of James was still the same. He was arrogant and condescending. He was nothing if not reliable in his behaviour.

Gulliver had come over to investigate when James followed me into the kitchen, and I saw out of the corner of my eye his efforts to be friendly. James pushed him away with his foot. I'd better watch closely. Any harmful move toward Gulliver, and James was out on the street, ear first. But Gulliver, smart dog that he was, just glared at James, turned his back and trotted over to sit by my chair. My dog was a clever one. Able to distinguish idiots at first sniff. Good!

"What can I do for you, James?" I offered him the cream and sugar.

"I take it black," he announced.

"Fine." I said, a little amused. I checked my watch again.

James took the hint." I've been talking to Harold."

I braced myself. Whatever scheme James and Harold had concocted, it wouldn't be for my benefit. Harold was Paul's youngest son and James's brother. He was a solicitor in the London and always seemed to fade into the background whenever I saw him—which was rarely. James was the dominant one and apparently successful in his work. Paul had told me James bought and sold steel. I imagine he did that at a desk. He had pasty white skin, and in spite of his over six-foot height, didn't seem tall. He had a slight stoop, even when he was sitting. He was still broad-shouldered, though, and I imagined those blue eyes matched steel for hardness. There was no joy in James, it appeared.

"What have you and Harold come up with?"

"We think you must realize Dad wasn't quite right in the head when he made his will. He couldn't have cut us out the way he did and given everything to you when he hardly even knew you." James spoke firmly. I believe he thought his words would convince me.

I had spent a month with Paul after mum died. We had our intense nightly talks, our laughter, our shared pain. Would James understand that time and the relationship I had with Paul? I doubted it. The boys had missed out on having a relationship with their father. I was glad I had that opportunity.

"Harold?" I didn't think a solicitor would agree with the notion that Paul was not competent. Paul had made very sure the will couldn't be challenged on those grounds.

James' mouth tightened. "Harold will agree with me."

I didn't consider them part of my immediate family. Had they loved Paul enough to support him in his grief? I wasn't sure. Paul's choice to leave me the money was very clear in his letter to me. Thankfully, it provided guidance for me with James.

"Well, your father was competent. Those affidavits from two physicians that accompanied the will showed cognitive acuity. You have a copy and there is no chance of upsetting the will on those grounds." I glanced at my watch again. I had about forty minutes before I had to get to the tour.

"Be that as it may," he said. "You must admit it is

only fair if you share the legacy with us. We are prepared to settle for one third each way."

"James, your father made it clear in his will that he wanted to me have the money. I am doing what he would want me to do," I said to him.

"Just to show there are no hard feelings," he went on as if I hadn't spoken. "I'll help you with investments. I know you aren't experienced in business, so I would be willing to invest your share for you and only charge a small commission since you are by way of being family."

Did he think I would have him invest it? I guess he did. I thought how sad he was as he had been alienated from his father. Paul had hinted as much to me. I wondered if Harold didn't want any part of James. I avoided him when I could and I would have to be very firm with him.

"I have business plans for the money. I am aware how motivated you are to 'help' me, but I have competent advice and some experience in business. I must decline your offer." I was starting to sound like a businessman now, even a bit like James.

I could see the flush rise up his throat and suffuse his face. It was time he left.

"I'm sorry, but I have a group of tourists to pick up, in about thirty minutes. I have a lot to do before I leave the house." I stood. Gulliver pasted himself to my knees.

James stood when I did and I escorted him to the front door.

James gave it one last try. "Give this some thought, Claire. You don't want to go to court. It would cost us all a lot of money."

In some ways, I felt very sorry for James. He was so unlikeable.

"There is no case to take to court, James. Goodbye." I shut the door and locked it.

Gulliver sat and looked up at me.

"You are totally right, Gulliver. He is obnoxious. I hope he'll never return."

I was glad Deirdre had suggested the annuities. I could tell James I had already invested the money so it was not available for him to take care of for me.

"Gulliver, James thought I knew nothing and saw himself as the one who should take over and be in charge. Mansplaining. It's an American term. Very apt when applied to James."

I shoved my arms into my jacket, grabbed Gulliver's leash and set off down my front walkway. Time was moving on, and Gulliver needed his last walk of the day.

I was almost past my van when something caught my eye. Something was odd. What was it? I turned and looked. The silver van listed toward me. My eyes followed the slant to the ground. Two flat tires.

"Crikey!" I felt heat rise up my neck. Who would do this? Surely, not James. It was beneath his dignity. He'd have to stoop to do it. Was there someone in the village who thought I was a threat? Did someone suspect me in Mrs. Paulson's death? Was there a village vendetta against me? Worrisome thoughts chased each other around my head. Then the immediate problem reduced all other speculation to minor status. Where was I going to get a van?

I called the rental company on my cell right there from the walkway and arranged a tow truck and a replacement van. The clerk informed me crisply that I could have it tomorrow morning.

"That isn't good enough. I have customers I have to pick up tonight. They have to catch a plane tomorrow. I can't wait until tomorrow. I need you to send it tonight."

She finally agreed to send the van tonight. After waiting what seemed ages, she came back with a time. Ten o'clock this evening.

"I won't be home, so leave the keys under the front tire."

"We can't do that."

"Yes, you can."

She agreed she could.

Now, what was I going to do about getting the ladies in all their finery to the ball tonight?

I worried the nail on my thumb and thought. Who has a van? Jack at the pub has a van. I called the pub.

"What's up, Claire?" I could hear the buzz of voices and the clink of glasses.

"Jack, I need your van tonight," I blurted out.

"What happened? Are you all right?" I heard his concern. That calmed me a little.

"I'm fine. An idiot slashed my tires, and I'm waiting for the tow truck and a replacement van, but I need to get my ladies to the ball."

"No kidding? Your tires? Someone from the village? This isn't much of a welcome to you. Just a minute."

He was away from the phone for a very short time. "Claire, no problem. Look, you must be running tight on your schedule. Why don't I nip over with it?"

"Thank you, thank you." My gratitude was heart felt.

"Will twenty minutes from now suit you?"

"It will."

I rushed Gulliver around the block, fed him and went upstairs to change.

A lot of the pleasure in the ball and my enjoyment of my new rented clothes and shoes had leaked out like the air from the tires with the worry about the tow truck, getting a new rental van, and Jack delivering his van in time to pick up my ladies. If Jack arrived within an hour with the van, I would be able to coordinate everything smoothly. If he was late, I didn't know what I was going to do—taxi or a couple of taxis, I supposed.

I heard the swish of the tires on the street in front of the house. I peeked out the narrow window beside the front door and saw the tow truck.

I grabbed a raincoat from the closet to cover my finery, picked up my bag from the hall table and rushed outside. My cloche hat with the curling feather must have seemed a little odd. The driver, a young man of about twenty-five, gave me one quick glance, but didn't comment.

"Nasty that," he said, looking at the van.

We studied the two flat tires.

The driver bent down to examine them. "Slashed. See that?"

I could see the sharp line in the tire.

"Deliberate like."

I nodded.

"Got any surveillance cameras around?"

I shook my head.

"Might want to install some if you've got enemies like this."

He had a point.

He unraveled a chain—the clank of machinery

sounded loud on this quiet street—and began to hook up the injured van.

I shook myself. "Just a minute."

I opened the doors and checked the interior for any forgotten articles. I found a bag of wool and a five-pound note. I took the lease contract from the glove compartment and then handed the keys to the tow truck driver along with a twenty-pound note in gratitude for his quick service.

I took the contract, the wool and the five-pound note and scuttled back into the house.

Make up. I needed make up. I dashed upstairs and hauled out my arsenal. This was supposed to be a light-hearted night of romance and frivolity. Two men wanted to dance with me. Where was my excitement? I was supposed to enjoy putting on make-up, fussing with my hair, even adding a little perfume. I applied the make-up with record speed. The hair was fine. Forget the perfume. If I was going to enjoy myself tonight, I was going to have to work at it. I had definitely lost my care-free mood.

THIRTEEN

THE CHUG OF the Volkswagen engine had me flying to the front door. Jack had brought his van to my house in precisely twenty minutes. Amazing.

"Sorry about the junk in it," he said.

"No problem." I scanned the back where a crate of empty wine bottles crowded a spare tire and some boxes. There was still enough room for my ladies and, just as important, enough seat belts. It was a mess, though.

I drove Jack to the pub and promised to return the van after the ball.

"Just drop the keys through the mail slot if I've closed." He waved and jumped out.

"Thanks. I'll do that." I was grateful. Very grateful.

Jack's van had a manual shift, but I learned on those, and I had driven them when I lived in Europe. I felt odd dressed in my finery, driving a working van, a little like Cinderella in her ball gown sitting in the pumpkin. I returned to my house.

Where did I stash my blankets? I rooted through my hall closet and grabbed my MacIntosh while I was there. Gulliver padded after me staying out of my way but watching my mad dash through the house. I found the blankets, surprisingly, in a box market "Blankets", picked up some cleaning supplies and a rag and flew back to the van.

I wiped the seats with the cleaner and stored Jack's tools in the back. I left the floor dirt, as I couldn't take the time to vacuum and using a broom on it would just send dust everywhere. I threw the blankets over the seats and tossed the cleaning materials into the back. I removed my Mac, shook it outside the van, folded it and placed it on top of the tools in the back. Finally, I brushed down my green velvet dress, shook myself and drove to the Badgers. I was five minutes late—a minor miracle.

The ladies were gathered in the lounge of the B & B and in the process of being admired by the Badgers. In costume, they were fascinating.

Faith wore a mid-calf chiffon dress with beading in a double line down the front draping over her curves. Its pale rose color set off her brunette and gray hair. A long string of artificial pearls dangled past her knees. Her shoes were low with Louis XIV heels. Katherine's figure suited the 1920s boyish look as her dress fell straight to the hem without much interference from any feminine distinction. I imagine she rarely wore a dress, but she looked almost ethereal in this one. She had a headband and a large feather in shades of silver and blue, and her shoes were a shiny, blue leather with T-straps. Aurora was her regal self in the maroon velvet with no trace of tears or any other signs of stress and Marybelle was elegant in a straight, black, ankle-length gown with black and rose-coloured beads forming an intricate pattern from neck to hem. There was a delicate beaded rose at her waist. She had a black satin wide ribbon around her head with long tails hanging down. My own green velvet dress had metallic silk embroidery over the tunic top and a flower applique in deep green and turquoise on the left side. The draped silk rippled around my calves. The small cloche had a matching applique flower. I had been sure I'd knock off anything more elaborate.

"Photos. Photos!" Marybelle demanded and five cameras emerged from clutch bags. We spent another half-hour taking photos and admiring each other before we loaded into the van, and I drove to the church hall, transformed tonight by industrious members of the Mystery Book Club into a 1920s nightclub.

The women were impressed with the decorations.

"Isn't this remarkable?" Faith said. "Just an ordinary church hall and, with a few sheets, tables, lamps and flowers, it looks like something out of *The Great Gatsby*."

Mary Greenwood who had sailed up to stand beside me beamed. She wore a pale lavender taffeta gown with an overdress of black lace. Her shoes, low-heeled, matching lavender with bows, were definitely frivolous. I'd thought she was a bit plump with a stocky build but tonight she was beautiful. Did everyone in the 1920s look this lovely in such marvelous clothes? "We did work hard," she said with satisfaction.

"You did a proper job." I reached into my purse, found the five tickets I needed and passed them to her.

She glanced at them then waved us further into the room. "Just keep them. You'll need to hand them in at the supper."

"Supper," Katherine said. "Do you suppose it will be lobster?"

"Lobster would go with the décor," I agreed. "But I doubt they could manage it on the ticket price."

"It's *always* chicken," Aurora said. "Luckily, I like chicken."

I glanced quickly at Aurora. She seemed content even with her difficult afternoon. She looked happy at the moment.

"There's a vegetarian choice for you," I said to Katherine.

Robert came up to greet us just then, and I introduced him to the group. He had already met Katherine. I was surprised to find I was presenting the women with some pride, as if I had personally been responsible for such interesting and entertaining company.

Aurora studied him. "You must be Sherlock Holmes."

"I am, and you?" He bowed, doffing his elaborate hat.

"I'm Queen Mary from the Rhys Bowen novels." She inclined her head, imitating the present monarch.

Robert bowed again. "The *Royal Spyness* series?"

"That's the one."

Robert wore the typical Sherlock Holmes outfit with its deerstalker's cap, tweed jacket and pipe. Around me, I saw a Miss Marple, several Phryne Fishers in truly elegant dresses and one Mrs. Jeffries with ruffled cap and pinafore. Surely, she was pre-1920s. I turned back to view Robert. While we surveyed him, he surveyed us.

"You are an elegant crew. Who are you?" he asked Faith.

"I am Belinda even if I'm old enough to be her grandmother." Katherine said.

"I'm Georgiana's mother, Lady Rannoch," Marybelle informed him.

"Now, Mother," I said. "You know you divorced daddy years ago, and you've had a couple of husbands since. You can't be Lady Rannoch anymore."

"I am still Lady Rannoch when I want to be and don't you forget it," she said in character. Then she grinned.

We laughed.

"What is the joke?" a voice said at my elbow.

It was Mark, dressed impeccably in a dark tux.

The ladies smiled at him.

"Hello, Detective Inspector. You are looking handsome tonight," Marybelle said.

Mark bowed.

"What series are you from? Katherine asked.

"I heard you discussing your plans at lunch in Wallingford, so I decided to fit into the Rhys Bowen series."

"Darcy O'Mara." Faith said. "You even have the same profession. Welcome to our cast of characters. You need to meet your love interest, Lady Georgiana here." She waved her hand as if introducing us.

My cheeks burned. I haven't blushed since I was fourteen. It was the dress. Or the 1920 manners or something. I could feel the fire blaze on my face.

"Lady Georgiana, could I have this dance?" Mark bowed again.

I hadn't noticed the band had started playing, and couples were on the floor.

"Lady Rannoch," Aurora said, turning to Marybelle, "may I have the privilege?"

"You may, your majesty," Marybelle said, and they followed us out onto the dance floor.

I saw Katherine and Faith take over a table for six near the buffet. My charges were all settled. I turned to Mark.

We danced easily together. People of our generation learned formal waltzes—our mothers insisted. Although I hadn't waltzed in years, I hadn't forgotten.

The band played some slow waltzes and then
switched to "Five-Foot-Two." I darted a quick look at
Mark. He shrugged and started a modified jive. He was
easy to follow, and we jived our way through the song.
We stopped when he had his arms around me in a turn.
He didn't complete the turn just pulled me a little closer
and leaned down. Was he going to kiss me on the neck?
In public? I started to stiffen, then relaxed. Why not?

His lips were close to my ear. "I got the toxicology
report."

I turned, his arms still encircled me until I was fac-
ing him.

"And?"

"Yew poison."

"Not Fentanyl?"

"Nope."

"Yew. Is it hard to find?" Then I remembered how
many yew berries I'd seen in my walks.

"No, easy. Anyone could make a toxic tea."

We exchanged a long look. Mark squeezed me a little, and I stepped back.

"I'd better join my ladies," I said.

"I'll be back," Mark promised.

Robert was sitting with my group when I arrived
and had apparently just returned from dancing with
Katherine. Of all things, he was discussing flying with
Katherine. It turned out, both had at one time earned a
private pilot's license.

"Over the desert is where to fly," Katherine said. "It
looks so green from the air over Tucson. Not the same
as other deserts where the ground is parched and brown.
Tucson is a desert full of cacti, Palo Verde trees and
mesquite—all green. It's magical. And there isn't much

air traffic around you so less danger of collisions,*and* it's usually sunny."

"Weather's a problem here," Robert said. "I've spent more time sitting in airports drinking coffee, waiting for the weather, than actually flying."

"That seems to be true most places," Katherine agreed.

"Look at us," Aurora said. "Here we are the characters from a mystery novel, sitting around a table at a mystery ball. We ought to be able to solve the mystery."

No one mentioned Mrs. Paulson's murder specifically, but I'm sure it jumped into everyone's mind.

"If we were going to solve a murder, we'd have to ask ourselves what was the motivation?" Marybelle suggested.

"Greed, revenge or jealousy," Katherine agreed with Marybelle's earlier explanation.

We were quiet for a moment. It did not seem to be appropriate to discuss Mrs. Paulson's murder when her friends and neighbours were within hearing distance.

I smiled at everyone. "Having a good time?"

They smiled back and nodded and let the topic of the local murder subside.

"Claire," Robert said. "Want a turn with me?"

"I'd like that." It was odd how the manners drilled in my youth by a sixth-form games teacher stayed with me. There were correct ways of asking for a dance and correct ways of accepting it. I didn't know what the ladies would discuss while I was gone, but I hoped they would speak quietly if they discussed Mrs. Paulson's murder. They were considerate women. I think they would be discreet.

Robert was light on his feet for such a stocky man.

"Your ladies are interesting," he said.

"They are." I warmed to him. I liked these women and appreciated his acceptance of them.

"You must meet all kinds in the tour business." He guided me smoothly through the waltzing crowd of elegantly dressed dancers. I kept glimpsing bits of brocade, some lace, some knee-length pearl ropes. In the history of this country, even the history of this town, 1920 wasn't far in the past.

"Some of them are pretty difficult, but this crew is exceptional."

"I get clients like that too. Some of them are warm and wonderful, and some of them are real pains."

I smiled. "I suppose it keeps us from thinking *we* are exceptional and wonderful when there is always someone who doesn't like us."

"Yeah, and who complains about us." I expected vets often dealt with demanding owners. He'd have physical problems tied up in emotional stress. It could be messy.

Robert danced with Faith next. Everyone seemed to be enjoying the ball. Mary was dancing with Thomas. Barbara Manning was supervising the laying out on the supper table. Mrs. Taylor, Rose's mother who worked in the post office, was encased in gray taffeta. She was waltzing with a small, slight man—and she was leading. Her husband, maybe? I didn't see Rose here tonight.

At one point, Aurora and I were the only ones sitting out a dance. She looked a little sad.

"Everything okay, Aurora?"

She turned and gave me a beautiful smile. "Oh, yes. You're thinking of my son, John."

I nodded.

"He's a courageous man, my John. Most people give

up, you know, but he's still fighting. Now, with the new medications, he's winning." The smile increased in wattage.

I couldn't help but return it. "I'm glad." I squeezed her hand. She smiled.

"I can see you're genuine. Thank you." She looked around at the dancing crowd. "Don't go through life without friends, Claire, particularly women friends. When women are described as a gaggle of geese, it's more positive than negative. Geese help the weak one fly, protect it and nurture it until it's strong. That's what family does and that's what women friends do. Value them."

"Agatha Christie said women should stand together," I remembered.

"It was her Miss Marple who said, 'What I do realize is that women must stick together—one should, in an emergency, stand by one's own sex.' I think we need to do more than *stand* by our women friends. I think we need to spend the time and effort necessary to allow them to be happy and grow." She leaned over and patted my hand. "That's enough philosophizing for tonight."

I thought about my circle of friends. I hadn't put a high value on keeping friends. I'd moved so many times it was hard to make the effort. Perhaps, at this new point in my life, I should pay attention to relationships. Occasional loneliness is part of being human, or so I'd thought. Other than Deirdre, I didn't have a circle I could count on. I hadn't realized what I was missing. I envied Aurora and her crew, their love and support for each other. Maybe the American culture emphasized creating friendships more than the British. Or maybe,

I hadn't realized how much friendship could be important in my life.

Mark returned just before the supper announcement and asked me for another dance.

We waltzed again. I noticed that the band played more and more sedate tunes as the evening wore on. Most of the crowd was well over fifty. I expected the band knew their audience.

Mark held me close and I relaxed. That little frisson of excitement I'd felt earlier was still there. I wondered if we'd do anything about it. I wondered if he had a wife somewhere. I hoped he did not. I was fast becoming dreamy, and I had only had one glass of wine.

Mark danced me behind a potted palm and kissed me.

"Oh my, that's nice." I reached up and pulled him down for another. We were heading into our third very satisfying kiss and a vision of Mark and I slipping out the back door and spending the rest of the night at my house had just flitted through my fuzzy mind when I heard a voice directly behind me.

"I will *not* have that interloper in the library."

I froze.

"Now, Barbara. Claire is a nice woman, a hardworking woman, and she could use the library to help her business." That was Thomas speaking.

"We are not required to support her business."

"But we are required to be kind in this world, Barbara, and it would be a kindness to allow her to examine the artifact and a kindness to me to get some help in the cataloging."

Thomas' gentle voice was firm. I imagined teenagers were persuaded to do their homework and upset parents were pressured to give Charlie another chance. Barbara might even listen.

There was a brief silence. Mark and I didn't move. Our mood had definitely shifted.

"You must keep that woman out of the library, Thomas. You must move the library to my house. If you don't do those two things, I will demand a financial audit and check every piece of information you have on the club finances. You wouldn't like it."

Thomas was obviously thinking that over. Finally, he said. "You can do that if you like, Barbara. It will cost the club money to hire someone, but I would be happy to turn over everything to the person we hire. You will have to have a reason or the rest of the board won't go for the expenditure." Again, his voice was gentle. I wondered if he ever lost his temper. I couldn't envision it. I wondered why Barbara didn't want anyone in the library.

"I'll find one," Barbara said grimly, and they moved away.

I let my hands trail down Mark's arm, but otherwise stayed still.

"What do you think?" I was whispering.

"I think something's going on there."

"Maybe Thomas stole something?"

"Or Barbara thinks he did."

I thought about it. "Maybe what they need is not a financial audit, but an inventory audit. It might not show if a folio was missing, but it would show missing pages or gaps in the dates of letters."

"You think they might need an inventory to make sure everything they have recorded is still there? Is there anything valuable there?" Mark asked.

"Both Barbara and Thomas say there isn't anything valuable in this Agatha Christie collection, but
Thomas hasn't finished cataloging the collection, and
there might be something. I know she must have written letters to her sister. Maybe she even wrote about
those days she went missing. Many people believe she
orchestrated her disappearance. Evidence has come up
years after supporting that view. But some people don't
believe it. She said she had amnesia." I was thinking
furiously about what Thomas might have hidden and
getting more and more excited about the possibilities.

"So there might be something."

I shrugged. "It's a long shot. There might be nothing." I had a quick thought that if my costume made
me the real Georgiana Rannoch, infused me with her
intelligence and observation skills, I would solve this
mystery. I decided I'd do so if I could.

The band leader announced a break for supper. Mark
and I stepped out from behind the palm and walked
back to our table.

"Our table is first in line," Aurora said happily. "Did
you arrange that, Claire?"

I shook my head. "No, that's just plain luck."

Mark and I followed Aurora and the other women to
the buffet and picked out a substantial supper. No lobster, definitely chicken, but a nice selection of salads
and desserts. And wine. The women were happily into
their second or third glass.

"This has been a great trip, Claire. We were talking
about making it a two-week trip next time," Faith said.

"Could we go down to Cornwall and check out the
sites for Carola Dunn's Eleanor Trewynn series?" Aurora suggested.

"And Veronica Black's *Sister Joan* series?" Mary-belle said.

"And Janie Bolitho's Rose Trevelyn?" Katherine said.

"And then maybe up to Yorkshire?" Faith added.

Before they could start on the mystery writers from Yorkshire I agreed. "Love to. I need about a three-month lead time to set everything up."

"We might bring few more people. How many can you take?" Katherine was likely the organizer.

"I can take eight in the van. More than that and I need a bus and that limits the places we can go." I would prefer to keep my tours small.

"Eight is good," Katherine said. "Four was great."

I don't know if they are always this agreeable. Maybe it was the wine and the good food but perhaps the high-fashion costumes encouraged everyone to act with good manners. "Civil behaviour creates civil discourse" as my mother used to say. Everyone seemed determined to show their good side—except Barbara. But perhaps she didn't have a good side.

FOURTEEN

My INTREPID PARTYGOERS hung in until the hall closed at one in the morning. I drove them to their B & B and left Jack's van at the pub, dropping the keys as instructed through the mail slot. I walked home in my low heeled 1920s, classy shoes. They were cream-colored and the strap closed with a pearl button. I felt elegant striding along the pavement, my gown swishing around my calves, a wool scarf wrapped around me keeping out the cold. It had been a lovely evening in spite of its rocky start. My anger at the vandal had receded, and I thought of the ball with pleasure. The ladies had been happy. Mark had kissed me again before he had answered his cell phone and left the ball. I felt elegant, happy and desired.

Now, if the new van was parked in front of my house, all would be copacetic. It was. The van stood in its magnificence at the side of the street. The moonlight glinted off the shiny, silver bonnet. Lovely. The street was deserted. I expect everyone was home and in bed. A few willow leaves whispered as they stirred in the slight breeze. I knelt on the pavement, careful of my gown and felt around the front tire for the keys. There was nothing on the passenger side. If they hadn't left the keys, I was going to lose my temporary rosy view of the world and swear.

I walked around the van to the driver's side and again

arranged my gown so I wouldn't be kneeling on it and fished around for the keys. Eureka! There they were. My fingers closed on the fob.

"Miss Barclay?" a voice said behind me.

I jerked and hit my head on the wing.

"Mrs. Taylor." I hadn't heard her approach. I staggered to my feet and blinked. There she was, splendid in grey taffeta.

"Are you all right?" she asked and peered closely at me. "Too much to drink there, love?"

I rubbed my head. "No. No." I held up the keys. "The rental company left the replacement van and the keys behind the front tire." I had to give her some explanation for groveling on the ground.

"Oh, I see. I see. You didn't tear that lovely gown now, did you?"

"No." I brushed at my gorgeous green finery and examined the skirt. "No, I don't think so."

"Such beautiful gowns there tonight." She glanced down at her own.

"Yes, it was a great occasion. Yours is very appropriate as well—very 1920s."

"Well, thank you. It turned out quite nice."

I gave her more praise. "It did. Very elegant."

She smiled and waited until I joined her on the sidewalk.

"Mr. Taylor is staying behind to help clean up. I thought I'd walk home." She paused. "What happened to your other vehicle?"

"Someone slashed the tires."

"In Ashton-on-Tinch?" She was indignant. Lady Macbeth with her "What, in our house?" couldn't have produced more umbrage. "That neer-do-well boyfriend of Sarah Andrews! It must be him. I told her he was no good. One of the Wards from below the river. Getting above himself with those university courses. A lot of nonsense. Wards! That family was always a pestilence."

"Uh, Mrs. Taylor. I don't think it was Jay." She was unfair. I felt a fierce need to defend Jay. I didn't want her spreading a story about him and tried to think of a way to deflect her. I thought of James and sacrificed him. "It could have been a relative of mine who wanted money from me and wasn't happy when I wouldn't give it to him." I didn't like telling Mrs. Taylor my business, but it was better than having her spread lies about Jay and Sarah. I didn't name him, so I wasn't being unfair to him or slanderous.

She absorbed the information in silence for a moment then said, "I see. Relatives, hmmp." She nodded briskly as if storing that particular piece of information away in a safe place. I imagined she'd soon dump it in the gossip pool.

"Put ice on your head," she said and trotted off, taffeta rustling into the night. I did as she suggested and then went to bed.

I was up early and loaded my costume into its plastic storage cover and into the van along with Aurora's knitting and the five-pound note. Gulliver hopped into his crate, and we were off. As I drove away, I saw a lorry with a small digger on the flat deck pull into my driveway. Peter and the destruction crew. It would be a mess of dirt when I returned.

The ladies, predictably, were ready with their costumes in individual containers and their luggage by the door. I opened the rear door, and they loaded everything into the van. I left them to it while I handed

Carol Badger my credit card and thanked her for giving the women such a good time. She assured me she would be happy to accommodate more of my customers.

Then Aurora had to return to her room to look for a lost ring.

"She'll find it," Katherine said, "and it's faster to let her look on her own. If we try to help, she'll slow us down by talking."

I had built fifteen minutes into the schedule for a delayed start, so we would still be on time. Aurora was back with her ring in ten minutes and climbed into the van.

I reunited Aurora with her knitting and the ladies asked me to donate the five-pound note to a street person as they couldn't decide who owned it. They started talking as soon as we were underway and rehashed the highlights of the tour all the way to Heathrow and were busy trying to solve Mrs. Paulson's murder as we approached the departure gate.

"I think she must have been dealing drugs," Marybelle said. "She probably died of Fentanyl poisoning. Lots of that around. Sampling her own wares maybe. That stuff's deadly."

I felt a little guilty at not telling her Mark's latest information on yew poisoning but didn't think he'd want me to broadcast that piece of information.

"You need to take a good look at the one who benefits. Detectives always do that," Katherine said. "It's only logical."

The person who benefited was Mary and, through her, Thomas. I didn't like the thought.

"No. No. Maybe that Jay everyone is so down on slipped into her house and…."

And they were out the door.

In the flurry of goodbyes, no more was said about Mrs. Paulson's murder.

"You come back anytime," I said to them. I so enjoyed their company and seeing how they cared for each other.

"We will," they chorused and were gone through the revolving doors. I was smiling as I pulled into the rental agency. I traded the replacement van for a smaller hatch back. My next tour, the first for my own company, wasn't for a month. I would need to buy a van soon. I detoured to Guildford and returned the costumes. They had been perfect.

I left Heathrow and drove, not home, but to the museum in Wallingford. I hoped Mrs. Hancock would be available and the recalcitrant Louise at home so would not have to talk to her.

I stopped at Hurley just before Henley to let Gulliver prance along the river. The Thames is constrained by locks here and the grassy park alongside them was almost deserted. I still didn't trust him off leash, so he had to content himself with sedate exercise.

Because the roads were fairly clear, I made good time to Wallingford. I pulled up close to the museum entrance, powered down the back windows an inch or two, opened the roof vent and presented Gulliver with a chew toy. That should keep him happy while I was gone. In any case, he'd sleep. The temperature had cooled to about 15 C which was about 60 F, so he wouldn't get overheated. I poured some water from my thermos into a dish and left it with him.

Mrs. Hancock was in and so was Louise. This time

Louise simply sniffed before she knocked on Mrs. Hancock's door.

"Miss Barclay, so lovely to see you." She was as gracious as she had been previously. She peered behind me. "No tourists?"

"Not this time. I wondered if you had a moment to help me on some research? I can call back…"

"But you'd rather not?"

"True," I said.

"Come in. You're making my day better." She gestured to her desk where rows of index cards on long steel rods reposed in narrow oak drawers.

"I'm transferring records into our computer. Very boring."

She indicated the chair I should sit on and resumed her own. "What do you want to research?"

"Agatha Christie's missing eleven days."

"Aha! That fascinates everyone."

"I've read Cade's book, and he makes a good argument. If Agatha asked the jeweler in London to send her repaired ring to Mrs. Neele at Harrogate *before* she left on her escapade, she *planned* the jaunt. She didn't suddenly suffer from amnesia and wander up to North Yorkshire."

"Yes," Mrs. Hancock agreed. "She had money and didn't draw any from her bank, so it seems reasonable that her sister-in-law Nancy Watts was in on the planning and gave her money." She stood up quickly. "Follow me."

We walked briskly from her office, down the hall and into a large conference room. Filing cabinets lined the walls and a long table surrounded by chairs took up most of the room. A computer squatted in the centre of the table. It smelled like a library—a little musty with a hint of leather. It was warm as libraries always seemed to be, and I felt my shoulder muscles relax. It had been a busy few days with the American ladies.

"Sit down," she gestured at a padded leather chair. I put my steno notepad and electronic notebook on the table.

"Let's look. What do you know so far and what are you looking for?"

"I know the theories put forward by Andrew Norman on the possibility she suffered from a fugue state. His work was in 2006 so eighty years after the fact. He was supported by the speculation of two psychologists Pujol and Kopelman who thought she could have had amnesia of the post-traumatic variety. There is a lot of discussion in the literature on brain function and learned explanations of neuron activity in such a state. Then there's Andrew Wilson in 2017 who thought Agatha tried suicide when she abandoned her car close to the quarry and then was ashamed of her attempt and hid out. I'm most convinced by Cade's reasoning—that her escape was planned as a weekend shake-up for her wandering husband. According to Cade, she wanted to embarrass him and perhaps raise the possibility that he had murdered her. She hadn't expected the public search and world-wide concern and didn't know what to do about it so just hid out at Harrogate. It's all contradictory and intriguing." I had spoken quickly, because I was sure Mrs. Hancock knew all that.

"It is," Mrs. Hancock said. "and it is over ninety years ago that it occurred yet we are still taking about it. The London Main Library hosted a discussion just this year on 'The Eleven Missing Days: come and find out'."

"After all this time." It was amazing that one short period in a woman's life could fascinate us today. Of course, she was brilliant and gave a huge impetus to the mystery genre. Scholars could study her for years. I read *The Pale Horse* when I was twelve and I've been hooked on the genre every since. Partly, because the characters are intriguing and partly because there is usually humour and wit in the writing. Justice prevails and the world is orderly. I relax into the environment of the protagonist and, for the time I'm reading, I can trust the world is sane.

"Quite an enigma, our Agatha," Mrs. Hancock said. "What particular interest do you have?"

"I want to find any letters she might have written to her sister Madge or possibly Nancy Watts to plan this caper."

Mrs. Hancock nodded. "Interesting idea."

"Have you heard of any letters, Mrs. Hancock?"

"Carla," she said absently, "I'm Carla."

"I'm Claire."

She booted the computer. "I've wondered, but I haven't seen any."

I had another idea about letters. "I think she wouldn't have spent eleven days at Harrogate hydro without writing *someone*. People in her day wrote letters to each other all the time. She must have written some."

"That's reasonable," she nodded, still hitting keys on the computer. "How could we find them?"

I'd thought about that on the drive here. "Isn't there an antiquities market? I mean a place on line where people buy and sell such old letters—a kind of special category on ebay. I thought you might have access to those sites."

Carla stared at me for a moment. "You mean I could look on professional sites and special interest sits to see if anyone is selling such letters?"

"Could you?"

"Perhaps." She clicked he way through websites. I sat silently, waiting for her to connect with a source.

"UK. UK." Carla muttered to herself. "So many American historical artifacts, undocumented and without provenance. Disgraceful. Too difficult to sift through them to find a credible source." She clicked on. "I need a UK site. Ah, here we are." The computer hummed. Muted traffic noise drifted through the leaded windows.

She was quiet while she peered intently at the screen.

"I'll leave you the public sites to research, Claire. There are lots of them and someone might put out Christie's letters on those easily accessible sites. I'll look at the professional sites where I need to register as a librarian. Just a minute." She looked up and to the right, obviously searching for something in her mind, then clicked in some letters. "Password," she explained. "Hmm. Hmm."

I waited.

Finally, she heaved a sigh and straightened. "I don't see any sales pending on these sites, but I'm going to a conference next week, and I'll ask around and try to find a whiff of a sale which would tell us there were such letters. Sometimes, the sellers don't advertise them or even indicate they have such artifacts because they already know where they are going to sell them. They may even have an exclusive with this buyer that says they can't sell it to anyone else. It might be a private collector or even another museum."

"You'd think any seller would approach you as you have the Agatha Christie Museum."

"Sadly, our budget might not compete with a private collector. Agatha Christie is very popular. Many people collect her first editions and any articles they can find about her."

"Anything to do with the missing eleven days would be avidly pursued?"

"Absolutely, and by me if I could afford it." She looked up and smiled. "I'll ask around. It's the best I can do. Sorry."

I sat back. "Wouldn't it be exciting if we could find something?"

Her eyes lit and she grinned. "Oh, yes, I'd love the experience of discovering it and I'd be shaking with excitement when I first read such a letter. What if she admitted to planning to go to Harrogate? What if she admitted to involving her sister-in-law—all to make Archie sorry he was such a jerk?"

"What if?" I agreed. I know my voice rose. That discovery would be exhilarating.

She almost squealed.

I laughed. "It would be thrilling."

She sighed. "Yes, but it's unlikely there are such letters. If we did find them, I couldn't afford them."

I though about my fortune. "Well, I could probably add to your bid."

She looked at me, possibly revaluating her first impression of tour guide, modestly dressed, driving a rental van. These accoutrements did not scream money.

"You could?"

"I could."

"Well, I'll pursue this with fervor. I'll search the web and call if I find anything."

"If you find anything then I'll help you buy it. If I find it, I might offer it to my local mystery writers' club. Is that agreeable?" If I found letters in the mystery club's library, they would belong to the club and the club would have to make decision about selling them. They would probably stay in Thomas' library.

"I'd rather the letters were here."

"They might be safer here," I agreed, thinking of Barbara and her obvious need to hold the artifacts close.

Carla grinned. "Let's find them first."

We shook hands and promised each other to do our best. Even if we never found anything, the chase would be an adventure, and perhaps Carla might become a friend.

Gulliver was asleep when I returned. I shut all the windows and vents and drove out to Thatcham where I detoured only a few blocks from the Bath Road to let him out near the lake. The ducks tempted him, but I kept him on leash.

Carla had the drive of a scholar, the intensity of purpose that allowed scholars to focus on a question and look for answers. She'd do her best at the conference, and she might find someone was buying or selling Agatha Christie letters.

FIFTEEN

WHEN I ARRIVED HOME, Peter was supervising the operations of the small digger. A row of dirt rose like a dyke in front of the machine. Beside the dyke, lay a bush with a few orange rose blossoms almost defiant against the mess behind it. Peter must have ensured that the rose bush was excavated and set aside. I hoped he'd replant it. I waved at him. He nodded and turned back to the machine.

Rose was cleaning the house.

"Don't let that dog in the kitchen. I just washed the bloody floor," she said.

I took Gulliver up to my bedroom and let him arrange himself on my bed. I caught the phone on the second ring. It was Deirdre.

"How was the ball? I have to know but make it quick. I'm due in court in six minutes."

"The ball was a pleasure. The costumes were a hit and the ladies had a wonderful time."

"Did you?"

"Have a wonderful time?" I thought about the ball, the glitzy decorations, the music, the elegant costumes, the magical atmosphere. I thought about Mark. "Yes."

"Tell me."

"Mark kissed me," I blurted.

"Ohhh," she said slowly. "So?"

"Honestly, it's nothing. Probably the atmosphere or something. I really don't know him well."

She was quick to question me. "Does that matter?"

"Of course, it matters. I don't even know if he can sing."

There was silence, and I realized what an inane comment that was.

"I get it," Deirdre said. "Evans. He's Welsh, or his name is Welsh, and they sing, usually but…"

"It just one of the *many* things I don't know about him."

"Ah. I see. Relax, Claire. You'll learn. Take a moment. There's no rush." She sounded as if *she* was the older sister.

I let out a sigh. "Thanks, Deirdre. I know I'm making too much of this."

She laughed. "Beats nothing. Got to go." And she disconnected.

I shook my head. I *was* getting ahead of myself. One kiss does not make a relationship. I was not fifteen. I was being ridiculous. I finished my work and headed into the kitchen.

Rose was in full spate, cleaning and talking. "My mum said she saw you last night."

I nodded.

"She said someone ripped up your tires. And she wants you to know that the pizza delivery guy, the cousin of Suzanne who lodges in mum's house, saw a man take a knife to those tires. Mum talked to Suzanne this morning, and she told her about him."

I turned, giving Rose my full attention. "What did the delivery boy see?"

"He saw some guy rip up your tires, and the kid cell-taped him."

"He what?"

"The kid took a picture of him on his cell phone. A video like," Rose explained.

Aha!

"Does your mother know the boy's name?" I asked. Trust Mrs. Taylor to take her bit of information, cast it out into the sea of gossip and haul in a marlin.

Rose fished in her jeans pocket. "Right here. Anthony Chan."

I took the paper. "Tell your mother many thanks. I'll let the rental company know about this. They'll probably get in touch with Anthony."

Rose marched past me to the hall closet and hauled out the vacuum. I left her to go to my study and call Anthony. He agreed to send a copy of the video to the rental company and to me. I promised him twenty pounds for his efforts. He sent the video attached on my email. It was a little grainy, but the perpetrator was clear. James! Part of me was relieved there was no village vendetta against me and no unknown person trying to do me harm. But to learn that it was Paul's son? I was appalled with James and his behaviour. The rental company could deal with him. I'd let them know who was starring in the video.

Rose was dusting up a storm along the stair railing. "Bad doings in the town. Slashed tires. My mum's that upset. She says nothing good comes of foreigners coming here—excepting you of course. Dodgy, they are."

"Does she mean this," I glanced at the paper, "Anthony Chan?"

"No. No. Not Anthony. He was born here. Nice kid.

Others." She wafted her hand vaguely, as if to include vast populations. Mrs. Taylor, however helpful she'd been to me, sounded like a difficult woman.

Rose went on. "I'm here to tell you all is not sweetness and light in the town. No, it's not. That Barbara Manning who's so high and mighty her head should freeze, she's real mad at Thomas and Mary for keeping the club library in their house. Seems she wants it. Must give her some kind of snob points or something. I heard her tell her friend Mrs. Anderson on the phone when I was cleaning at her house that she isn't going to stand for it much longer." I assumed she meant Barbara was going to move the library or ask for an audit on the finances. Either of those might put pressure on Thomas.

The salient piece of information I got from this was, that if Rose got this information from overhearing a phone call, I should never have a phone conversation in Rose's hearing.

"The Greenwoods are going to take a holiday. Nice for them. They've got money though. Real money. They're travelling to Portugal this time, I think."

I can only take so much of Rose's prattle. I collected Gulliver and went for a walk, taking my cell phone.

Once past the noisy digger, I called the rental company and relayed Anthony's name and the fact that he had taken a video of the perpetrator. It would be better if they got the video from Anthony than from me. Anthony could attest to where and when he took it. I also gave them the identity of the person in the video, James. The company thanked me and said they would pass the information on to the private investigators they retained for fraud cases. Good. It was out of my hands now.

It was another beautiful, bright day and Gulliver and

I walked alongside the river, partly to get the exercise and partly to get away from the roar of the digger. It had been working near the street, so I expected it would soon depart, and Peter would get into the trench and cut out any offending roots left behind.

Gulliver satisfied his curiosity about the ducks feeding on the grass—they move when you chase them—and barked at a squirrel, although he hadn't a hope of catching it. I saw Robert's clinic and decided I'd pick up some dog treats for Gulliver. Deirdre said I should buy them from the vet's office and avoid the imported kind that can make dogs sick.

Sara was sitting at the reception desk.

"Hello," I said.

"Oh, Claire, hi. How was the ball?" She stopped what she was doing and waited for my report.

"I loved it. Did your dad enjoy it?"

"Yeah, he said those women you brought to the ball were fascinating." She frowned. "He doesn't get out enough."

I wasn't sure if that was an insult or an observation, that the women were fascinating because he met so few, or the ball was a rare outing for Robert.

I remembered Mrs. Taylor's condemnation of Sarah, and Peter's accusations of theft, but I couldn't believe them. It seemed to me there was a bit of jealousy involved here. Sarah was young, good looking and secure with a father's support and a choice of careers ahead of her. Both Peter and Mrs. Taylor had not had those advantages and had lived all their lives in Ashton-on-Tinch. They might think she was spoiled, and it was their duty to criticize her. Sarah had visited Mrs. Paulson on the day of her murder, but I didn't see Sarah as a killer, either. She seemed a friendly, well-balanced young woman. I doubt she'd care enough about Mrs. Paulson to kill her. Still, I wondered why she'd been there.

I asked her.

"Oh, yeah. The detective asked me that one. I'd cleaned for her a few times, and I wanted my money before I went to the uni. She always paid, but sometimes she was late, and I wasn't having that."

"I wish you'd arrived a little later, and we could have discovered the body together."

Sarah laughed. "I don't. For one thing, then I wouldn't have collected my wages and for another she wouldn't have invited me to tea. I'm not classy enough."

I pocketed the treats and left her. Sarah was not a likely murderer. She had no reason. Mrs. Paulson was no threat to such a confident young woman. I crossed her off my suspect list. At the rate I was going, no one would have enough motivation to have poisoned her.

I headed toward Thomas and Mary's house. I would bear in mind I wasn't omniscient and couldn't know if they were desperate for money and saw murder as a way of getting it or simply a nice older couple who had been friendly to me. In any case, they had no motive to murder me. Perhaps they would be home and allow me to have a look in the library. Their street gave me just as much pleasure today as it had when Katherine and I walked along it. The roses were fading fast but still colourful. I approached the front door this time. Thomas and Mary were home and willing to let me into the library.

"We can put your little dog in the kitchen with Gracie. She's an old and lazy beagle and could do with some stimulation." Mary reached for Gulliver's leash.

She looked much different today in her jeans and shirt than she had last night in her 1920s finery.

"Mary, I heard you were a friend of Mrs. Paulson's. I'm sorry," I said as I passed her the leash.

She took the leash, looked at me and paused for a moment.

"Oh, that's nice of you. I'd known her a long time. She was a friend of my mother's. When my mother died, I kept up the visiting. She was a habit."

"Not so much a friend, then?"

Mary snorted. "It was like trying to befriend a hedgehog."

"All prickles?"

"Yes, all prickles." She thought for a moment. "Still, I miss her. She was admirable in her way, involved, productive. She accomplished a lot. Yes, I'll miss her."

I thought Mary was genuine, and I was a little ashamed of prying.

"Thanks for keeping Gulliver occupied," I said. "I'll leave if he howls." I don't know why I keep expecting him to howl. The only time he did was when the fire sirens sounded. I suppose I don't know enough about dogs to predict his behavior.

Mary led Gulliver toward the kitchen. Thomas escorted me down the beautiful oak-paneled hall to the library. It was similarly oak-paneled, with tall, narrow windows and floor to ceiling books. What ever damage had been done by the fire wasn't obvious now, but there was a faint smell of smoke.

"This section is the mystery books section." We

walked over to an alcove where two filing cabinets stood at either end of four shelves of books.

"There are a lot of books here." I felt a little inadequate, and I know that was a simple thing to say. What did I expect in a library?

"Yes, and more papers and letters in the filing cabinets," he said.

I looked around me. "This is a beautiful room." Sunlight warmed the wood walls. Books in muted colours filled the shelves. It was a large room so easily held a few easy chairs, some occasional tables, a long library table with chairs around it all on a handsome, faded jewel-tone rugs—an elegant but comfortable room.

"We like it very much. It's temperature controlled. I am fortunate to be able to pander to my obsession with books."

We smiled at each other, united in our love of books.

"Now, what would you like to look at?"

"I'd like to see your catalog and then anything to do with Agatha Christie."

"Oh yes, Agatha. I haven't gotten around to cataloging what we have yet. I'm still on the *B*s I'm afraid. The *C*s are next."

He showed me a ledger, an old-fashioned, accounting book, with the titles of the books in elegant copperplate writing.

"Oh my." This was not what I expected. I suppose I thought the catalogue would be on a computer file.

He smiled as if reading my mind. "Isobel Paulson wanted me to put it on computer, and I recognize the validity of her request. I just haven't done much about it yet."

"Thomas," Mary called from the door. I hadn't heard

her walk down the hall and she startled me. "The restoration people are here. They want you to tell them what you think was damaged."

"Coming, my dear." He turned to me. "Please excuse me. Examine anything you like." He followed Mary to the back recesses of the house.

Examine anything you like? Good. I would. I turned to the filing cabinets. I thought that any letters, and it was letters I was interested in, would be filed somewhere in the cabinets. There was nothing under "Christie" and nothing under "Agatha." Would it be under her married name "Mallowan?" Yes! I pulled out a thick file of letters, magazine clippings and notes. With the file in my hands, I carefully checked the space where they had been sitting. No loose papers left there.

I brought the file to the library table and sat down. My heart was beating fast and my mouth was dry. Maybe, just maybe, there was something exciting here.

There were a couple of magazine reports of her disappearance in 1926, one of them dated 2003. All Christie scholars had worried that to death. A magazine article wasn't likely going to offer me anything. And then I saw it—a letter starting "Dear Madge."

My hands were shaking as I smoothed the paper. I bit my lip. This could be huge or it could be mundane. I took a deep breath and began to read. She was telling Madge about the progress of *The Seven Dials Mystery*. "I have so many characters running through this story I've had to make a list and consult it often."

I took a moment to remember the plot of *The Seven Dials Mystery*. There *were* a lot of characters: Ronny, Bill, Jimmie, Bundle, Lorraine and, of course, Superintendent Battle. She must have had quite a time remembering who did what and when.

She talked about Madge's health and the repairs on her house. It wasn't an earth-shattering letter, but it was charming, and it showed how much she cared for her sister. There was a second letter. I noticed the date was some five months later.

The letters hadn't been hard to find. I wondered why Thomas hadn't mentioned them. If he was only at the Bs, it would be a long time before he got to the Ms.

I heard him approaching the library door. He was talking to someone. I closed the file and turned it over so the title "Agatha Mallowan" was hidden.

Barbara Manning swept into the library. That woman demanded attention. She was energetic and even majestic. Her salt and pepper hair brushed back and up, gave her an impressive two or more inches.

"Claire Barclay. What are you doing here?" Her tone was so imperative I wanted to say, "Stealing the silver," but refrained.

"She's interested in the Mystery Club library and has graciously offered to help me with the cataloging," Thomas answered quickly.

"No one except members can examine the library and you," she glared at me, "are not a member."

"I am a paid member," I said, remembering how quickly Mary had taken my money. Then I was irritated with myself for being defensive.

"You haven't been accepted," Barbara snapped.

"I am the membership chair," Thomas said firmly, "and I will see that her membership is accepted. In the meantime," he said over Barbara's attempt to interrupt, "I will give her permission as a special guest."

I was astounded by Thomas's resolute stance. I suppose I thought a man so gentle and polite wouldn't be strong, but he was. It might have something to do with a career that forced him to face teenagers at the comprehensive school for many years. They would require firmness, even a resolute will.

"You can't do that." Barbara was like many women who should be running their own business, but because they didn't have that opportunity, ran the lives of everyone else.

"Indeed, I can. I am doing so. Now, I suggest, Barbara, that you come with me to my office and discuss what you came to see me about. We will leave Claire in peace to pursue her studies."

Short of wrestling with him, there wasn't much Barbara could do. What made me wildly curious was why did she care if I examined the material?

After they had both disappeared down the hall, I frantically searched through the file but didn't find any more letters than the two I had already seen. I snapped pictures with my cell phone even though I knew they wouldn't be clear. I read the letters quickly, took some notes and swore I'd come back soon. I didn't think Barbara would leave me in the library for long. She was obviously in a mood, and I wanted to be out of her line of fire until she calmed down. I was tempted to tear through all the files right now, but I needed to be systematic and I would likely be interrupted soon. Thomas had been gracious in allowing me to look at the artifacts and would probably give me access to the library again. I'd come back when I had time to search the files. What a discovery! I didn't dare share it with anyone.

Two letters from Agatha Christie with a five-month gap between them! Where were the missing letters?

I sat at my kitchen table the next morning still bubbling with excitement but trying to stay calm enough to enjoy my coffee. Gulliver had been out for a quick pee and back, eaten his breakfast and was staring at me. His communication was clear. It's walk time.

"Just wait, Gulliver. I want to think."

Letters were missing from Madge and Agatha's correspondence. They might not be *missing* from Thomas' library. They may never have been there and could be reposing in someone else's library, but the tenor of the first letter in particular showed this was on-going correspondence. Agatha had referred to her last letter, so I assumed she was in regular correspondence with her sister. The two letters were dated, *Thank you, Agatha*, five months apart in 1927. She asked Madge to check whether the servants' staircase had a landing, another proof that *Chimneys* and *The Seven Dials Mystery* were set at Abdney Hall, her sister's mansion. *The Seven Dials Mystery* was published in 1929. Allowing for writing, revising, editing and publishing it made sense that Agatha would be writing it in 1927 and asking her sister for collaborative details at that time. There was also one tiny reference to Agatha's friendship with a man. This was after her escape to Harrogate, but perhaps she mentioned it. She didn't marry Max until 1930.

I felt a chill up my arms. How exciting to find those missing letters. I put the coffee cup down with a bang. Gulliver cocked his head.

"I must tell Thomas about them. It's his library, after all, but not when Barbara is around." I would tell Thomas since it was his library, but I wouldn't tell Barbara even though the artifacts in the library belonged to her club. Ah well. I wasn't always logical.

"Imagine what might be in that correspondence," I challenged Gulliver. He rolled onto his back. No comments were forthcoming from him.

Agatha might have mentioned something about the lost ten days in 1926. Was she with a man? She was estranged from her husband. He was asking for a divorce. Everyone thought she was so distraught by his demand for release from the marriage that she succumbed to a fugue state and was temporarily amnesic about those days. Why shouldn't she have disappeared with a man and worked out her bitterness at her husband with someone else? That seemed more reasonable than temporary amnesia. A naughty ten days. That would be amazing. Unlikely too, but still worth pursuing.

"Oh, Gulliver. This is going to be exhilarating. I'll probably have to spend hours and hours reading through material to find more letters. What if there aren't any more? Does that mean someone stole them? Or they have never been there?"

I clipped on Gulliver's leash, grabbed a jacket and a scarf. The late September sun failed to warm. I stopped talking aloud to Gulliver, but I continued to think about those letters.

What might she had discussed with her sister? Poisons? Christie had been an apothecary's assistant during the First World War. She knew about poisons. "Give me a decent bottle of poison and I'll construct the perfect crime," she is supposed to have said. Maybe she set out ways to use the poison from yew in those letters? Yew poison featured in one of her novels. I think it was *Pocket Full of Rye*.

If the letters were missing, it didn't mean they had been stolen. I reminded myself. They may have been separated years ago and disappeared into the collections of others or into Lady Margaret (Madge) Watts' wastebasket. I imagined a maid picking up the contents of the wastebasket and dumping those precious letters into the fire. I consigned that maid to a lifetime of scrabbling in a dump looking for the letters before I reined in my imagination.

SIXTEEN

WHEN GULLIVER AND I returned from a quick scamper down to the river and back, a black mid-size car was parked in front of my house on the opposite side of the road. I looked at it intently. If James was determined to have another go at me, I was going to give him short shrift. The man was barmy.

It was Mark. He opened the driver's door and stood. "Hi," he said.

I smiled.

Gulliver tore the leash from my hand, dashed across the road and barreled into Mark's legs. That could have been a disaster if a car had been coming. I'd have to hold the leash more firmly.

"Want coffee?" I called and walked over to pick up the end of Gulliver's leash and hold it tight.

Mark squatted down, ruffled Gulliver's hair and fondled his ears. Gulliver wiggled in ecstasy.

"Sure. Do you have time?" He gave Gulliver a last pat and stood.

"My ladies have gone. I have a hiatus right now." I turned, and he followed me into the house. He settled onto a chair in the kitchen with Gulliver on his lap while I made another pot of coffee.

"You grind your own beans?" Mark seemed incredulous.

"I lived in Seattle," I sounded a little apologetic, so

firmed my voice. "They make the best coffee there and, when you've had the best, it's hard to settle."

Mark nodded. "Especially for some of that weak, milky stuff they serve you in some places."

The scent of coffee was almost as good as the taste. I poured us both a cup and then told Mark about my discovery at Thomas's library.

"Exciting," he said.

"Very," I agreed.

He was quiet for a moment. "You need to be careful, Claire. Just put your discoveries on hold for a while because Thomas isn't off my suspect list."

"Thomas?" I said in disbelief. Gentle, quiet Thomas? Still, Barbara had thought Thomas was hiding something, and Mark was suspicious of him. I should consider that rational. But Thomas wanted me to research in the library. He wouldn't encourage that if he had something to hide, would he? "Really? Thomas?"

"I realize he's not a strong suspect, but Mrs. Paulson had his name on her calendar. She had an appointment with him the day following her murder. Mary inherits, so Thomas stands to gain from her death. Mrs. P. was trying to move the mystery club books and artifacts from his library."

I liked Thomas. "She might have had an appointment with her dentist as well and you wouldn't suspect him of murder." I didn't want one of the nicer men of the world to be suspected of murder. And he thought he might be suspected of arson as well. He didn't need this aggravation.

"I know it's a tenuous clue, but just be careful and, maybe, stay away from there until we get this solved."

"Huh! Do you have any evidence that Thomas is in-

volved?" Now, I was suspicious of Thomas. He could
have removed any letters and stored them in another
place, his bedroom, his kitchen, anywhere. That way
he would be happy to have an inventory, because although the letters would appear to be missing, no one
could say they'd been in the file to start with. I wasn't
going to say that aloud.

"No. His fingerprints don't even match the ones we
found on the table in the gazebo or in the kitchen. So,
you're right, he's not a strong contender. I don't know
why Mrs. P. was trying to get the library relocated.
Maybe she was just bloody-minded."

"Barbara also is trying to get the library into her
house," I said.

"Yes. Strange that. Why would they want to move
the library? Thomas's place is perfect."

"Yes, but Thomas gets to see all the scholars who
come, and Thomas gets to have the prestige that goes
with the artifacts. I bet both of those women wanted
to be the biggest hen in the hen house." Egos grab for
satisfaction in some unusual ways as I have found out
from my work running tours.

He regarded me for a moment. I could almost see
the wheels in his head turning while he contemplated
my opinion. "Could be. I need evidence. I wish I could
take everyone's fingerprints, but I have to have probable cause. I have clear prints on the gazebo table and
on a kitchen cupboard that don't match the deceased.
I'd love to match those. I have Thomas' prints because
his name was in the appointment book and that was sufficient reason. I can't go around asking everyone Mrs.
Paulson knew for their fingerprints."

"Constrained by law?" I took a long sip of delectable coffee and watched him.

"That's right. I need yours, though." A frown traced a faint line on his forehead.

"What? My fingerprints? Why?" I put my cup down with a bang and slopped coffee on the table. I jumped up and grabbed a dish cloth and wiped up the mess.

"You were there," he said, calmly drinking his coffee. "I have probable cause. Come by the station tomorrow if you can and the tech will take them."

I said nothing. I had my back to him as I rinsed out the cloth and hung it on the tap. The silence must have conveyed my disapproval.

"Does it bother you?"

"It does a little," I said as I returned to my seat and my coffee, "as if I was a criminal. I know. I know," I said as he started to speak. "It's just for elimination. My fingerprints will be on the floor."

"Did you touch the table?"

I thought back to my discovery of Mrs. Paulson's body. The light had shone on the tea set on the table, but I hadn't touched it. "No," I said.

"Good. Nasty business, poison. You should stay away from those mystery club people until we get this cleared up."

I objected. "I'm not going to avoid the library. Honestly, Mark. This could be the most exciting discovery about Agatha Christie in ninety years. Where was she during her stay at Harrogate? That's what everyone wants to know. Maybe I'll find a letter that tells me. She developed a whole new genre. I love her writing!"

"It's better to just stay away from there," he advised.

I returned to my enjoyment of the coffee. "Mark, you

are asking me to stay away from the library? I wouldn't be in danger there. The books aren't going to hurt me. Libraries always feel safe. There might be more letters from Christie there. Her letters are so important. Thousands will want to read them. Definitely, *I* want to read them."

He considered me for a moment, perhaps recognizing the futility of giving directions without any power of enforcing them. "Then be careful."

I nodded. "That I can do."

Odd. That little argument with Mark felt comfortable. It sharpened my wits for a few moments and then I relaxed back into comfort. It was good to be able to argue and not have it be about who would win an argument which had happened in my past relationships with men.

"Did you find Thomas' fingerprints on the table in the gazebo or the kitchen?"

Mark shook his head. "No. He might have worn gloves."

I refused to believe Thomas had anything to do with Mrs. Paulson's murder.

Mark drained the last of his coffee, rose and poured himself more.

"That was a great 1920s ball. No emergencies until late, good music and a new beginning." He toasted me with his coffee cup.

"Perhaps," I said.

"Cautious, are you?"

"I am at times."

"Okay. Not a bad stance to take. You need a little information about me, I think." He looked out the window at the garden then turned back to me. "I was married for ten years, and I've been divorced for twelve. No children. No present entanglements. What about you?"

That was succinct. I could reciprocate. "Pretty much the same. I had a ten-year relationship and parted about ten years ago. No children. No present entanglements."

I hadn't asked for any involvement with Mark. I was sure I hadn't sent out any messages that Deirdre called "invitational vibes". Mark was simply happening to me. Part of me wanted to run. Part of me was fascinated. He was intelligent, had a sense of humor and liked my dog. Tick, tick, tick on the plus side. I hadn't been looking for a romance. I was getting used to my life here in England again. I was starting my own business. I needed to pull back here. I couldn't say all I was thinking. Then I met his eyes, those patient waiting eyes. It was time for honesty.

"Uh, Mark, I'm not looking for romance. I think it's a bit of a minefield, and I am reluctant to start anything."

"Okay." He stood.

I felt a sudden deflation. That was it? No more discussion? That's all it took? He was leaving. I stood.

Not leaving. He reached over and pulled me close. "How about we start slowly?" Then he kissed me. The tingle started low and built. I hadn't forgotten how to kiss a man. He was pretty much an expert.

"You'd think we wouldn't have these feelings at our age." I sighed—with contentment, I must say.

"Still seem to be there."

I drew back a little in his arms and smiled. He did have the deepest brown eyes.

I was a little bemused as I watched him get into his car and pull away from the curb.

I put the coffee cups in the sink, shook myself and

headed to my office. I caught up on my correspondence, worked out the schedule for my tour next month and made up a list of accommodation sites to call and make sure all were still in place. I needed to get to the bank and ensure my savings and personal accounts were separate from my business accounts and which of my two VISA plans was the most advantageous, so I could collect travel points and get discounts on hotels and airplane tickets.

I made my supper—breast of chicken, squash, potatoes and string beans. The house did not have a dining room, but I didn't expect I'd ever use one. The kitchen was large and contained a small table by the window where I ate my meals and a bigger table that could open up to seat eight at the end of the room. It was all I needed.

Gulliver and I took a short walk up to the church hall and visited the cemetery. Gulliver's mandatory twice a day walks were going to ensure I got to know my new town. Headstones hold history. "Sacred to the memory of Mary Smith, aged 23 yrs and her daughter Ruth Smith, aged 2 days July 2, 1821". No question, childbirth was dangerous then. I speculated which of the Smiths buried here were relatives of poor Mary "aged 23 yrs". Was Harold Smith, "b June 1820 d August 1880", her son? Did he grow up without a mother? Did he acquire a step-mother?

The sun was setting when we returned home, and Gulliver found a soft spot on the sofa beside me while I watched the news and cursed the government. I read for an hour, and then we headed for bed.

I had been aware of cars arriving on my street and peered out once to see people on the Stonning's walkway. They were having a party. They definitely were having a party. It was fairly quiet when I went to bed about eleven, but I awoke to loud music at two. The wall in my bedroom, our common wall, shook a little. Gulliver raised his head and looked his inquiry.

"Just a party, Gulliver, but one that probably won't quit soon. I might as well get up. I won't be able to sleep through it."

I liked a glass of wine or a cup of cocoa when I woke at night. I slipped on my dressing gown, tucked my feet into slippers and prepared to philosophically endure the neighbours. Gulliver accompanied me to the kitchen and then decided he had to go out into the garden to pee.

I opened the door and stood there, waiting for him. The music was raucous, crashing over the high wall and resonating in my garden. Conversations were taking place at shouting volume. I heard snatches of conversations. "I told him what he could do with his damn job!"

"She thinks she's got it all. Bitch." There seemed to be a lot of animosity over the fence. The party had spilled into the back yard, and I could see a red glow. They probably had heat lamps in the garden. Nice for the partygoers, but it encouraged people to stay outside and was hard on the neighbourhood.

A voice quite close to the fence said, "That nosy bitch, Paulson, complained to the police about us last time. She won't be complaining anymore."

I stood there stunned. Who was that? I listened.

"Hey, Patrick. It's your own fault for living in this backwater. They like it quiet here."

"She's got it quiet now." Then the voices receded as they wandered back to the house.

Patrick. Patrick Stonning. My neighbour.

I didn't call out to Gulliver, just snapped my fingers, I didn't want anyone next door to know I was listening, and Gulliver, attentive dog that he is, trotted back to the kitchen. I shut the door softly.

I sat up in bed sipping my drink and worrying about what I'd heard. Should I tell Mark about it? Was I living next door to a murderer? When would Patrick Stonning have had the opportunity to kill Mrs. Paulson? Was he just happy she wasn't going to complain about his partying? Even with the wine, I wasn't going back to sleep any time soon. I slipped on my woolly robe and slippers, took my wine with me and headed for my office. I might as well do some research on Agatha Christie while I was awake and while the party was in full swing.

There were hundreds of entries for Agatha Christie. I read only the ones that talked about her missing days, but there was a score of those. Her contemporary journalists seemed to have been very hard on her, talking about the way she had wasted everyone's concern and effort and should be charged for the police time. There seemed to be several belief camps—those who thought she definitely had amnesia and those who thought she was orchestrating a publicity stunt. I didn't believe that story. She hadn't liked the limelight so I don't think she would have staged this for publicity. She was more likely to be motivated to upset Archie, the straying husband. It did result in more book sales, though. If she'd planned it for publicity, it would have been brilliant. There was one article that said her publishers knew where she was. They may have capitalized on her pique.

I moved my search over to Google Scholar and was immersed in the scientific explanation of the fugue state when the computer died, and all the lights in the house went dark.

I raised my head and looked around. While I had been engrossed in studying, the wind had risen. I could hear it now. It was so dark I couldn't see a thing, but I could hear. The trees near the house scraped the windows. A whoosh of wind hit the window. Something rattled. It was eerie. Gulliver crept onto my feet and huddled there.

Did I have any candles? There were some in my bathroom near the tub. I felt my way along the wall to the door, along the hall to the stairs and then held onto the bannister to guide me up to my bathroom. Gulliver followed me like a ghost.

A crash from behind the house stopped me momentarily. I suppressed flashbacks from horror movies I'd seen. No zombies. No supernatural demons. It must have been the trash can. No doubt a wind this strong could toss the cans around. There would be a mess in the morning. I felt for the candle and the matches I kept alongside it. Finally, I had some light.

Gulliver whimpered.

"It's just a storm," I told him, partly to reassure myself. I'd not yet weathered a storm in this house. I returned to the lower floor and checked all the doors to make sure they were secure. I did the same to the windows. Everything was tight. I left the candle on the kitchen table and moved to the front window. A little light came from a street lamp a few houses away. The wind whipped the willow fronds hanging from the trees along the street like dancing strings, rolling up and then tangling as if they were alive—crazy acolytes dancing to the wind god. Then the rain came, torrents of it, slashing at the windows, pounding on the roof. Through the sheets of rain, I saw figures, most of them holding flashlights, stagger down the Stonning's walk. The party was over.

I was glad I couldn't hear what they were shouting at each other. It was probably profane. I watched for some time as the partygoers found their vehicles, piled in, turned on their headlights and drove away. The headlights illuminated the street and the trees along it. The rain on the pale-yellow willow fronds glittered. The wind was still tossing them through the air, so the spectacle seemed to be a magical display of light and movement. It amazed me that the leaves weren't stripped from the trees. The roses would not fare as well. I doubted there would be one left with petals.

I thought about Mrs. Paulson. She'd drifted away like the rose petals, gone in a moment. No resurgence for her next spring. Does that mean I should gather rosebuds while I may? I left that metaphor as too difficult to contemplate.

The dark power of nature, shook me a little. My house seemed solid, but it was just a house. It couldn't protect me from everything. I was about to leave the window when I thought about the trench the digger had created in my front garden. Would it fill up with water? Would it run back into the house?

I dashed into the kitchen and grabbed the candle. There was no basement beneath my house, but there was a space about three feet deep where the plumbing pipes ran below the floor. I stored a few boxes there. I searched through the kitchen drawer and found a flashlight with batteries. I returned the candle to the table and, gripping the flashlight, opened the door of the cleaning closet, moved the vacuum cleaner and pulled up the trap door. I removed it and propped it against the stairs. Then I took the flashlight in one hand, braced myself against the floor with the other and stuck the flashlight and my head into the space.

Gulliver whined. He might have thought I was disappearing into a hole, head first.

"It's okay, Gulliver. No problem," I called back to him. He stopped whining.

There wasn't a problem. A couple of boxes. An oversized suitcase. No water.

I replaced the cover, put the vacuum back and shut the closet door. I'd check later, but it looked as though I wasn't going to get flooded.

Owning a home created worries. A flood would be a dreadful crisis to deal with. I wouldn't even know how to begin. With Peter, I expected. Then it would take a renovation company and a great deal of money. No wonder I'd put off home ownership until my forties. It wasn't just buying the house that took time and money, it was maintaining it. *Oh, relax, Claire. You're borrowing trouble.* There was no water in the crawl space. I was fine. One thing that worrying about the house did for me was drive any fanciful terrors from my mind. The practical present was enough to deal with.

I poured another glass of wine and returned to the front window to watch the rain decimate my garden. When the wind died, I headed for bed.

"That's enough disruption, Gulliver. Let's allow the world to get on without us for a while."

I wasn't responsible for storms, floods or other acts of nature. I might as well forget them. I'd limit my worries to what came up day to day: Agatha Christie's missing letters and Mrs. Paulson's murder. I had to also figure out what I would tell Mark. That was quite enough.

SEVENTEEN

ON SUNDAY MORNING, the weather eased. No rain, just low-hanging clouds and the threat of drizzle. I let Gulliver into the garden, but he was back quickly.

"You are a fair-weather dog, my Gulliver," I said as I petted him. "You'll have to get over that."

I checked the crawl space. There was no water. I'd check the trench and the front of the house after breakfast. Sunday breakfast was a leisurely cup of coffee and scrambled eggs. The grey light of the overcast morning fought with my cheerful kitchen and lost. Depression could stay outside. Inside, it was warm and cozy. I started a ritual of a relaxed Sunday morning breakfast over ten years ago and I enjoyed it. Lovely. No Peter. No noise. I swallowed the last of the coffee, surely the nectar of gods, and got ready for Gulliver's walk. Gulliver and I paused at the trench and peered in. There was water, but not as much as I had anticipated. With luck, it would drain away without causing problems. I'd promised to meet Robert at his clinic this morning at ten for a hike with the dogs into the countryside, rain or no rain. I'd packed a small thermos of coffee and another of water in case we didn't find a stream for Gulliver. An apple, a protein bar and a bar of chocolate were all I needed. This wasn't the wilds of the Pacific Northwest. Here, there was likely a tea shop nearby. I tucked a ten-pound note into my rucksack in case we found one.

But Robert was not standing and waiting for me at the clinic. Sarah was.

"Dad's got an emergency out on Clayton's farm. Something about a stuck calf. You wouldn't think there would be many calves born this late. Must have been a mistake of some kind. Or maybe a dairy cow." She was accompanied by four dogs that milled around her.

"The logic of all that escapes me," I said as we allowed Gulliver and the four dogs to get acquainted. She had Muggs and Jetty off leash and two Golden Retrievers on leash.

"This is Sally and Sparkle." She introduced me to the dogs.

"Sparkle?" I questioned the name.

"So help me, the names get worse. People are so cruel sometimes. They think it's cute to name their dog stupid names, and then the poor dogs are stuck with them. A six-year-old girl can say 'No one will call me Priscilla ever again. My name is Rilla.' That's what everyone will call her. But a dog can't do that. Ever meet a dog called Sir Lancelot?"

I shook my head.

"Or Princess Patricia? Or Rambo? That was a dachshund. Or Fluffy? That was an Alsatian. You'd think the owners would be embarrassed to name a dog that way. But no, they think it's clever to slap a cutesy name on the dog. Sorry, Sparkle." She petted the larger of the Goldens.

"Are they patients? Is something wrong with them?" They looked healthy to me.

"Not these. They are the dogs of some friends of Dad's who are on holiday. We board dogs once in a while. It's not good for some dogs to be in a vet clinic, but Sally and Sparkle are used to coming here and aren't upset by all the noise and activity. They're Goldens. Not much upsets them." She constantly petted the dogs.

They were certainly beautiful with a calm air as if they'd been sent from some celestial realm to keep an eye on us. We collected the Labs who came at Sarah's whistle and headed for the river walk. In a few minutes, we were out of the village and into the countryside. The air was full of moisture, but it was not raining. Sally had an oiled slicker with a wool scarf around her neck. She had sturdy hiking boots, probably waterproof. I wore an L.L. Bean rain jacket and boots. I wasn't sure if they were waterproof. I hoped so. I hated being wet.

"How did you make out in the storm?" I asked her.

"Oh, we were all right. Dad's place has good drainage. We get those sudden storms, more in the spring than in the fall, but we can get them all year. We blame Newfoundland for them."

"Newfoundland?"

"You know, in Canada. We always say Canada sends us bad weather, and Portugal sends us sunshine."

"Good to have someone to blame and good to have the storm over with wherever it came from."

I took a deep breath. Even on a dark day with lowering clouds, it was wonderful to be walking in the countryside. I smelled juniper berries and wood smoke—someone had a fire somewhere. The trail followed the rise of the land, and we hiked easily along a two-tire rutted road. Sarah let the Goldens off leash, and they ran with Muggs and Jetty—first ahead of us and then behind—but usually on the trail. I was not yet sure of Gulliver's ability to respond to my "Come" command so kept him on leash.

"There's a meadow up ahead," Sarah said. "You can let Gulliver off there, because you will be able to see him and catch him before he heads for the woods."

The meadow was perfect for dogs as hedgerows encased it. I unsnapped Gulliver's leash, and he shot like an arrow after the bigger dogs. His speed didn't last. He stopped after about twenty meters, hopelessly outclassed, like an eight-year-old boy on a professional rugby field. The other dogs came back and played with him, cavorting around him before tearing off again. He bounced after Jetty, ears flapping and feet splayed, almost galloping.

Sarah and I perched on a low stone wall to watch them but not before Sarah banged on the wall a few times and waited.

I remembered, then, from my childhood. Snakes. They liked walls. We have smooth snakes here, the brown non-venomous kind. Only adders are venomous, and they don't usually live in this part of the country. I didn't want to share my seat with a snake whatever kind it was. I'm well aware that snakes are not inherently evil, that prejudice and social conditioning have persuaded me they are repulsive. I can accept that intellectually. Emotionally, I react with instinctive horror when I see one. I'd probably scream. None appeared.

"Tell me, Sarah," I said as I settled on the wall, "why is it unusual to have calves at this time of year? You told me your dad had to attend a calving, and it was unusual."

Sarah brushed some moisture from her coat as she answered me. "Farmers usually breed so the calves are born in the spring. That way the mothers get good grass and can produce lots of milk."

"That's logical. And dairy cows?"

"We have dairy herds in Hampshire, but not many nearby. Dairy cows are bred all year because the farmers want to have milk all year. You have to breed cows to get them to produce milk."

"Again," I said. "Logical. Thanks."

"No problem."

She stood and called Muggs and Jetty. All the dogs came with the obedience duo. We patted them and gave each dog a treat.

"Reinforces good behavior," Sarah said.

"Are you going to be a dog trainer or write about dogs?" I asked her.

"No," she glanced at me. "I'm going to be a physician."

"Oh," I said nonplussed. Her father certainly didn't have any idea of her ambitions. He thought she wanted to be a writer. I had seriously misread her, and she realized it. No point in apologizing. It would be too complicated and embarrassing.

"What kind?"

"First a family practitioner and then a specialist in endocrine problems." She said it calmly as if she was committing herself to a two-week course in basket-weaving.

"I have no idea what that entails except it sounds like years of work and dedication. Good for you."

She smiled. "I haven't told Dad yet, so don't you tell him. I'll need his support, and I have my own strategies for getting it. I expect he'll be so relieved that I'm not going to live in an attic and get tattoos that he'll help with the living expenses."

"I see. No, I won't tell him. In any case, we aren't on those kinds of terms."

"I didn't think so."

We were silent for a moment. This conversation was oddly intimate.

"What about Jay? You have a relationship with him. Where's it going? I mean in terms of your ambitions, wouldn't involvement with Jay hold you back?"

"We'll manage it. He's going to be a surgeon. The biggest problem with surgeons is their ego. If Jay starts getting that ego inflation, things might change."

Jay? A surgeon? Mrs. Taylor was going to be surprised. Again, I'd underestimated someone. This time Jay. I felt as if I had been walking on a firm dock and now the planks were gone. I had no idea there was so much ambition in a couple who appeared to be merely marking time in life.

"Uh, shouldn't you be in university right now?"

"Monday," Sarah said. "This is my last walk with the dogs. I'm glad I got the chance. I miss them when I'm studying, but I don't have time for them at the uni."

I wondered at her vaulting ambition. She seemed a determined young woman. She'd a good chance to accomplish all she set out to do. Life offered young women so much more now than it had when I was her age. My ambition had been to get away from home and become independent. I'd thought that as long as I could be on my own, making my own decisions, I could control what happened to me. I wouldn't have to depend on unreliable parents who did not keep their promises. Home meant responsibilities, work, worry and a kind of helplessness. After Mom married Paul, I wanted to visit home but not live there. I had accomplished independence and I was now making a home for myself which was something new for me. I hadn't had Sarah's long-term vision. Still didn't, I expect.

We walked to the end of the road where a gate barred any further vehicle traffic. A smaller gate at the side allowed walkers to continue. We found the trail and walked up the hill to the lookout point. From here, the rolling downs of Hampshire stretched in front of us. Even on this grey day the scenery was idyllic. The light green of the pastures with the occasional yellow crop contrasted with the deep green of the hedgerows, scoring the land into parcels. It was wonderful to be home again. The harsh call of a flock of rooks rose from a copse nearby. They always sound as if they're quarreling.

We poured water for the dogs who lapped it up then settled on the grass around us. Jetty stretched out her black body as close to the cool earth as she could manage, her red tongue accenting what I'm sure was a grin. Muggs was all bright eyes and red tongue as his chocolate coat almost disappeared into the grass and earth. The two Goldens sat, heads up, staring into the distance like a pair of Chinese dragons guarding a temple, dignified and almost immobile. Gulliver with his black and brown markings looked like a particularly colorful mop. His hair was going to need a thorough brushing when we got home.

Sarah and I sat on a wooden bench and extracted our lunch from our bags. I sipped my coffee and Sarah her tea as we observed the clouds scudding across the hills miles away from us. The mist settled on our jackets. I had a hat with a brim that I had bought in Seattle, the centre of practical rain gear, and I pulled it out and fixed it firmly on my head. Let it rain. Sarah pulled out a Tilley hat, and we headed home.

We didn't talk much because the rain had begun in earnest, and both Sarah and I were focused on getting home quickly. I stopped at the trench in my front garden. Even with this new rain, the water had dissipated. Good.

Once Gulliver and I were safely inside my house, I toweled him dry and brushed his hair to ensure it didn't form mats. Then I ran a bath for myself and soaked away the chill of the walk.

It was about three when the doorbell jarred me from my doze on the sofa. I shoved Gulliver off my lap where he'd been enjoying a sound sleep and blinked myself awake on the way to the front door.

A well-dressed, almost dapper man of about fifty stood on my steps. Gulliver leaned against my legs but didn't bark.

The man thrust out his hand. "Patrick Stonning, next door."

"Oh hello, Patrick." I shook his hand. "Come in. It's nice to meet you."

He took two steps into the foyer, but no further.

"I should have come over earlier. My wife, Rita, she said we should come over and introduce ourselves and make nice with the neighbours and all that, but we never did and so now I've come because I think you had a listen to a bunch of crap last night, and I'm sorry it was so loud."

"Oh." I processed that speech given at high speed and without a breath.

"Patrick, do you have time for coffee?"

"No. No coffee. No tea. No nothing. Thanks all the

same. We're heading back to London. Both working, you know. We have to be there in the morning. Bright eyed and all that so we're off. Just…sorry."

I put my hand on his arm to stop his nervous prattling.

"It's okay, Patrick. I'm okay with a little noise once in a while. You can have your parties. It's okay."

He stared at me. I dropped my hand. There was a brief silence. "You mean that, don't you?"

I nodded.

"That's cool. That's really cool. Thanks."

"Not too often. But occasionally is fine."

He backed out my front door and gave me a salute. "Okay. We're good. Thanks. See you 'round."

That was Mr. Patrick Stonning. I peeked out the front window to see a woman of about my age, a little shorter, very slim with long blonde hair and wearing leggings and a tunic top with a down vest over it. That was probably his wife, Rita. I couldn't see myself having chatty neighbourhood conversations with her, she looked fashionable, in a slightly Bohemian way. But, as Sarah had reminded me this morning, you can't always know from first impression what people are like. I wondered if she lived in that same breathless, agitated state as her husband.

Monday was not one of Rose's days with me, so I breakfasted in blessed silence with only Gulliver for company. Outside, Peter was back. This time without the digger. He had eased himself down into the trench about half-way from the house. I expected the problems with the roots in the drains started there. He wasn't noisy. He didn't even swear, just used the power saw periodically, cutting out the roots. Other than that, I heard only the clinks and thuds of a shovel. I left him alone.

I took a second cup of coffee with me to my study and was looking at the schedule for my next tour when that annoying doorbell jolted me into awareness. This time Gulliver barked.

I padded down the hall in my stocking feet and opened the door to Mark.

He looked me up and down and smiled. "A little different from your outfit at the ball."

I surveyed my jeans, T-shirt and ubiquitous hoodie that I was in the habit of wearing and shrugged. "This is the real me."

He turned to look at Peter.

Peter stopped with a shovelful of dirt in his hands and glowered at Mark.

"What's going on?" Mark asked.

"Drains."

"Oh," he said with complete understanding. I imagined drains were a problem all over the country. "Can I come in?"

"Sure. Want coffee?"

"Love some."

He followed me into the foyer and shut the door. As I turned toward the kitchen he reached out and pivoted me into his arms as if we were dancing.

"Hi," he said. And those warm brown eyes lit.

"Good morning," I said and kissed him.

He responded and drew back. "Nice," he said.

"Hmm," I said. Not capable of much else at that moment.

He followed me into the kitchen and sat at the table while I ground the beans and made fresh coffee.

"Want a bagel?"

"If you have some."

I pulled a couple from the freezer and put them in the toaster oven. They'd be ready when the coffee was.

Mark stretched out his legs and leaned back in the chair. "I've just been to the Greenwoods."

"Yes?"

"Thomas has been very sick."

I had a sudden sense of sadness. Thomas is one of the gentle men of the world. We need more of them. We don't need them sick.

"I'm sorry, but you're not a doctor. Why did you go?"

"Because his doctor thinks he was poisoned. Or at least he is not satisfied with the diagnosis and, I'd say, because of Mrs. Paulson, the doctor is over scrupulous and cautious."

"Was Thomas poisoned?"

"I don't know. Someone could have doped him. He could have taken something himself deliberately or he could just have picked up something accidentally. No way of knowing."

I attended to the coffee, brought the bagels, butter and jam to the table and fetched a couple of napkins.

"How is Thomas?"

"Getting better." Mark reached for a bagel.

"Good." I pondered on this news for a moment. "Someone could be trying to kill Thomas."

"That occurred to me." He sounded wry.

"I'm thinking aloud here not trying to teach you how to detect."

"Go ahead. I'm at the stage where I'm speculating and imagining almost any crazy motive." He yawned.

"We should have my American ladies here."

Mark grinned. "They had some wild ideas about Mrs. Paulson's murder, but I'd listen to them right now. If you can think of anything, go for it."

I tried to think of some kind of motivation. "If we postulate someone is trying to kill Thomas in the suspicious fire and then this illness, what does Thomas know? As far as that goes, what did Mrs. Paulson know that is a threat to the murderer? Does Thomas know he knows something?" That sounded vague when I said it aloud.

Mark didn't have trouble following me. "Doesn't seem to."

"Maybe Mrs. Paulson *did* realize that 'something' and maybe she was trying to blackmail the murderer with the knowledge. Maybe the murderer thinks Thomas is going to do the same to him?" I was starting to sound like Aurora.

"Or her."

"Most murderers are men." Almost all of them.

"Maybe, but I'm an equal opportunity detective."

That stopped me for a moment. "Okay, I agree. It might be a woman. I guess the question is: Who is so fearful of what Thomas knows he or she is trying to kill him?"

Mark licked the jam from his fingers. Why is that endearing? Thousands of people lick the jam from their fingers. It didn't make Mark special. I sighed. I was going to have to *think* about him because I was definitely *feeling* too much.

Mark continued. "We could be over-reacting, thinking Thomas is the subject of a murder attempt when he was simply ill from something he ate at the ball. A lot of the food was prepared in people's homes. That makes for a less stringent control of bacteria than you'd get in a regulated kitchen. Still, most pot-lucks and community meals are healthy enough. People are used to protecting themselves from bacteria and have high standards. Once in a while, though, we'll get an outbreak from a public gathering."

"Perhaps this isn't a murder attempt?"

"Perhaps it isn't. If someone else gets sick, it might have been the food at the ball."

I gave a thought to my ladies who were no doubt home now. I hoped they were well.

"But your instincts tell you it is," I persisted.

He nodded. "No evidence, mind. I might be just grasping at straws because I'm frustrated by lack of development on the Paulson case."

"Since you don't have any evidence, maybe you should trust your instincts?"

"That wouldn't go far with my Superintendent."

I understood. "He has to have logic and evidence. Yes, of course." Anything else would become prejudice and conviction by innuendo and bias.

"She," Mark corrected. "That's right."

I absorbed the fact that his Superintendent was a woman. I'd ask about her some time.

I told him what I had overheard from Patrick Stonning's place last night.

"Hmm. Not much there but I'll interview him."

"More and more interviews and sifting through hearsay and real evidence. And, meanwhile, you collect fingerprints, study the toxicology report and… Did you get a toxicology report on Thomas?"

"There is not enough reason for the department to spend the money. So, no."

"How very annoying." It would frustrate me if I was trying to figure out if a suspect had been poisoned and couldn't get the evidence I needed.

He nodded. "You have no idea how annoying. If I had an unlimited budget and no constraints on how I gathered evidence, I'd solve crimes every day."

"Of course you would," I said, I must admit, dryly.

He laughed. "But I do have to answer to the law, to my Superintendent and to the budget department of the Hampshire Constabulary."

"You can't be the Lone Ranger or Robin Hood sweeping in to right the wrongs of Ashton-on-Tinch?"

"Afraid not."

He kissed me goodbye at the front door. He tasted of jam and warm energy. Neither of us seemed willing to step into that hot area that we knew was simmering between us. We drew back as the spark ignited. It wasn't going to stay subdued for long.

He stepped out into the rain. I watched him hunch his shoulders against the increasing downpour. If he felt at all the way I did with a flush of body heat, steam should be rising.

EIGHTEEN

When Peter returned on Tuesday morning, he was accompanied by the trench digger, a machine with a bucket at the end of a huge arm and an operator's cabin perched between two elongated tires. Not normal tires, but rubber stretched around a frame to give a grip to the long track. The man running it was encased in the tiny cabin. The machine looked like a toy, but it made enough noise to be taken seriously. I watched while the operator maneuvered the dirt back into the trench over what I assumed was a repaired drainpipe. Peter stood, his hand on a shovel, ready to smooth the dirt and add a shovelful where needed. The operator glanced up after he dumped dirt at the side and before he directed the machine to take another bite. He waved. He was probably mid-twenties, bright red hair with long arms that made him look uncoordinated, but he operated that small machine with some delicacy. I smiled. He sent me a huge grin showing crooked teeth—a man happy in his work. I walked over to speak to Peter.

"Finished?" I asked.

"Just about."

"Nice tidy job." I surveyed the piles of dirt kept to one side of my garden.

"We'll put the rose bush back and smooth out the ground. I'll scatter some grass seed. No walking on it, mind."

"I'll remember not to. The bill?"

"I'll bring it by."

I thanked him and headed to the back of the house, taking Gulliver with me. I left the men to their dirt play. I know it was serious business that I would have to pay real money for, but it seemed to me they were having fun with mechanical toys in my front garden. I collected the material I needed from my kitchen drawer and joined Gulliver in the back garden.

"We are going to attempt to take a rose cutting, Gulliver. I should have done it before the storm." I hadn't, so I hoped there would be at least one rose I could cut.

The YouTube video had made it look easy. I checked my equipment. I had secateurs, exacto knife, small plastic bag and some tape. I would need a six-inch cutting from the bush with, at least, three rose buds on it. First, I needed to find my *Climbing Lady Hillingdon*. That was the rose Thomas thought admirable.

I headed down the garden path. Gulliver trotted alongside me. As far as he was concerned, everything was an adventure.

"This must be it, don't you think?" I gestured toward the bush growing thick on my back wall. Most of the roses had been stripped by the storm, but there were a few still flashing their lovely blossoms, yellow with a touch of deeper apricot at the tips of the petals—and so many petals. One rose was almost a bouquet. I could see why Thomas was enthusiastic. I found a branch that had several buds on it and cut what I thought was six inches. I took the exacto knife and scored the cut end, put a little soil in the plastic bag, stuck the cutting into it and wrapped it with tape. Done.

"Now, why should something so simple give me such satisfaction?" It had taken about three minutes.

Gulliver cocked his head.

"I don't know either," I answered myself.

I sent a quick glance around my yard. There was such a lot yet to do—rake the small lawn, dig up the weeds in the flower beds, tie back the overgrown bushes and prune some of them, but I didn't do any of it. What I did was go back inside, set the cutting by the door and change my clothes into clean jeans, shirt and hoodie.

"I won't be long," I told Gulliver as I prepared to leave for Thomas's house. "The book says I should leave you for an hour or so to get you used to it. Have a nap."

Peter had left the front garden tidy. All the mess was contained under the smooth dirt of the trench. I wondered how long it took willow roots to regroup and invade the drains again. Nature could be relentless.

I walked toward the river but turned off a block onto Cobbler's Lane. Thomas' house seemed peaceful. The sun lit the flintstone around the windows. I walked around the house to the front garden. The roses that had been so profuse a few days ago were sparse today, but some still bloomed red and pink against the stone. I rang the doorbell and waited.

Thomas answered the door. "Hello, Claire."

He was upright. He was coherent. "Oh good. You must be much better," I said and proffered the cutting.

"Yes, thank you. I am. What's this?" He took the parcel from me.

"It's *Climbing Lady Hillingdon*," I said. "You expressed an interest in her. Would you like this cutting? I hope she lives because I've never taken a cutting before."

"Do come in. Your little dog isn't with you?" He peered behind me.

"Not this time." I reached down and patted his dog, Gracie. She sniffed my hand, then turned and padded back down the hall.

"Well, isn't this a treat? *Climbing Lady Hillingdon*. Did you put some hormone stimulant on her?" He sniffed the rose. It reminded me of the way a wine connoisseur sniffs wine, with a certain elegant flair.

"No, I didn't have any."

"Why don't you come into the library and pursue what you want while I attend to this lady. I will be back shortly. Would you like tea?" He started down the hall. I followed. I'd rather have coffee, but my mother had trained me to be an accommodating guest, "Good manners start with kindness", so I said, "That would be nice."

"Mary is at work, so I am afraid it may take a little time for me to pot this young lady and make the tea. Make yourself comfortable and look at any of the collection that appeals to you."

I left my jacket over the back of a chair in the library. What appealed to me was the computer. Was there some kind of list of the artifacts? I shouldn't look. On the one hand I was abusing Thomas's hospitality by sneaking a look into his computer. Mum would not have approved. On the other hand, there was that rampant curiosity of mine. What if there was a stash of letters written by Agatha Christie? My conscience slid into idle mode and then shut down completely. I sat in front of the computer and clicked the mouse. The monitor lit and asked for my password. I thought about Thomas's interests. "Mystery". No, that didn't work. "Books". Another dud.

What was the name of his favourite rose? *Bienvenue*. I typed it in. Bingo.

I scanned the files for Mystery Book Club Library. Found it, clicked through until I found "Catalogue".

There *was* a list. Well, there was a file but that didn't mean there was a complete list in that file. It might have been started and abandoned. I hesitated and my conscience awoke. I could not investigate more. It wasn't ethical. I could see there were only a small number of bytes on the file. Even so, I wasn't going to look. I logged out of the computer. Thomas must be computer-savvy as most school teachers today use them. Maybe his insistence that he hadn't cataloged anything past the *B*s was not true. I would not look, but I would still try to figure out if there was motivation here for murder.

Thomas brought the tea and effusive thanks for *Climbing Lady Hillingdon*.

"I'm delighted to have her now. I have the perfect spot for her. She needs sunlight, you know."

"She's doing well in my garden." Now I was doing it, talking as if the rose were a person.

"I hope she'll do well in mine."

"I am sorry you were sick, Thomas. When did it start?" I wanted to know if he thought he'd been poisoned and how he thought it had happened.

"Just after the ball. I am afraid that someone must have contributed something to the pot-luck that caused this. I can't for the life of me think what it might have been, and it would cause a great deal of hard feelings in the town if I were to speculate."

I looked at him. "What kind of harm?"

"If, for instance I said I thought it might be the lamb pate and you brought the lamb pate, I would force you into defending yourself. Since I can't *know* it was the lamb pate, you would feel guilty, and others would blame you. That would be careless and unkind."

I nodded. "Yes, I see. A small community has to guard against that kind of gossip."

"It does."

It was heart-warming to find someone whose ethics were so fine he anticipated problems from careless talk. Few people were so responsible. My conscience awoke and smacked me. I wasn't nearly as fine a person. I had just been tempted to look at his computer. Thomas would not even have thought of it.

It was hard to accept Thomas and Rose as products of the same village. They had such different attitudes to gossip. Rose gave herself free rein on any wild surmise that flipped into her head and enjoyed it. Thomas probably saw every word he said about someone encased in a moral dilemma. I couldn't see him as a thief or a murderer—but I wanted the information on the computer because I wanted to know if there were any artifacts from Agatha Christie here that were being ignored or neglected. I enjoyed research in my work too and the shelves beckoned me to see what was stored there, but I couldn't see myself as a thief.

I wasn't going to find out anything about a possible poisoning if Thomas didn't speculate. I hope he had voiced some kind of opinion to Mark.

"You would tell the police if you had any suspicion, wouldn't you?" I asked.

"The police? About my illness? They talked to me, Detective Inspector Evans came by. It isn't a police matter, you know. Perhaps, a public health one. The district nurse will probably drop by to ask questions about the food. That will cause quite a stir with the ladies and some of the men who contributed to the meal at the ball." His brow furrowed, and he seemed genuinely concerned about that.

I didn't stay long. He'd been sick and I didn't want to worry him.

Robert called that afternoon and invited me to ramble with the dogs on Wednesday morning.

"I schedule a locum in every Wednesday morning so I can get some exercise."

"Sounds like a great idea." I'd like to explore the neighbouring countryside, and Robert would be easy company.

"Good, I'll come by with my vehicle and we will walk when we get there. Have you ever been up north of Basingstoke to Roman Silchester?" This sounded like a more elaborate outing than I'd expected, but it also sounded interesting.

"No, I've always meant to go there." I'd been to Chichester in West Sussex but not Silchester in Hampshire.

"I thought you might like to see it." He sounded pleased. I wanted to go with him, and I was looking forward to it. He duly arrived at my house at nine on Wednesday.

"This is nice, Robert. I missed a lot when I didn't have a dog and didn't have to get out and explore." I wondered what my life in Seattle would have been like if I'd had a dog.

He smiled. He was what I thought of as a "sandy" man with straw-colored and ginger hair, freckles and a muscular body. I suppose a vet who lifts calves and shoves cows around would develop muscles. Intelligent. Hard-working. Dedicated. All together an attractive man. He'd be good company. He was a member of the Mystery Book Club. Would he have any interest in Mrs. Paulson? He knew about poisons. He'd warned me about yew berries. Could he be an attractive killer? *Oh, slow down, Claire. You can't suspect everyone.* As far as I knew, he wasn't on Mark's suspect list.

"Silchester sounds intriguing," I said.

"Fascinating. You'll have to drag me away from all the explanatory plaques," he apologized in advance.

He looked at my small rucksack and then around the garden. Was something missing?

"Do you have a crate for Gulliver? It's much safer to drive with the dogs in crates."

Of course. I should have thought of it.

"I do." I handed Gulliver's leash to Robert and left him squatting in front of Gulliver having a one-sided conversation. I darted toward my car and pulled Gulliver's crate from the back.

We fitted it into the Land Rover's back seat. I tossed a treat into it, then lifted Gulliver in. He was momentarily distracted by the treat and then woofed a greeting at Muggs and Jetty who barked back their hellos. Once the Land Rover rolled onto the street, the dogs settled down.

"How did your emergency turn out on Sunday?" I asked.

"The calf took its time coming. First calving for the poor cow, but finally it went smoothly. Mum and babe doing fine."

"That's rewarding."

"It is. I don't get many calvings. Birthing usually involves dogs and cats. For calving, the farmers call on Black and Barley. They're large-animal vets. Occasionally, both Black and Barley are away, and I get the call. It's interesting."

He pulled out onto the busier road and we were soon making good time. We headed north through tidy pastures and cultivated woods, skirting Basingstoke and arriving at Silchester in about a half-hour. We parked the Land Rover as close as possible to the Roman ruins.

They were impressive. Walls once thirty feet high now were reduced to a mere ten to twelve feet, but they still enclosed the site of the old Roman town. We kept the dogs on leash as we walked along the walls, assessing how safe it was to let them loose. We weren't allowed inside the walls with the dogs, but we could see what a huge fortification it had been. There were panels containing information along the path, and we wandered along the perimeter stopping to read them. Robert, as he had forewarned me, was a compulsive reader of plaques.

"It says there was an Iron Age town here. Imagine that? Before the Romans. A couple of thousand years ago people built a permanent settlement, had their families here, worked, played and probably sang and worshipped." He raised his head and contemplated the surroundings.

I took a moment to image it.

"Deer hide tents?" I suggested.

"Maybe mud, logs and thatch?" Robert was right. I was mixing up my continents. Deer hides in ancient North America and mud and thatch in ancient Britain. I'll have to research this. The idea of thatch in the Iron Age was a little startling.

"That long ago they used thatch?" People used thatch

today to roof their houses. I'd known it was an old material, but I hadn't known it was that ancient.

"They had a sophisticated town before the Romans came. They planted gardens, ate off plates, kept livestock and brewed wine. The Romans would have felt right at home." He scanned the area around us. "There don't seem to be many people here today. We can let the dogs off leash." He bent and released his dogs. I did the same for Gulliver, trusting that, as Jetty and Muggs came on recall, Gulliver would follow them.

"The Romans built on top of an Iron Age atrebate around 270 AD," I read from the next plaque. "What is an atrebate?"

"That's the name of the local Iron Age tribe and village. It means 'inhabitants', I think."

I continued to read. "The Romans lived here from 247 AD to the fifth century."

I scanned the green fields, the fenced pastures and woods. "They lived here for two hundred and thirty years. That's generation after generation. Somehow, I thought of the Romans as just armies—men who stayed for six months and then went back home. But they must have settled here, had families, generations of them." I peopled the meadow with imaginary women and children playing near their homes.

Robert was quiet for a moment. "Possibly, they're our ancestors?"

"Are we standing on ground inhabited almost two thousand years ago by our ancestors?" I hadn't thought about how many thousands of years my ancestors had lived here.

"Maybe."

"How could we know?" It was an intriguing idea. Was I related to an ancient Roman?

"DNA mapping?" he said.

Now there was a thought. I had heard someone had done DNA mapping of the people of Britain to find how the Vikings had integrated and spread their progeny throughout the country. Why not do that for ancient Romans or even Iron Age people? Maybe I was Claire, descendant of Marianne, matriarch of the Iron Age clan?

We left the information plaques and followed the dogs along the straight wall that seemed to sweep before us for a mile. Jetty scrambled to the top of the stones piled there two thousand years ago. It was covered in grass and sod, so she wouldn't slip. Muggs followed her. I hoisted Gulliver up and the three of them investigated this strange elevated pathway. They had more trouble getting down, and Robert had to brace his dogs so they didn't fall as they dived for the ground. Gulliver just sat at the top, whining until I coaxed him to a lower ledge where I could pick him up and set him down beside me.

We walked to the amphitheater at the far end of the wall. They had it all, those Romans: the defenses, the agriculture—they even grew grapes—and their theater. It would have held a hundred or more. They had sat here, chatting with their neighbours, entranced by the play, sipping wine and nibbling on canapes. It might not have been such a difficult life. If they had the weather we did today, they would have enjoyed the blue skies, the brisk breeze but not cold and the hint of frost coming. I wondered if they wanted to go home the way many immigrants to Britain do, who, even after generations of living here, take holidays back "home" to Greece or Portugal or wherever they or their parents or grandparents came from. There would be no jetting home for a visit for these Romans.

We stopped at the Plough Inn for lunch. The sign said "We are dog friendly". I figured Robert knew all the dog friendly places. Three dogs were a bit much for the restaurant, so we left his two in the car and brought Gulliver in with us. The Plough was a Seventeenth Century building that kept its old character. My tourists would love it. I wrote down the name and the website information published on the menu.

We had a Guinness each and studied the menus. I ordered the soup. Robert had the sandwich of the day which was beef and horseradish. Gulliver slept at my feet. I felt cozy and relaxed. We ate in comfortable silence.

"Did you have a good walk with Sarah on Sunday?" Robert asked.

I had a perfect cup of coffee in front of me. I had warm soup in me, but I wasn't so relaxed I forgot Sarah's strictures about betraying her plans.

"I did. She is a lovely young woman."

He beamed. "I like her."

I laughed. "Good thing since you have a life-time together. You've done a good job with her."

"I worry, though. Did she talk about her plans?" He turned his coffee cup around in his hands.

"She did, Robert, but she asked that I not disclose them."

His eyebrows drew together. His eyes got larger. He looked alarmed.

"Don't worry. They won't upset you. She has her head screwed on very well that young woman. I wouldn't worry."

He was silent for a moment. His brows smoothed out and the lines at the sides of his mouth disappeared. "Thanks. I guess I will just let her make her own decisions."

"She will anyway, you know."

He nodded. "True enough." He picked up the cheque.

"Thanks, Robert. I enjoyed our walks. I'd like to do it again, but next time I get the cheque."

He met my eyes. "Cautious, are you?"

"Yes." He was attractive, personable and pleasant, but I didn't know him well. Time would reveal more and I was attracted to Mark.

He raised his eyebrows. "Want to take it easy, do you?"

I thought about it for a moment. "Let things evolve if they are going to."

He shrugged. "All right. Funny about lovers, isn't it? You never know whether you're going to click or when that might happen. Dogs aren't like that."

"No?" I was interested.

"No. They know right away. They are best friends immediately, or they are sworn enemies. It's instant."

"What about their relationships with their owners? Is that instant?"

He was quiet for a moment. "That's different. Some start with instant bonding and some develop that bond slowly. Some never get close, just have a mutually respectful attitude to each other, but not love." Robert must know something about love. Vets would know how important it was. I could learn something.

I thought about couples I'd known who didn't have that bond. "I agree. It is odd. Attraction seems to have nothing to do with age or common interests or common background."

"Nope. Just chemistry or quantum attraction or something."

I picked up Gulliver's leash and followed him out to the vehicle. "It's like that for people sometimes—instant attraction." I said. I thought of Mark and the way something certainly sizzled there.

"Once in a while," he agreed.

We drove home in companionable quiet, speaking only occasionally, commenting on the animals in the fields. I saw some llamas and a variety of sheep I'd never seen before.

"Those are Black Mountain Welsh," Robert said. "Most of the sheep in that field are Hampshire Downs, but someone must spin because Mountain Welsh have fine wool."

I looked for more of those sheep as we drove home, but never saw any.

I took Gulliver from his crate and then unloaded the crate in front of my house. "Again thanks, Robert, for the interesting day."

"Let's see what's up for next Sunday morning."

That would be a walk nearer home. "Sounds good," I said.

I toweled Gulliver dry—I expect I will be doing that for years—brushed him and gave him some water and a chew toy. He settled happily under the kitchen table, worrying that toy.

It was about five in the evening when James called. "Claire, this is James Malkin."

"Yes?" I waited.

"Did you think about what I said? You know Harold

and I have a right to some share of Dad's estate. You can't hope to win in court, and it only makes sense to settle with us now." I had to hand it to James. He was persistent.

I was firm with my answer. "No, your father wanted me to have the legacy he left me."

"You have no idea how to invest money. You can't know how to make it grow. I can make all of us have more money if you just do the right thing and spread the money out to us all." He spoke quickly and loudly as if speed and volume would convince me.

"No. I have already given you my decision." *If you think I'd give any money to a relative who slashed my tires, think again*, but I didn't say it aloud. I stayed calm.

"You have to reconsider. I need that money. Things aren't going too well, and Dad wouldn't want me to suffer." His voice had a whine to it now.

I took a deep breath and said. "Your father is not here and I had a letter from him, James. It said I did not have to give you the money and I'm not going to."

There was silence for a moment, then, "You are so selfish."

I slid back the bar on my phone screen and disconnected.

I stood immobile for seconds, the phone in my hand, my finger still on the screen. Everything blurred as if there was haze in front of my eyes. My heart raced. I knew I was breathing too fast. I was, I realized, very, very angry. Words flashed in my brain. He was such a lout and a larrikin. I distracted myself with "larrikin". It wasn't apt. James wasn't young, wasn't a social rebel and had better clothes than the definition implied. I concentrated on slowing my breathing. In for a count of five, out for a count of five, in for a count of six, out for a count of six. When I had successfully completed a count of ten, I walked into the kitchen and drank a glass of water. Then I called Deirdre.

"Deirdre, I'm sorry I know it's supper time, but can you talk to me? James, just called."

"Tell me," she insisted. I was so glad she was my sister.

I told her what he had said. I could feel my anger start to rise again. This time I felt a slow heat spread up from my chest to my throat. I concentrated on slowing my breathing. The flush subsided.

Deidre listened without interrupting and then gave instructions. "If he calls again, tell him his call constitutes harassment and you will report him to the police."

"Would the police take me seriously?" I asked. After all, they often didn't take harassment seriously.

"You sound funny, are you all right?" She always knew when I was upset.

"Yes. I'm fine," I reassured her. "Angry, but fine. Will the police take me seriously?" I asked again.

"I think so. Refer them to me if they don't."

Nice to have a barrister on tap. "I hope the insurance company studies that video and proves he slashed the tires on my van." It could make my call to the police about harassment taken a bit more seriously.

"What?" Her voice came to me as sharp as an icicle.

"I didn't tell you about that?" I supposed I'd been so busy getting the ladies to the ball and then to the airport the next day I'd forgotten to call her.

"No," she said with some steel in her voice. "What happened?"

I told her then.

"Promise me that if he calls again you will tell him you have nothing to say and to stop calling. Any more calls will constitute harassment," she repeated. "Got that?" She was very clear.

"I got that." I said obediently.

I felt better after that call. Deirdre always seemed so positive and sure of herself. It made me feel as if I had my own Roman army at my back.

The next day was Mrs. Paulson's funeral. I didn't send flowers. I hadn't known her well enough for that, but I was going to attend. The local Anglican church was only a short walk from my house, so I dutifully arrived at ten o'clock and entered to find a seat in a pew near the back. Several people jostled a little to give me room as the church was full to overflowing. The casket sat on a rolling trolley at the front near the steps to the altar and was draped in a green cloth with so many bouquets of flowers on it I wondered it they'd topple off when the casket was moved.

The choir contributed glorious music. I might start coming to church if I could hear them sing like that again with those clear high tones soaring into the nave. The minister praised Mrs. Paulson's energy, her concern for the community, willingness to help and, true to tradition, never mentioned her bossiness, nosiness and ferret-like qualities. I wondered if the people whom she annoyed most would miss her the most? They might notice some of the energy around them had disappeared.

The minister enjoined us all to pray and, after the prayer, invited us to a reception at Mary and Thomas' house.

Six men, most of them elderly, wheeled the casket on its trolley to the rear of the church. Not one floral arrangement fell. They must have been pinned to the cloth.

We filed past the casket as we left the church. I noticed the names on the bouquets "Ashton-on-Tinch Women's Institute", "The Garden Club", "The Hospice Society" and a lavish bouquet from the "Mystery Book Club". All the tributes came from organizations not from individuals.

I followed the attendees on foot as we only had to walk a half-block to Mary and Thomas' house.

Barbara was holding forth in the hall when I got there. She was haranguing Mary whose face was pale, and her eyes a little sunken. Was she more upset by Mrs. Paulson's death than I had thought?

"I should have had the reception! She would have expected me to do it." Barbara wasn't shouting but speaking in a low, firm voice.

"She would have appreciated your offer," Mary said, "however, our house is more convenient to the church."

Thomas arrived just then. "Barbara, can I get you some punch?"

Barbara allowed herself to be guided into the main sitting room where others were standing. I spoke with Mary for a moment and followed Barbara into the room.

There must have been sixty people there, moving slowly, drinking punch, coffee or tea, holding small crustless sandwiches. I took a cup of coffee and tried to keep it steady on its saucer. In Seattle, coffee was served in mugs and it was much easier to manage.

"Claire," a voice beside me startled me.

"Rose. It's nice to see you."

She looked different in her dress-up clothes—black tights, high, platform-heeled shoes, not a brand I recognized, multi-coloured tunic top and a small purple shrug over it. Chunky earrings dangled almost to her shoulders. Bangles on her wrists supported more stones.

"Good send-off," she declared with the confidence of a serious adjudicator. "Mrs. Paulson would have approved. Lots of flowers. Good choir. All okay."

"There was quite a crowd there," I said.

"Oh yes. She'd have expected the whole village to turn out. I bet the murderer was there. They usually show up a funeral, don't they?"

She looked to me for an answer. Did she expect to have knowledge of the usual behaviour of a murderer because I organized mystery tours?

"I don't know, Rose. Do you think that's true?"

She was quiet for a moment. "No. It's not likely in most places—cities, for instance. But it's likely here. You'd be noticed if you *didn't* show up at her funeral."

It was not in the best of taste to be discussing Mrs. Paulson's murder at her reception.

"Try one of these, Rose." I held up a tiny sandwich. "They have shrimp in them."

"I'd do that," she said as she jangled away.

PETER ARRIVED AT my door about seven-thirty with an envelope which contained his bill. I asked him to come in.

He stood in the foyer while I fetched my cheque book and pen and had a quick look at the amount. I kept my face straight. He had to pay the digger, after all, and he had spent the better part of three days at it.

"Peter, you said you were going to plant grass. Will it grow there?" I handed him the cheque.

"It's pretty much all that *will* grow there. Too much shade."

"Then I'm going to have to cut the grass. But then, I'll have to cut the rest of the front garden lawn anyway."

"True."

I couldn't see myself remembering to cut the lawn and trim the bushes.

"Peter," I said impulsively. "Can I hire you for garden maintenance once a week?"

"I'll think on it."

"Thanks."

He was silent for a moment then said, "You went out walking with that Sarah on Sunday."

"Yes?"

"She has some funny friends—and relatives."

I controlled my face. "Good night, Peter."

After he left, I had second thoughts about the wisdom of asking him to work weekly at my house. He would likely do a good job, keep my roses pruned and my garden tidy, but I would have both he and Rose pouring village gossip into my ears.

NINETEEN

Rose arrived in the morning with her cheerful barrage of constant chatter. Gulliver and I escaped into the sunshine. I had a lot of work to do in organizing the next tour, but I could take an hour off. We walked along the river, past Robert's clinic and up the hill above the Tinch. The view from the top was worth the climb. I saw rolling downs and the late rapeseed crop startling yellow in small fields. Below me, the river wound a placid path with its guard of bright yellow willow on both banks their fronds trailing in the current. In Seattle, the Tinch would be called a stream, not a river, and it would have been paved over or diverted into a culvert years ago. Here, it continues as it had for centuries, feeding the land and creating life—evidence that even a small life force matters. I felt knitted into the landscape, as if the soil was familiar to me, part of my life. I suppose everyone makes connections to their landscape when a child, and it stays hidden, perhaps for years, but always there. Perhaps, even appreciation of foreign lands is tied to childhood experiences. My love of the chestnut trees of Luca might be connected to the lofty chestnut trees that perfumed the area outside my infant school in the spring and provided me and my friends with those lustrous, brown conkers in the fall. Whatever the reason or the emotional imperative, I felt as if I was soaked into the Hampshire landscape. The sun was warm on my face, but I was glad of my quilted jacket as the breeze had an icy edge.

"Okay, Gulliver. Let's go home."

He pulled his nose from an enticing hole and cocked his head, waiting, I imagined, to see what I was going to do.

"Gulliver, come." I pulled a small tidbit of dried liver from my pocket. He dashed to me and managed a momentary sit. I gave him the treat. If I remembered to give the same command and reward, the book assured me, he would learn to come on recall.

The temperatures dropped even more as we neared home. Next time, I'd wear gloves.

Rose was working upstairs, so I retreated to my study and didn't see much of her until she was ready to go about noon.

"All's good for another week," she said.

"Thanks so much." I handed her the cheque. "You do an excellent job." She did.

"It suits me," she said and hovered by the door.

She was usually dashing off to another job. "Where are you going now?"

"It's Barbara Manning's afternoon. I'll run by to see if she needs anything. She won't want me to clean because she's been sick. Had you heard about that?"

I shook my head. Whatever it was, I hadn't heard it.

"She was sick. Gut slopping sick. Just a pale ghost of herself, you wouldn't credit it."

"Oh, I'm sorry. Was it the flu?" She hadn't looked well at Mrs. Paulson's funeral.

"*She* blames bad food. But me, I think someone's poisoned her. Lots of that going around."

I glanced at Rose. I wasn't sure if she was reporting facts or inventing drama.

"Food poisoning?" I suggested.

"Maybe," Rose said. "She's getting better, so she keeps saying, and she was at the funeral." Rose seemed a bit disappointed. "Said I should come over for an hour today and run some errands for her, because she's recovering but doesn't want me around for the whole afternoon."

"Maybe it was the flu. Some of the new viruses can be severe." If I was attempting to divert Rose into a more acceptable cause of Barbara's sickness, I failed.

"Be that as it may," Rose sniffed. "I say poison." On that note, she finally left. It could be the flu. The trouble was, like Rose, once I suspected poison in one incident, I suspected it everywhere.

I put in a couple of hours on the computer running down changes requested by one of my upcoming tourists. She planned to meet the tour at the airport, not arrive with them. As long as I had her cell number, I could coordinate that at the airport. Gulliver padded into my study, gazing intently at me a couple of times and each time I obeyed his silent command and let him out into the back garden for a pee. So far today, he had a clean record in the house. I'm not sure if he really has to go out so often or if he has me trained to let him out when he feels a need for a change.

I made myself lunch and let Gulliver into the garden again. I considered my garden wall—lovely old stone, still with some roses offering colour. I should take another cutting to Thomas. What if the first one didn't work? And I wanted to get back into that library There must be letters either from Agatha Christie or about her.

I rang the bell on Thomas's house about two.

Again, he answered the door and glanced at my package. "Claire, what do you have this time?"

"I'm such an amateur gardener, Thomas, I thought I'd better make another cutting to be sure you had a viable *Lady Hillingdon*."

"Now, that is thoughtful of you. We have a much better chance of getting a strong start if I have a couple of cuttings. Come in. Come in." He gestured his invitation.

"How are you now, Thomas?" He looked brighter, more energetic. His pale eyes lit as he examined the cutting.

"Much better, thank you. I'll be back to work next week. Can I get you tea?"

"No, thanks. It's a little early for me. I would like to spend some time in the library, though, if I may?"

"Come through. Where is your little dog?" Thomas held the potted rose cutting close to his chest as if protecting it and started down the hall.

I followed him. "Gulliver is getting 'at home' time again. The book says he needs to be left alone for an hour or two a day to get used to it." I didn't want to have to watch him every minute in this house full of antiques that included antique carpets.

"Very wise. But he is most welcome here."

"Thank you." I'd bring Gulliver visiting when he was reliably house trained.

"I will go get a pot for this lovely girl. You know your way?" He motioned toward the back of the house.

I nodded. I moved toward the library and Thomas to the kitchen.

I went to the filing cabinets, removed the file with the Christie letters and spread them out on the table.

Although I was thoroughly engrossed in reading that tantalizing letter to Madge, I heard Thomas in the hall and looked up as he entered the library with Gracie, his beagle, padding along beside him. I showed him the letters.

"What do you think, Thomas? See, there are two letters one dated in March and one in August. It seems by what she says in the last letter there were others in the time between them."

He fondled the beagle's ears while he read the letter. "People wrote to each other often in those days. Sometimes daily, but often every week. They had the post twice a day then and once on Saturdays." He sounded wistful.

Email is definitely faster than post, but twice a day mail was remarkable. "It's reasonable to suppose, then, she wrote many letters to Madge between March and August."

"Oh, yes. I would think so." Thomas pushed his glasses up further on his nose and raised his head so he peered through the bottom of the lens. Bifocals were in my near future. Gracie dropped to her stomach, lay her head on her paws and closed her eyes.

"Yes, I'd say she most likely wrote more." He nodded.

"Do you have them here? Filed elsewhere?" I held my breath.

He studied the letter for another moment. "It's possible, but not probable." He hadn't seen them or he was not telling me.

Thomas smiled at me. "Letters like these appear in many collections. You'll find few collections contain all the correspondence. You might find two here, two in Wallingford and two in someone's private collection. It is rare to find them together." To Thomas, this was interesting, but not intriguing or captivating.

"Rats." I let my disappointment show.

"You can look, though. There might be some. I don't want to discourage you. Sometimes artifacts are misfiled, dropped into a filing cabinet out of order or hidden behind another notice or letter. It's worth checking through what we have. Of course, you will be creating an inventory as you go. Could you note in the ledger if what you are reading is recorded there? That way we could catch any not documented."

I felt a little nonplussed. That would slow me down but I had offered to help Thomas and the Mystery Book Club. Thomas wasn't inviting me to use the library for my own aims, but this could work out for both of us.

"Certainly."

Thomas picked up the letter, reading it again. "You know this is interesting. I hadn't realized there *were* letters here written by Agatha. Very nice to have at least two."

"Would you need to insure them?" I asked.

"Hmm. Probably not any more than my household insurance. They may not have much monetary value— she wrote a lot of letters, but they are of historical interest."

I wasn't so sure about that after being around mystery readers and their love of Agatha Christie. There was an active, avid and voracious public for Agatha, her writings and her life story. Thomas was the treasurer of this club but he might not know about how Agatha Christie was viewed in the mystery reader world. I hoped he knew if any of this collection was valuable.

I suspected Mary did most of the work of the treasurer and maybe knew the collection as well. Did Thomas have all of the information about the collection? Had Mary removed the letters? Were any artefacts moved? I couldn't ask those questions without sounding like an amateur detective. I couldn't resist one, though, and asked "Did you have the collection valued by an estate insurer?"

He shook his head. "We should do that, but first we need an inventory."

I smiled. "Yes, first we must have an inventory. I can help with that."

"Thank you. Isobel Paulson had started listing our artifacts. That's her writing in the ledger. I worked on it occasionally, but, as I said, I didn't get far, just through the *A*s in the filing cabinet. Isobel didn't work chronologically. She simply picked out a file and delved into it, recorded what she found and picked another the next time she came. I tried to put a list into my computer, but I've barely started."

"Did that bother you that she didn't work in alphabetical order?"

"Well, it did. But, if you think about it, no harm was done by working that way. She documented everything so it amounted to order in the long run. But…"

"But?"

"I have to go over everything. Volunteers are often neither consistent nor accurate. Sorry," he apologized.

I was, after all, a volunteer.

"I can see you'd want to check everything." If I were Thomas, I wouldn't be able to resist looking at everything in the library. "It would take you some time."

"Since I am still employed full time at the comprehensive school, I don't have a lot of time to spare. The library then has to wait." He looked around with satisfaction. "I plan to retire at some point and I will be able to investigate everything here."

Not if someone poisons you before you get a chance was my first thought. Was he absconding with Agatha Christie's letters? Would he tell me they were *not* valuable even if they were? I now wondered what I would find in the filing cabinets and what might be missing. If he was stealing letters and selling them, was he also committing murder to protect his source of income? What was I doing alone with him in the library? Mark would think I had lost my mind.

"What's the matter?" Thomas asked.

I must have let some of my consternation show on my face.

"Gulliver," I said. "I realize I've left Gulliver long enough. He will start chewing the mat and getting into the garbage. I'd better go home." I mentally apologized to Gulliver. He had not yet chewed the mat or gotten into the garbage.

"Ah yes. Puppies. We haven't had one for years." He fondled the beagle's ears again. "They are energetic and inquisitive." It was hard to imagine Gracie had been energetic at any time in her life.

I managed a smile. "Thanks so much, Thomas."

"Anytime. Come sometime when Mary is home. She'd like to get to know you."

I repeated my thanks and rushed home.

Gulliver was sleeping on my bed and, apparently, content to have been left alone.

I checked my emails and answered a woman from Boise, Idaho, who was interested in joining a tour. I studied tentative dates and areas of exploration and sent her a reply giving her my schedule and rates. She was looking at next summer and I had only the broad outline for that tour up on my website. Then I pulled a piece of paper close and wrote the names of the people I thought could have poisoned Isobel Paulson.

Thomas made sense in terms of logic, but as I thought about him now I was home I couldn't see him as a killer. I expect he escorted spiders from his house with gentleness and care.

What about Barbara, that miserable woman? There was not much reason for her to murder anyone, much less Isobel Paulson. It could be that I wanted her to be a murderer. She wasn't a promising suspect. I just didn't like her. I would have to cultivate acceptance and develop the village spirit, accepting everyone as Thomas did as part of the whole.

I took Gulliver with me and marched off to the post office. Unlike Seattle, where post offices sold stamps, money orders and took in parcels, this post office did all the business of mail carriage, but also sold groceries, hardware and a few flowers. I left Gulliver tied to the dog post near the door. The book on dog training said I should leave him for short periods and then reward him if he didn't bark.

I bought multi-colored calla lilies. They were pretty and cheerful and came in a clear vase. Barbara wouldn't have to find a container for them.

"They'll look lovely, they will, in your house." Mrs. Taylor said her bright eyes staring at me inquisitively.

"Thanks," I said without revealing Barbara's house as the destination of the flowers as, in my mind, the village gossiped enough.

Gulliver hadn't barked, so he got one of the liver treats that now seemed to be a permanent part of my wardrobe as they were in all my jacket pockets. I managed to untie Gulliver without dropping the flowers and headed toward Barbara's house. She lived near Robert's clinic at the end of town in a pretty chocolate box, thatched cottage surrounded by neat topiary and formal Italian style landscaping on a miniature scale. It was an odd landscaping choice for a house which seemed to call for roses and columbines. I wouldn't like all this chipped rock and neat brick edging, but it probably wouldn't take much maintenance and would always look tidy. I suspect any wayward daisies would be plucked out the minute they popped out of the ground.

I had not called ahead to find out if she might be too sick to cope with a visitor. I wasn't going to stay long, in any case. I looked for somewhere to tie Gulliver. There was a wrought iron railing on the porch with projections that should be strong enough to hold a small dog's pull. Once he was secured, I rang the doorbell.

Barbara pulled open the door. She looked pale but no longer gaunt.

"Oh," she said. "It's you." And frowned at me.

I stood on the porch and offered my flowers. "I heard you were sick," I said.

"Oh." She looked a little less annoyed. "This is nice of you. Come in."

I walked into a foyer as severely decorated as the yard, yet in the house, it was more attractive. Black and white tiles brightened the floor. The walls were white but with lovely watercolors softening the stark effect. Sunlight poured down from a high skylight above. She took the vase and scrutinized the flowers. "Very nice," she said of the flowers. She looked at the vase. "Wait here. I have something better to put them in."

I waited. I couldn't stay long in any case because Gulliver had limited patience. She made me feel like a delivery person instead of a villager. She returned with the flowers in a beautiful, cream-colored vase.

"Now," I said. "That really complements the flowers. It's lovely."

She smiled, actually smiled. "Yes, it's antique. Here, you might as well have the clear vase."

I took it and told her I could use it.

Gulliver started to bark.

"I'm sorry, Barbara. That's my dog, and he is only learning to wait for me. I'll have to go now. I hope you continue to improve."

"Thank you for the flowers." She was gracious now and opened the door for me. "I do appreciate them."

Gulliver stood on his hind legs and pawed the air, breathing fast and indicating as clearly as he could he thought I'd abandoned him. I petted and reassured him that I would never desert him. I untied him and did *not* give him a treat because he'd barked even though I was glad he barked as he got me out of the house. I held the vase by the neck and walked home with dog and vase.

Mark was waiting in his car and joined me on the walk. I handed him Gulliver's leash and the vase and fished for my keys.

"Busy day?" I asked.

"So, so."

He followed me into the kitchen. I unleashed Gulliver. Mark set the vase on the counter.

"Coffee?" I asked.

"Love some. Got anything to eat?"

"The days of the sweet girl providing sustenance for her handsome hero are over." I only cooked if I felt so inclined and it was good for him to know it now.

"Duly noted." He laughed.

I grinned and got the coffee ready. "How's crime?"

"Other than two fights at a mall between gang members—belonging to the same gang which is unusual—some counterfeit fifty-pound notes circulating, a couple of hate crimes that seem to be politically motivated and no new information on Mrs. Paulson, life is normal. How's the day going for you?"

"I visited Thomas because he's been sick. I just can't see him as a murderer."

"He isn't likely, I agree. But you never know. Any tours scheduled?"

If he wanted to change the subject I was fine with it. Or maybe he was interested in my business.

"Not for a month. I'm still setting up my business. I'm calling it British Mystery Book Tours. My old company is willing to send clients my way as they haven't got anyone to take my place. They'll stop once they hire someone, but it's a good boost to have business at the moment." I appreciated that generous help.

"Time to visit the sick then." Maybe he did want to talk about it.

"Yes, I saw Thomas, and I visited Barbara this morning. She's been sick also. That seems odd. Both of them."

"It does. I hope I'm not missing something. Like a maniac deciding to poison the Mystery Club members." I hoped that wasn't the case as I was now a member.

"You knew they had been sick?"

"I did."

"How sick were they?" I poured the coffee into two mugs. It smelled wonderful.

"They weren't poisoned with yew poison that's for sure, or they would be dead."

"It might be the work of the murderer. Maybe a warning? Maybe…" I was out of ideas. "You need some kind of a break in this murder, don't you?"

"What I need is fingerprints. We have fingerprints from the table, from the kitchen cupboard and on the cup, which may belong to the poisoner, but I can't take fingerprints from everyone unless I have probable cause. I have Thomas's because he had an appointment with Mrs. Paulson and that constitutes sufficient cause, but his fingerprints don't match. I'd love to have Barbara's Manning's fingerprints."

I stared at him for a moment and then turned to look at the vase on the counter. He followed my gaze.

"She handled the vase, so help yourself," I said.

Mark sat up straight. "Your prints and mine will be over top of hers."

"Then there's Mrs. Taylor at the post office who handed it to me."

"Who?"

"Mrs. Taylor. 'Helen' is her first name. Rose's mother. Short, dark."

He brought out his tablet and entered the information.

"It's a long shot because there might be so many prints on there we won't be able to distinguish Barbara's," he said.

"You held it last, me before you and Barbara before me. It might not be too hard." I was more optimistic.

"It's worth a try. Thanks." He leaned over and gave me a quick enthusiastic kiss. "Got a plastic bag for it?"

I found one, and he inverted the bag and draped it over the vase, managing to enclose it without applying any more fingerprints.

The fine lines around his eyes deepened, and he looked more cheerful. "You'll need to stop by the station and have your fingerprints taken for elimination."

I hadn't gone to the station and been fingerprinted. "I see the reason, but I don't much like the idea of it."

"I'll have to do the same, so you are in the best company."

"It'll be messy."

"No. You're out of date. We have a new digital camera—no ink."

I shrugged.

"Claire, remember someone did poison the old harridan and might be inclined to play free with lethal means with others, including you."

"Why me?"

"You've been talking to suspects on my list. People who murder are not necessarily your most balanced and reasonable citizens."

He leaned closer and looked me in the eye.

"Be careful."

I gazed back at him, understanding his concerns. "All right. All right. You too."

He put his coffee mug in the sink and was letting himself out the front door when I spoke.

"Mark?"

"Yes?"

"Do you sing?"

He turned back. "I do. The Constabulary Choir. Baritone. Do you like music?"

"I do."

"Do you want me to sing for you?"

I nodded.

He took a step toward me and stopped, the door still open behind him. He sang "All Through the Night," a Welsh lullaby of tenderness. My mother had sung that to me when I was a child. I felt the same comfort I'd felt then. His rich, low baritone filled my hall, soaring to the ceiling and ringing in the air. He dropped the volume and ended in almost a whisper. By then, tears were trailing down my cheeks.

I sniffed. "Thank you."

"Thanks for the vase." His voice was upbeat.

You'd think I'd given him gold.

TWENTY

FULL BOXES OF household goods are demanding. They are almost alive with authority, issuing a peremptory command, "Deal with me". I had stuffed boxes stashed in rooms. Some might hide in closets for years, but I had emptied the ones in the bathroom, my bedroom and most of those in the kitchen. Now, the stack in my study needed attention. On Saturday, I spent the morning sorting. Not only the boxes there screamed for attention, the built-in bookshelves cried for the books. I spent a happy couple of hours reacquainting myself with my library and organizing it. I had no idea I owned so many mystery books. I resisted the temptation to sit down and get more intimately acquainted with my favourites and resolutely shelved them. I don't know how a librarian can keep from frittering away her work hours, reading what grabs her fancy. Libraries would be a hazardous environment for me, like a pharmacy for an addict.

By noon, I had everything in its proper place and looking cozy. It wasn't just the comfort of the books around the walls, the promise of hours of pleasure, it was their colour as well. The blues, yellows and reds of the paperbacks brightened the dark blues, greys and browns of the older, hard-cover books. I dusted my hands and surveyed my little kingdom. Very satisfying.

I let Gulliver into the garden and back yet again then tided the kitchen. It didn't need much because Rose had been thorough. I was just thinking about leashing Gulliver and heading to the post office for some stamps and some garlic—I noticed they had some in mesh bags when I was there last—and dropping into the community policing station to present my fingers when the doorbell rasped its usual harsh demand.

James stood on my doorstep. The man was ubiquitous with the same stoop, the same frown and the same petulant attitude.

"You should answer your emails," he snapped.

Not a good start to any conversation with me.

Gulliver barked and shoved his nose toward James.

"Keep that mutt away from me. Little dogs are the worst. They bite your ankles and everyone feels sorry for the dog."

The thought of James being terrorized by a little dog, a Shiatzu, for instance, a fluffy mop nipping at this tall beanpole of a man, distracted me so much that I backed into the house as James entered without consciously deciding to let him in.

Once he was in, I motioned to him. "You might as well come into the lounge." I had my cell phone in my pocket. I'd call Deirdre if James got nasty—or Mark if he got threatening.

Gulliver was still barking and growling at James. I didn't know how to stop him, so I just picked him up.

James began. "I'm trying to make a living, and you're taking too much of my time. If you'd answer your emails, I wouldn't have to drive down here."

I hadn't answered his emails. I had decided not to. I put Gulliver down, and he immediately ran at James barking and complaining that this man should not be here.

James pulled back his hand.

I raised my voice. "Behave yourself. Do not hit my dog, James." I had a fireplace but I didn't have a poker, but I'd find something to protect myself if necessary. Both the man and the dog stopped. Gulliver crept back to sit beside me and stopped barking. James let his hand drop.

"Now, what is this about?"

"Harold and I are going to take you to court to get our share of the money. Think about that. All that money unnecessarily going to barristers. If you'd settle with us now, we wouldn't have to waste money."

I hadn't sat down or invited him to be comfortable, and I wasn't going to. I wanted this man out of my house fast.

"You go ahead and bring an action, but you know you're wasting money. Paul's legacy is legal and court-proof. Besides, I put most of the money in an annuity."

I put *some* money in an annuity. But I didn't owe James the details of what I was doing with the money.

He stood stock still. His pale face turned almost paper white. His shoulders dropped even further. His six-foot-two height shrank in front of me. A flush rose to cover his face and his blue eyes widened.

"You!" He erupted.

"James, you have to stop trying to get money from your father's legacy," I said. "You were caught on video slashing the tires on my rental van. I have turned that video over to the rental company who will turn it over to the insurance company who will turn it over to the police.

"You can't do that!"

"I did do that."

James straightened his spine and rose onto the balls

of his feet. How could I have been so stupid as to make him angrier? He was bigger, stronger and less in control than me. Where was the poker? I didn't have one. Mace? Hair spray?

I tensed and Gulliver jumped to his feet, barked and dashed toward James.

"Shut up! Shut up!" He yelled at the dog.

"James, I want you to go now." I said as matter-of-factly as I could. One of us had to remain calm.

"Shut that dammed dog up."

"I can do that," I said firmly, "but you must leave now."

Surprisingly, he did. He stomped down the hall and out the front door but turned on the walkway to shout back at me. "We *will* take you to court."

I shut the door and locked it. I walked slowly into the kitchen and dropped onto a chair. Gulliver leaned against my knee. I gathered him onto my lap and sank my face into his silky fur.

"That was nasty," I murmured.

I remembered those old days when the Friday night pub closed and my dad would be in a rage. He'd stagger home to hit the first one handy. We never knew what would set him off. I realized that, like James, he used anger to clear us out of his way. Maybe I was standing up for myself with James because I couldn't with my dad for so long. Whatever it was, overt anger like James' made me angry and scared. It was why I was looking for poker when he voiced his anger at me.

Gulliver licked the tears I hadn't even known I was shedding.

"I hit my Dad back you know, Gulliver, when I was eighteen. I was moving out. He came home and smacked Deirdre across the face. She was eight years old. I hauled back a fist and hit the old bastard in the diaphragm. My friend Eugene at school taught me how to punch. I just hauled back and plowed. He dropped like a dead weight. For a minute, I thought I'd killed him. I was glad. I was really glad." I remembered that moment of intense satisfaction. "Then he got his breath back. I told him, if he ever hit Deirdre again, I'd kill him. I don't think he ever did. I should ask her and find out. She never complained to me so maybe he did not hit her. I wish I'd stopped Dad years earlier. I don't know why I didn't."

Gulliver snuggled into my arms and whined a little.

"James comes across like my dad—but in better clothes." I said to myself. "I've got to stop shaking. Let me make some coffee."

I didn't feel like lunch but sat by the window drinking my hot comfort.

I was calmer now. I'd talk to Deirdre later, but right now I wanted an hour of quiet time. I'd take Gulliver for a walk. How had I managed my emotional life without a dog?

The cold demanded my winter jacket, hat, scarf and gloves. Gulliver was quite fashionable in his winter sweater of red and white. It seems affected to dress dogs as if they were toddlers, but it was cold and Gulliver was small. We walked down by the river and watched the ducks hover near the shore, looking for handouts. There must be some place I could buy seed for them. Probably at the post office. The quiet of the village worked its magic, and I calmed.

I walked to the police station, more properly called the Community Policing Office located near the church.

The police support worker was a young woman who seemed willing to help me and squatted down to pet Gulliver.

"Hello there, you handsome young lad," she said.

I smiled and explained my visit. "Detective Inspector Mark Evans asked me to come in and have my fingerprints taken for elimination purposes."

"Oh, good of you to come in. Could you step into the small office," she pointed, "and I'll bring the forms we need."

Mark was right. It wasn't messy. Community Special Officer Mayne—I read her badge—took pictures of my fingers. She gave me a form to sign which gave the Constabulary of Hampshire permission to do whatever they liked with the prints and delete them from the files in three years if not used.

About four in the afternoon, Patrick pushed my discordant doorbell. He looked harried. His dark straight hair flopped in front of his eyes. He pushed it aside impatiently.

"Claire, can I talk to you? My drains are a problem. Sarah called, so I rushed down here today."

He followed me into the kitchen still talking as he claimed a chair.

"We weren't going to come down this weekend, but Sarah called, as I said, and she's right. There's a backup in the downstairs loo. So gross. I don't know anything about plumbing. So I saw you had your drains excavated. Who did you use?"

He paused and looked at me.

"Peter Brown," I said.

"Is he any good? Expensive? I hate paying for something that should have been done years ago, but sewerage! Ugh!"

I took moment and said, "I think so. He seems competent and, yes, expensive, but perhaps not relatively expensive. I mean I've no idea what other plumbers charge. He's local, and he came when he said he would."

"Oh good. Good. I'll probably call him then. What's his number?"

I was momentarily stymied. "You know, Patrick, I don't know his number. I left a message for him at the pub, and he came around to the door. He did call me once to ask about the date for the digger. Just a minute."

I fished my cell phone from my pocket and scrolled down my phone log.

"Here it is."

Patrick had a pen in his hand and wrote the number on the cuff of his shirt. I didn't think men did that anymore. He was only about forty-five but seemed a mixture of an older man in his outfit of jeans, dress shirt and jersey and a twenty-year-old with his rapid-fire speech.

"Okay. Okay. I'll have to get on it. It's inconvenient. I've got two authors coming to town. I have to get back to talk to them."

I remembered Patrick was a publisher. Meeting with authors sounded glamorous.

"Both of them are absolute bores," Patrick said, revising my fantasy. "But they write brilliant books. It's as if they are split personalities. Remarkable, really."

He stood and almost galloped to the front door. He was pulling his cell phone from his pocket as he went.

I imagined the conversation between Peter and Patrick. The one so taciturn, the other so voluble. I hoped they would be able to understand each other. After sup-

per, I left Gulliver at home and walked to the church hall
for the meeting of the Mystery Book Club. I met Mark
at the door. I immediately thought of the Welsh lullaby
and the tenderness in his voice last night and smiled.

"Are you attending this?" I hadn't thought he would
have time for leisure activities like book clubs.

"You bet." His voice sounded energetic.

I glanced at him sharply. His eyes were alight. He
leaned toward me and spoke softly.

"Thanks for the vase."

"What did you get?" I hoped for clear prints.

"Mrs. Taylor at the post office tells me that she pol-
ishes all the vases every morning so, of course, she gave
you a clean vase. She was indignant that I was questioning her housekeeping expertise." He looked amused.

"So," I whispered impatiently. "You got them?"

"I did, four sets, so you'd better get into the station to
have yours taken, or my Superintendent will be wanting to have you in for questioning."

"I did it today, but my fingerprints won't be on Mrs.
Paulson's table or cup."

"I'll find out."

"They aren't," I insisted. "And Barbara's are?"

"I can't prove they're hers until I take hers directly.
Because those on the vase match the ones in the kitchen
and on a cup, she will have to explain herself."

Another person joined us at the entrance, so we
stopped talking.

Barbara might have a good excuse for having her
fingerprints in Mrs. Paulson's gazebo, on her kitchen
cupboard and on the cup. She might have visited earlier
in the day. I heard they'd known each other since they
were very young, after all. It was reasonable to think

Barbara had tea with Mrs. Paulson. They hadn't been friends, so was tea likely? Perhaps. Tea was possible in all English social situations.

There were about twenty people at the meeting which is a fair turnout for any sized town. I'll give Barbara credit as she ran an efficient meeting. She had recovered from whatever she'd had. We went through the secretary's report and the treasurer's report. Thomas gave that one, but I saw him look at Mary a couple of times and hesitate as if checking to make sure he had the figures correct.

When we got to new business, Mark stood.

Barbara regarded him as an intrusion to her running the meeting.

"Yes?"

Mark spoke clearly. "I move the Mystery Book Club hire an inventory auditor to do thorough cataloging of the books and compare it to any records available." So that's why he was here.

There was a silence for a moment while everyone absorbed what this meant. Then Mrs. Taylor seconded the motion.

"Discussion." Barbara said.

There was silence.

"Well, *I* have something to say." Barbara was belligerent. "This is an affront. It isn't necessary and almost accuses the custodians of the library of fraud. I won't have it. And no motion can be accepted from someone who is not a member of this club. You, sir, are not a member."

Mark sat impassively. He had planted the seed of doubt in the minds of the members there. Was something wrong with their library?

I felt like a traitor to Thomas, but I stood. "I am a member and I will put forth this motion."

Barbara glared.

Mrs. Taylor again seconded it.

"Discussion." Barbara was forced by Robert's Rules of Order to allow discussion.

A few people asked what this would mean and what information the results would give the membership.

Then an older man at the back stood and said, "It's a good idea. We can get someone to poke around in the library and get some notion of what we have. Isobel Paulson, poor soul, wanted that—was insistent that we check into what's on our shelves—so maybe it would be a nice tribute to her if we did it."

That swayed the voters, and they voted in favour of the audit.

"I don't believe," Barbara said, "that an audit is necessary, but since the club seems to want it, and I am obliged to conduct the will of the membership, I would like you to consider that we don't need to hire an auditor to do it. We could use club members."

A small wave of discomfort rippled through the audience. Barbara had accepted the vote, but she was attempting to direct the audit. The members knew her well and thought getting her cooperation was dicey, and this was as good a compromise as they were going to get. There was silence, and finally the man from the back stood again.

"Good enough. Maybe we could have a committee of people who know how to catalog books. Thomas does, for sure."

Again, there was silence. Then Thomas stood.

"I would be happy to help and I suggest Claire Barclay who, although she is a newcomer, is very skilled in investigating files and would be very useful."

I was thankful I hadn't copied the files on his computer. Although I'd been tempted, I hadn't done it. Maybe he'd show me the files.

"And maybe Robert Andrews," Mary added.

Robert was at the back so I hadn't seen him arrive. He stood to respond to Mary's request. "Sorry, I can't spare the time right now."

Barbara grabbed the subject back. "Thomas and Claire Barclay should be enough along with me, of course, as president. Acting president," she corrected.

I glanced at Mark. He nodded.

"Fine," I said. This wasn't the audit Mark was hoping for, I was sure. Thomas and Barbara were on his suspect list. I suppose it was my job was to make sure they didn't take or hide anything that might portend to the murder.

The meeting continued and the entertainment committee presented a skit from Charles Finch's *A Beautiful Blue Death*. It took only two actors to read the climax scene between Lenox and Claude, but they did it with passion and intensity. The audience sighed in appreciation at the conclusion and gave the actors the respect of a moment's quiet before clapping.

I turned to Mark. "Did you like that?"

"Yes. It was well done. I wish I could tie up a case as competently as Charles Lenox." He sounded wistful.

"Are you staying for refreshments?" I hoped he might walk me home.

"No. I'm working. I'll call you."

I nodded and turned away to the refreshment table.

Mark was a detective and his job would never be predictable.

Mrs. Taylor was helping herself to a substantial meal of biscuits, cakes and a token carrot. I filled a cup at the tea urn.

"The coffee's decafe," she said. "It's always decafe at night." It would, no doubt, be weak.

She was a comfortable looking woman who dressed in a loose jumper and jeans.

"That's fine," I said.

"Are you going to get at that library then?" Those dark bright eyes assessed me.

"Yes, I am." I wasn't looking forward to working with Barbara.

"It would be good if you could give a report at every meeting, casual like, you know. Just let us know what you are doing and if you found anything."

It occurred to me I wasn't the only one who wondered what was in that library. If Mrs. Paulson had been insistent that the artifacts and books should be catalogued, many people might be curious.

"That sounds like a good idea, Mrs. Taylor. We should do that, thanks for the idea."

"Helen," she said.

"Helen," I repeated. She was right about asking for a report. The membership should know what we find—if anything. But I wondered what kind of mess I was getting myself into. It would be a fabulous opportunity to look for those letters of Christie's yet I'd have to spend time with the sweet Thomas and the difficult Barbara. It would not be pleasant, and it might even be dangerous.

TWENTY-ONE

IT WASN'T THOUGHTS of the coming audit that irritated me when I arrived home. It was thoughts of that rat James. I let Gulliver into the back garden—he was almost reliable now in the house. I huffed around my kitchen then called Deirdre and reported on James. I had a fine time.

"I'll draft a stinker of a letter and warn him off." She was indignant on my behalf.

I tried to imagine James' reaction when he got the letter. He might be cowed, furious, or he might feel the letter was a challenge. His reaction might cause me problems, but I must stop his continued idea he was owed some money.

"Thanks. I won't let him in the house if he comes again." I *definitely* won't let him in the house. I'd put my faith in Deirdre's ability as a barrister to put an end to this siege of his.

"He'd better not come anywhere near you. Are you sure you aren't going to weaken and give him money?" Her voice was sharp.

"No fear. You know he was going to hit Gulliver? What kind of a monster does that?"

There was silence on the phone, then Deirdre laughed. "If I can't rely on you to protect yourself, I can rely on you to protect your dog. Right?"

"I'll protect myself, but I'll protect my dog too."

She was satisfied, and I went to bed convinced we'd routed James.

Barbara called early in the morning and demanded my presence at an audit meeting at Thomas's house tomorrow at two. I agreed. We might as well get started on the project.

Shortly after, the doorbell announced Patrick on my front step, bouncing a little on his feet in a flurry of worry and jangling nerves.

"I've got to get back to town, and you won't believe the problems I'm having with the sewer."

"Oh, what a shame. You too?"

"Come out. Come on. You have to see this."

I hadn't been paying much attention to the sounds from next door as I knew Patrick had Peter working in the front garden, and trenches don't interest me a great deal.

I followed Patrick outside and over to his front garden. The usual digger had arrived, but unlike my tidy single ditch, Patrick's front garden sported multiple ditches criss-crossing the entire area.

"Look at it! Just look at it! They can't find the pipe."

"Isn't it at the side of the house the way mine is?"

"No, it isn't." He pointed. "That's where they first dug."

I saw the straight ditch a mirror image of the last week destruction in my garden.

"Where does the town plan say it is?"

"What plan? No one made any plans? The idiots who laid these pipes years ago didn't leave any drawings of even written description of where the pipes are. There are no drawings for any sewer connections in town. You'd think the pipe layers were setting up business for a century. Everyone will have to hire a digger to tear up their property from end to end to find the pipes. Employment for years. A home-grown make-work project."

I looked over at my garden, Neat now, with the rose bush replanted. I'd been lucky.

"I'm so sorry, Patrick. This is really a mess."

"It's a mess. It's a catastrophe. It's ridiculous. And you know why we are having so much trouble with the drains?"

I did know why, but I could tell Patrick wanted to lay that out for me. "Why?"

"Because Paulson, Mrs. Bloody-minded Paulson decided to plant willows along this street. Those pestilential trees are invading the pipes. Squirreling through the rain-soaked land and tearing into cast iron pipes. It's like an alien invasion."

"Oh, surely not, Patrick. Tree roots are, at least, natural." Patrick's normal discourse seemed to be hyperbole, but 'alien invasion' was a bit much.

"All right. I'll grant you 'natural'. A natural invasion from Mother Nature. The roots are running through the underground, reaching out to grab the wallets of everyone on this street. And they picked me out from the rest of the home-owners."

I could understand his frustration, but I doubted he was targeted by the fates.

"If we want to stop this from happening again, we need to get rid of the trees."

"Can we do that?" I liked the look of the trees on the street.

"No, we bloody well can not! You need a permit to cut a tree, even on your own property. Even then, you have to hire an arborist and prove it's diseased."

He glowered at the willow tree. "I'd like to poison the lot of them. Or introduce a disease that is specific and deadly."

"Sorry about this, Patrick. It's a problem."

"The plumber can't find my drains. He's digging up my front garden looking for them. It's ridiculous. Look!" Patrick made an extravagant wave of his hand to indicate the dirt, piles, trenches and general mess. "That's a huge amount of money, not to say, a huge visual abomination. And I can't be here to supervise this. I have authors to meet, catalogues to get out, artists to pacify."

"It's very difficult for you, Patrick. I can see that." I appreciated his irritation, but he'd be better off taking a calm attitude. He had to deal with this mess somehow.

"Sarah's just away at university. Robert is too busy to help out here. Everybody's looking after their own lives. It's inconvenient." He surveyed his garden one more time, grimaced and turned back to me. "Can you supervise for me? Just look over and make sure they aren't taking out the front steps or smashing windows or anything. Let me know if there are decisions."

"Can't you do that on the phone with Peter?" I didn't want to take on the responsibility of his plumbing problems, yet I wanted to be a good neighbor.

"The phone?" Patrick's voice rose. "The phone? When I'm standing right in front of Peter Brown, he hardly says a word. I have to *guess* what he's thinking. It would be impossible to even get an inkling of what he was telling me over the phone."

He had a point. I imagined Patrick holding the phone to his ear and listening to Peter's silence.

"All right," I said but very reluctantly. "Tell Peter to

talk to me if he has any concerns, and I'll look over the garden every day—when I'm here," I added that proviso. "I'm sometimes away."

"Excellent. Excellent." He rubbed his hands together. "Just leave a message with the receptionist, Alexandra. She'll let me know. I'm grateful. Very grateful." He hurriedly handed me a business card, sketched a half-salute and darted back inside his house.

I stood there for a moment, bemused. Oh, well. Peter would not pester me with decisions. I expect he would carry on as if no one was watching him. Patrick blamed Mrs. Paulson for his problems. Was he a suspect for her murder? No. She had died before he discovered his drains were plugged.

The next morning started badly with rain lashing the kitchen windows and making Gulliver's trip to the back garden a reluctant necessity. I dried him with a towel I now kept handy.

"What a wild day." I peered out the window over my sink at the deluge. It would be cold and wet for our walk. I knew I had rain pants somewhere and Wellingtons. I'd dig them out. Gulliver had a new raincoat.

I saw that Patrick and his car had departed for London and his publishing business. I peered over into the garden and saw Peter lowering a sewer pipe into the first trench he had dug. I expected the criss-crossing trenches were unnecessary, perhaps a reaction to Patrick's hectoring style of supervision. Left alone, Peter would likely conclude this job today or tomorrow. I reminded myself to be polite to Peter.

Gulliver looked gorgeous in his red fitted coat, and it would keep him fairly dry. We set off in the rain, suitably outfitted and walked up behind the town into the

hills. The rain lightened a little into a steady drizzle.
Gulliver didn't seem to be interested in sheep but got
excited when he spotted a bird. The birds entranced me
as well. I heard a willow tit, the four clear "eee" calls.
I studied the hedgerows and low buses and finally saw
the flick of feathers, then the black cap, white throat,
dab of black beard and the tawny gray body. A beautiful bird, but elusive. I felt lucky to have seen it. The
great spotted woodpecker was much easier to discover.
He gripped the bark of a tall tree, pecking loudly and
squawking his short whistle call. I heard the high twit-
ter and long whistle of the tree creeper, but I didn't see
it. I'd read that the song birds were diminishing in number and a cull was going on to get rid of sparrow hawks
and crows. That seemed absurd to me. It was probably
the increasing population of humans that was affecting
the song bird habitat.

Gulliver cocked his head and looked inquiringly at
the shrubs and trees but didn't attempt to search them.
He didn't react much to sound, but he definitely reacted to movement. If a bird flew up in front of him,
the chase was on.

I turned back toward town and, in the clearing air,
appreciated the spectacular orange-red of the oak trees
in the park on Robert's side of the Tinch—ancient, glorious and enduring.

Just before two, I left Gulliver with a chew toy,
locked the door behind me, peered into Patrick's yard
to see the digger smoothing earth back into the trenches,
the job finished in hours. I hoped it had all worked out
for Patrick. I trotted down the street to Thomas and
Mary's house.

In the short time it took to cover the distance, the

storm blew in again. Dark clouds rolled over the Downs bringing torrents of rain. I arrived at Thomas and Mary's door, my rain jacket streaming water and my hair plastered to my head.

Mary answered the door. "Oh, my. Here." She handed me a small towel, and I rubbed my hair, absorbing as much moisture as I could. I toed off my Wellies. My thick socks could act as slippers.

"No dog?" Mary asked. She was her usual, relaxed self in jeans, a shirt and hoodie.

"Not in this weather and too distracting," I said. "I may have to go home to let him out, though, depending on how long we'll be working." Gulliver would be a great excuse to leave if the meeting became uncomfortable.

"Still a puppy, isn't he? They need to go out often. You can bring him back here if you find you need to."

"I love your house, Mary," I said, as I followed her down the wood paneled hall.

"It was my uncle's house. He left it to me."

"Lucky you."

"Yes," she turned and smiled at me. "I quite like it, especially in a storm such as today's. It seems safe and secure, even if it creaks a little."

I listened for a moment but didn't hear any strange noises.

"My father was such an unreliable sort, capricious I suppose you could say, never could stay at anything and moved my mother and me from pillar to post. My uncle was the opposite, so respectable and predictable he was boring. No creativity in the man at all, except his garden. I find it restful. Perhaps I am as predictable as Uncle Harry. We've been here quite some time now."

"I like it." It was a big house and lovely but it wouldn't suit me. I'd have to have Rose every day in a house this size.

I followed her to the library and took a moment to appreciate the smell of furniture polish, the patina of the wood panels and the feel of the soft, thick, blue rug. Libraries had always been a safe place when I was young as there was no noise, no violence, just a calm centre. I could investigate whatever I wanted in the library without criticism and I could look up the trajectory of planets, the sex life or lack of it of the earthworm, the reason for World War II or home remedies for acne. Anything I could think of, I would likely find something about it in the library. There was something about a library that made my neck and back relax. I felt at peace as if I was cocooned from the world in this room. The new libraries with glass, long ash tables with chrome legs, high counters that displayed "Welcome" in jarring red paint did not give me the same sense of belonging. I appreciated this collection of books on high shelves, the antique furniture and heavy, elderly drapes in this house.

Mary stood by the door, looking around, probably checking as the hostess that all was well.

Thomas and Barbara were seated at the long table where they had begun organizing the books. They were a contrast. Thomas with his grey hair, grey sweater, blue eyes hunched a little over the papers. Barbara, although not as tall as Thomas, looked taller because she sat stiffly erect, her black hair piled high on top of her head, her scarlet sweater a dramatic statement. She would not be easily overlooked in any room. Her silver bangles dangled from her wrists and jingled as she moved her hand.

Thomas had spread the ledger open on the table and piled some books in front of him. Barbara had a notebook, a pen and a frown on her face. Thomas gestured to the chair beside him.

"Welcome, Claire. My, you are wet."

"It's pouring out there."

Barbara didn't say anything as I assumed she had managed to arrive before the rain and was immaculate and dry. She was making no secret of the fact she didn't want me here. I decided to ignore her attitude as a legitimate member of this committee.

"Do you think we can put these records in a computer file?" I asked. "It would be too easy to have the ledger disappear." Was the fire here last week an attempt to burn the ledger? I hadn't thought of that before.

"We don't need that," Barbara said.

At the same time, Mary said, "Good idea. It'd be easy to check on something and easy to send files to others. You should do that."

"Can you operate the computer, Claire?" Thomas asked, neatly deflecting Barbara.

"Everyone can operate a computer," Barbara said. "Five-year-olds can operate a computer."

Behind Barbara's back, Mary raised her eyebrows as if to say 'What a difficult guest!'

"I can, indeed, operate a computer as I do so in my work every day." I answered Thomas and touched the keyboard. The computer sprang to life. Thomas reached over, typed in his password, scrolled to the library files and pulled up the catalog.

"I started a file," he said apologetically. "But I don't have much in it."

I knew that, as there were very few bytes in that file.

"I'll record them as you and Barbara find them," I offered.

So that's what we did for two hours while the storm raged outside. Mary was right about the way the house creaked. I heard groans from the floor above us and rattling of loose shutters. I wondered if my house made storm noises. If so, I hoped Gulliver was sleeping through it. Thomas pulled a book from the shelf and read out the pertinent information to me. I created a template, so I didn't have to type in "Title, author, date of publication, condition and donated by" every time and recorded his reports, questioning the spelling occasionally. Barbara also pulled books from the shelves and read out the information to me. I could keep up with the two of them, because they had to put the books back, and that took a few moments. We got into a work rhythm and managed to get quite a lot done, although it was going to take many weeks to go through it all. It surprised me that we worked so well together. It was as if tension had eased because we were united in a task. While the storm seemed to be dumping the ocean from Newfoundland on us, there was only a little wind and our electricity remained constant.

Mary left us and returned a couple of times. Gracie stayed, sleeping on a dog bed near the fireplace, occasionally snorting or coughing.

I typed constantly but kept an eye on where Thomas and Barbara were getting the books. I watched to see where on the shelves they were pulling out the books and if either of them was hiding anything. I compared what I was typing into the computer files with what Mrs. Paulson had recorded in the ledger. Thomas had the most opportunity to steal from the collection or to hide artifacts. He would know where everything was and could easily keep us from finding such purloined items. That didn't make Thomas a murderer. So far, everything Barbara and Thomas reported to me matched what was in the ledger or was something new which I added. It became apparent we were going to have to finish the whole collection before we knew if anything was missing. Even then, some letters or books might not have been cataloged. After two hours, my head ached. I hoped Gulliver was sleeping.

I was grateful to see Mary arriving with a tray of sherry and cake. I decided I would leave after I had some cake but only if Thomas and Barbara stopped. It was important to have all three of us doing the work together. Mark also expected me to supervise this process.

"Very nice, Mary. Thank you," Barbara said. The words were gracious, but patronizing.

"How are you doing?" Mary asked.

"Very well." Barbara answered for the three of us.

I stretched and yawned. "We're getting some good records established, and we certainly have some interesting books," I said.

"Why do you suppose that Detective Inspector wanted this audit," Mary asked.

Barbara snorted. "He is looking for a motive for Isobel's murder. As if the books could tell us."

"Oh." Mary was quiet for a moment and then said, "Who do you think murdered her, Barbara?"

"Who knows? She had some odd friends. Maybe someone from her past."

"She *had* a past?" I asked.

Barbara shot me a glare. I didn't react.

Barbara had the floor and continued. "Everyone has

some kind of past. Isobel was quite the flirt. She flirted with my husband before we were married. Almost married him herself, but I put a stop to it."

"I hadn't heard that," Thomas said. "I never saw her that way."

"She was always pulling everyone and everything toward herself. Like some kind of giant magnet."

I thought that could describe Barbara. We often don't like in others what we abhor in ourselves.

"You'd known her since you were at school?" I finished the last of the entries, saved the file and shut down the computer.

"Of course." Barbara sipped her sherry but continued, "I wasn't surprised she died. Although, I thought she would have died from a surfeit of bile."

Thomas choked on his drink. I turned to him with concern but saw the twinkle in his eyes. He was trying to contain a laugh. I smiled.

How odd that the four of us were sitting in this eighteenth century elegance, partaking in a sherry party and discussing murder.

TWENTY-TWO

THE DOORBELL RANG with a much more musical chime than clattered in my house. Gracie lifted her head. Mary left to answer the door. We heard the murmur of voices then Mary's footsteps returning to the library door.

"Thomas, the restoration people are here. They were supposed to come earlier, but the storm held them back."

Thomas glanced toward the window. "Has it stopped?"

"It's abated a little. In any case, they have arrived, and they need a decision on the bedroom wall. I know what I want, but you need to back me up. They are hoping to put in something substandard." She spoke directly to Thomas and didn't look at Barbara. I don't suppose Barbara would require backup with any worker and was prepared to tell Mary how to manage the tradespeople. I suspected that avoiding eye contact with Barbara was Mary's way of forestalling criticism. It worked, because Barbara didn't comment.

"Coming, my dear." Thomas stood. "Please excuse me," he said to us.

"I'll take Gracie into the back garden," Mary said. "She needs to go out, then I'll join you upstairs."

I was beginning to understand a little about the interactions of these three "friends". Mary and Thomas were polite to Barbara but slipped around any direct confrontation. It was a good strategy and I would keep it in mind.

I helped myself to a glass of sherry and some cake and put them on the table near the filing cabinet. I'd been wanting to get into that filing cabinet all afternoon. This small break was my chance. I left the sherry and cake on the table and walked over the cabinet. I opened the middle drawer, pulled out the Christie letters and showed them to Barbara. I went over to the table where we had been working and splayed the letters in front of her. If she was a true Christie aficionado, she would be thrilled.

"There must be more letters," I said.

Her eyes widened. Then she looked away, took a deep breath and turned back to me. The silence lengthened.

"Very enterprising of you," she finally said.

She showed no surprise. "Did you know about this?"

"Of course."

She *had* known about them but wasn't happy that now I did.

She sniffed. "I thought you might discover them. Inevitable given your penchant for nosiness that you would find them. You are a researcher—*some* kind of researcher, so I understand—researching sites and travel destinations. You'd know how to look. I thought of that." She raised her head and glared. "I won't have it. Snooping into the filing cabinet. Unearthing the letters. They are none of your business!"

She was focusing on the fact I'*d* found them—not on their existence. She *had* known about them. Was she keeping them hidden until the missing letters were found? That would make the whole set of letters much more valuable than just these two. What was the problem with the letters?

"They're records, aren't they?" I asked. "And they are legitimate records of the club."

Barbara grabbed the letters from me, marched back to the filing cabinet, thrust the letters into the drawer and slammed it shut. She turned and almost spit at me. "You are far too busy ferreting out information and passing it along to the constabulary. Peter Brown told me you gave the vase you so kindly brought to me to your detective friend."

I should have remembered that Peter, who noticed everything, was working in my yard when Mark arrived. Peter was like a sieve, everything that poured into him also poured out. He'd told Barbara.

"Looking for fingerprints, I hear." Barbara was seething. What might defuse this situation? Empathy? Reason?

I could understand she thought I'd been sneaky. Truth to tell, I had been sneaky. Peter must have seen me carrying the vase into the house and Mark coming out with it. Peter and Rose should be town criers. I decided to tell her what I knew.

"Detective Inspector Evans is looking to eliminate suspects," I said. "If you didn't kill Mrs. Paulson you have nothing to worry about."

"If I did?"

Silence stretched for a long moment.

"Then I expect you'd better worry," I said slowly.

In that instant, I abandoned Thomas and Mary as suspects. I had been so wrong about them, concocting motives and opportunities and ignoring Barbara. They were just what they appeared to be—civilized, ethical and reliable. I kept my voice calm, but asked a question. "Why did you do it?"

She looked around, walked over to the door and shut it. I mentally measured the distance between where I was standing and the door. She returned to stand by the table. "I can tell you because I can just deny this. No one would believe you in any case—you're an outsider."

That wasn't true. They might not believe me, because I didn't have any proof. I didn't think the constabulary was prejudiced against outsiders. Besides, she couldn't claim I was hand in glove with the constabulary and then aver they wouldn't believe me. Her reasoning process was unravelling.

She stood quietly for a moment. "Isobel Paulson suspected what that detective suspects—that artifacts are missing."

"Are they?"

She said. "Of course, they are."

She said that so calmly that it slid into my mind smoothly and it took me a moment to absorb the dreadful loss to scholarship. Letters. Agatha Christie's letters. I was silent.

"How do you think I keep my house looking so lovely?" She turned and paced between me and the door, her body rigid, her posture impeccably straight, only her hands, jerking a little, betrayed any sign of emotion.

All right, she'd stolen important letters. That was bad enough, but she also just admitted to killing Mrs. Paulson. What was she going to do to me? She was intent on talking. I could deal with talking. I couldn't prove any of this, and she would know that.

"I was in an impossible situation. Isobel was supposed to be the poor one. I married her fiancé, you know." She glanced at me to be sure I understood.

I nodded, fascinated yet unnerved by the long-ago twisting of the love lives of Barbara and Isobel.

"Marshall Manning was rich and going to get richer. I had no intention of being poor. It wasn't hard to turn his head toward me and get him to the registrar. Isobel married that local boy Ernie Paulson who worked on the railroad. She was supposed to have a life of near poverty, and I was supposed to have a life of wealth." She nodded to herself and to me emphatically.

I didn't say anything for fear of the breaking flow of words, and also because I couldn't think of anything to say to such a colossal ego.

"It worked like that for many years, but then Marshall got dementia. If I'd recognized it earlier, I would have taken the power of attorney into my hands, but he was too far gone when I got the diagnosis. By then, he'd given away money and made poor investments. He couldn't give permission for the financial power to pass to me and I had to live under the auspices of the Official Solicitor and Public Trustee. Do you have any idea how demeaning that is? I had to account to a snotty little public servant for every penny I spent. They took thirty percent of the estate for 'administration'." She spate out the word. "Those last two years under their thumb were terrible, until Marshall died…providentially." She paused.

I waited. I wondered if poor Marshall had been helped out of this world. She didn't elaborate.

"Then Ernie Paulson died, and Isobel inherited his investments. He had a good pension which she got and years of investments which he hadn't even told her about. Now, she was the rich one, and did she let me know it! Offering me concert tickets. A ride in her new car. Sickening. I wasn't having that."

I understood it galled her, but I couldn't find one ounce of compassion for her. I rather thought Mrs. Paulson's wealth was some kind of nemesis. Barbara had snatched her fiancé, after all, but I wasn't about to offer my opinion.

"So you took the letters from the collection," I said.

"Of course, I did. Anyone would have. Those letters written by Agatha Christie were just sitting there ignored. I knew how to get money for them. The Internet sale sites are quite easy to use. I covered my tracks very well. You won't find any record of them here." She sounded smug.

I had no idea how long Thomas would be away or what plans Barbara had for me. I took a tissue from my bag and wiped my hands.

"I see. How long have you been taking things from the collection?"

"Oh, several years," she said offhandedly.

I put the tissue back in my bag and scrabbled around with my fingers to find my cell phone. Mark's number was speed-dialed on "9" on my phone. I felt for the lower right-hand part of the screen and pressed it. The sound was off. I hoped there was enough charge on the phone to make the connection. I couldn't hear the phone dialing, but I could feel some vibrations, and then they stopped. I spoke quickly.

"Since I'm here in Thomas' library with you alone, Barbara, why don't you tell me all about it?" I spoke clearly and, I hoped, loud enough for Mark to hear me— if he picked up the call.

"I will, because you won't be around to report on me."

That was chilling. What was she planning? It was the middle of the day. Thomas, Mary and the restoration man were nearby. In spite of what seemed to be a protected environment, I was getting more and more uneasy about my safety. I would have figure out when to scream.

I doubted Mark could hear Barbara's voice through my bag. He might hear me, though, and, with luck, realize I was in trouble. Whatever he did or didn't hear was irrelevant right now, I couldn't rely on him to save me. Nor could I rely on him to understand the situation even if he *did* hear me. I'd better make plans to extricate myself. Barbara turned on me with what sounded like hatred.

"You are so rich, so privileged. You don't know what it's like to come to the end of the month with no money to buy food."

She saw herself as a victim in an unfair world. I *did* know what it was like to live close to starvation, but the truth didn't matter. She wouldn't consider she'd been wrong about me, because, of course, she couldn't be wrong about anything. There would be no reasoning with her. How could Barbara injure me or kill me? Put something in my food? In my drink? I eyed the sherry glass. With one sweep of my bag, I knocked it over.

Barbara laughed. "Very good. That was my first plan, but not my only plan." She reached into her bag. "You have just postponed your death. I have a spray here. It will do just as well, even better. So sad. Someone so young, having a heart attack. We will all miss you." She smiled. "I *always* have a contingency plan."

She was terrifying—so logical, so implacable.

She pulled out what looked like an ordinary bottle

of nose spray, the kind everyone carries in the winter when colds abound. She held it up, shook it, put her finger on the spray and started toward me.

"Do you carry poison just in case you want to kill somebody?" I wanted to keep her talking, and I wanted to stay alive. Was it nerve gas? Cyanide? Some kind of contact poison. Snippets of newspaper stories and TV reports of poison raced through my mind. Contact poison seemed totally possible.

"Of course not. I carried it today because I wanted to kill you. You, specifically. I'd planned to walk home with you and kill you in the lane. That would leave only Thomas and me to do the audit. I can manage him. The lane would have been private and I can't afford to wait now."

I gawked at her, almost paralyzed. What could I do? Scream, run, hit? Standing still was not an option.

I backed away. She wasn't in a hurry, just kept moving forward. I edged toward the fireplace. She was three steps away from me and raising her arm to spray me. I grabbed the poker with both hands and swung mightily, knocking the spray from her hand and striking her arm in the process. I heard a crack. The poker jerked almost rebounding out of my hands, but I kept hold of it. Barbara screamed and clutched her injured arm. Good. I hope I broke it. I tightened my grip, ready for another attack.

Mary and Thomas rushed in. Barbara and I must have appeared to be a tableau—Barbara clutching her arm, me standing at the fireplace with a poker in my hand. I'd forgotten to scream.

Mary stopped in the middle of the room and turned her head back and forth, as she tried to see if there was anyone else or anything else precipitating this scene. I saw her notice the spilled sherry and head toward it, her housekeeping actions no doubt instinctive.

I shouted at her. "Mary, don't touch the sherry glass or the sherry. Barbara may have poisoned it. Don't touch it. There's a spray bottle somewhere. Don't touch it either, but we must find it." I shouted those orders but didn't take my eyes off Barbara, the poker still at the ready. Thank God, this was an old house with a real poker-equipped fireplace.

It never occurred to me that Thomas and Mary might not trust me.

"She tried to kill me," Barbara said, whimpering a little. "She attacked me with that poker. I think she broke my arm."

Thomas started toward Barbara, his face showing concern.

Mark burst into the room. I thought for a moment he was an apparition.

"What do you need?" he said to me.

"The spray bottle. On the floor somewhere. Handle it carefully. I expect it has yew poison in it—or some other poison."

Barbara erupted in rage. "How could you stop me? How could you possibly stop me? You are an outsider!" She screamed at me. Thomas stepped back.

Mark raised his eyebrows and glanced at me. "An outsider, eh?"

"Restrain her," I snapped. "For God's sake."

Mark spoke into his phone. I thought he ordered a police car and two men.

"There!" I spotted the nasal spray near the table on the rug.

Mark whipped out an evidence bag and encased it in plastic.

Barbara stamped her foot and then reacted as she jolted her broken arm. She screamed and stopped moving. Her voice, though, was strong and full of rage.

"This is intolerable. That interloper has no rights here. *I* do. I have a right to whatever I can find in this collection. I'm entitled to it. I have worked for this club for twenty years. No one else cared what was here."

Mark nodded keeping his eyes on her. "Is that so?"

Barbara ran on in full spate. "No one cared except Isobel. *She* just wanted to thwart me. She knew I had been taking letters and books from here for years and selling them. But would she keep quiet about it? No. She was going to report me. I knew she would make me beg her to not tell the police or the club. I needed money and she didn't. Her with her fancy income. I didn't take too much at a time. No one but Isobel suspected me. She should have kept quiet. It was her own fault."

Fury had given her strength. She stood tall and magnificent, dark eyes flashing, her hair lacquered into its regal braid on top of her head but her face blotched with red spots. We stared at her, stunned and silent, even Mark who must have heard some bizarre confessions was quiet.

It was possible that the almost regal atmosphere of Thomas and Mary's library lulled Barbara into thinking she was having a civilized discussion with equals. She looked eager, even desperate, to display her intelligence.

"I was the one who developed the buyers, who knew how to sell and not be detected. She spoiled it all just the way this interfering outsider," she pointed at me, "spoiled it all. They both found out by studying the

collection. No one studies the collection. The membership just wants skits and entertainment. There were no
scholars until her." She jabbed her finger in my direction. "Thomas was too lazy to catalogue the library."
She sent Thomas a scornful look.

"How did you know there would be letters?" I said
softly, anxious not to distract her from her story but
wanting to understand.

"I knew Agatha would write to Madge about the precise references to Abney Hall. A scholar would figure
that out. Or someone with an overblown curiosity. I did
not want anyone in the library." She cradled her broken
arm, but she stood straight and defiant.

"Why didn't Thomas find it?" Mark asked. Did he
want to know if Thomas had colluded with her?

Barbara almost smiled. "He was working under my
direction. I advised him to work chronologically, and he
hadn't gotten to 1927 yet. When he did?" She shrugged.
"He'd have an accident. But he might never get there.
He's very slow."

I heard Mary gasp.

"Why poison?" I said. I thought I knew but wanted
to hear what she'd say.

"It was all there in the letters. Agatha told Madge
how to conduct the 'perfect murder' using yew. I just
followed her directions. She gave very detailed directions. She'd worked in a pharmacy, you know."

I nodded. I had known that fact.

"No one should have known about it." She glared at
Mark. "How did *you* find out?"

Mark kept his voice steady and calm. "Not through
the letters. I got your fingerprints from the vase, and

they match the fingerprints on the cup and on the cupboard door at Mrs. Paulson's."

Barbara hissed at me. "You did this to me. You got in the way"

Mark resumed talking in a slow, steady voice. "That was enough probable cause to get access to your bank accounts. You have been getting periodic income no one can account for. HM Revenue and Customs would have inquired about it eventually. That was enough evidence, along with your attempt today to kill Claire Barclay, to bring you in, detain you and charge you."

"You can't do that," Barbara whispered. I think she just realized she was going to be arrested. She looked shocked as if she couldn't believe she was no longer in charge.

Mark gave her the official caution. "You do not have to say anything. But it may harm your defense if you do not mention when questioned something which you later rely on in court. Anything you do say may be given in evidence."

"I won't go." Barbara said firmly.

We all heard the siren approaching the house.

"What," Mark said, "was Isobel Paulson doing that made her a threat to you?"

Barbara almost spat out her explanation. "She was doing what Claire Barclay was doing, searching through the manuscripts looking for discrepancies. Nosy. They were both too nosy for their own good."

"You might want to take the sherry glass and test it for poison," I said.

Mark pulled out another evidence bag and encased the sherry glass.

"Waterford," Mary whispered.

That was expensive crystal.

"You'll get it back." Mark assured her.

Mary shuddered. I don't suppose she wanted it back.

Two police officers appeared at the library door. Barbara was suddenly silent. The two officers, one tall and broad and one short and broad, conferred briefly with Mark and then escorted Barbara from the library and presumably into the police car. We stood for a moment in silence after she left as if in respectful tribute to the death of a dominating personality, or perhaps we were just dumbfounded at the extent of Barbara's callousness. In my case, it might have been a profound relief at being alive.

Mark turned to me. "Are you all right?" He took the poker from my hand—I had forgotten I was still holding it—and leaned it against the fireplace. He pulled me close and hugged me.

I froze for a moment and then leaned into him. "How did you get here so fast?" I spoke into his jacket. The speed of his arrival bothered me.

"I was already on my way. After I talked to the bank manager, I was heading to Barbara's house and then realized you were working here in the library today. I got your call just as I was approaching the house."

"At least, you came in time." I took a deep breath.

"I ran." he said simply and hugged me again.

"Thanks."

He closed his eyes. "I have a feeling you will make my heart stop many times."

I tried a smile but didn't quite pull it off. "Those letters." I sighed. "I can't believe they are gone."

It was almost physically painful for me to think that the letters which had been hidden in this collection, had been discovered by the unscrupulous Barbara and whisked away before scholars could study or report on them.

"Those letters she sold. They went to private collectors and we'll never find them." I moaned.

"Probably not," Mark said.

TWENTY-THREE

MARK HUNG YELLOW police tape across the library door and we adjourned to the kitchen which was small and cramped. The cooker crowded the sink, and the refrigerator pushed into a nearby pantry. The counters were stacked with containers and papers. What saved this kitchen from being impossible to use was a comfortable sitting room at one end. That was where we assembled.

Mark directed Mary and Thomas to sit on the easy chairs. They sat straight. Mary's hands were folded in her lap They looked calm and ready for questions. Mark sent me a sharp, assessing look and left me huddled in one of the overstuffed chairs nearby. He pulled out a hard-backed chair for himself and settled across from Mary and Thomas. They were older than me. I worried they have might have been be experiencing shock, but they appeared strong.

"Tell me what you experienced," Mark said to Mary. "from the time you opened the door to Barbara until we left the library."

He had his notebook and tablet in front of him. I think the tablet worked as a recorder for the interview, because he gave his name, rank and time and then Mary and Thomas's names.

Mary spoke hesitantly at first and then more smoothly as she talked and reported what she'd seen and heard. It calmed me to listen to her and imagine the events as she'd seen them.

"I think Barbara is a little mad," she concluded.

I would guess Barbara was more than a *little* mad.

"Possibly," Mark said.

Thomas reported his own version of his day which included a mild argument with the restoration man. Thomas was a surprisingly firm character. Because he seemed so gentle and retiring, his resolution surprised me. His verbal tousle with the restoration man about the work which was to be done in the bedroom and the costs involved showed he was not always acquiescent. He didn't confront either, just gave directions in a determined voice.

"I couldn't believe she was so homicidal," he said. "I was no help to Claire," he nodded an apology at me, "no help at all."

"Understandable," Mark said. "Luckily, Claire takes action on her own."

"Not something I want to do often," I said. "I was grateful the poker was handy."

Mark closed his notebook and slid the bar on his tablet.

"Thanks very much. I wonder if you could get Claire a cup of tea."

Tea? I glanced at him.

He correctly interpreted my glance. "Or coffee. She's had a difficult day."

What an understatement.

Mary jumped up and began to assemble the coffee.

I expected Mark to interview me next, but he shoved his tablet and notebook into his pocket and crouched down in front of me.

"I can't take your statement," he said. He picked up my hand and rubbed it between his. I hadn't realized I was cold. I shivered. He continued a gentle, comforting rubbing.

"I'm not a disinterested official," he said, smiling a little. "I'll call a constable."

What a time and place for some kind of declaration? I couldn't process it as my brain was overloaded with adrenaline and wild reactions. I took a deep, slow breath. Then another. I just couldn't answer.

The constable arrived. Mary let him in. He looked to be a teen but was probably twenty-four. He was tall and as thin as a heron with his beak-like nose. What a thing to think of in this situation. He smiled and his bright blue eyes were kind.

Mark hugged me and then got up to leave. "I'll be over later."

"Okay," I said.

Mary handed around the coffee in mugs. I took a sip. Wonderful.

The constable had his own tablet, recording device and individual notebook. He sat on a chair beside me and dictated the date, time, his own name, "Michael Emmett", rank, "Constable" and then leaned toward me.

"Tell me what happened, madam, in as orderly a fashion as possible, if you please."

I leaned forward, cupping my hands around the hot mug. The warmth seeped through my fingers and up into my shoulders. I felt them drop as I began speaking.

"She's barmy." I said.

"Yes, madam. What happened?" He was polite but persistent. I realized my opinions were not important here.

I started at the point where Mary left the library and

reported everything from that time on to when Mary and Thomas appeared. The constable typed silently. He occasionally prompted me with: Then what happened? What did she say? Could you repeat that? He took me painstakingly through the afternoon.

Thomas sat listening but said nothing. Mary brought shortbread and left it where we could help ourselves. I was ravenous and grabbed two. I drank the coffee, stuffed in the shortbread and rattled off the events of the afternoon as I remembered them. When I had finished relating everything I could remember, the constable offered me a stylus to sign the statement on the tablet.

"You'll have to come to the office, read the hard copy and sign it," he said, "but we have this to be going on with."

I thanked him. He unfolded his long legs, stood, nodded to Thomas and Mary and left. I sat there for a moment, just staring at the floor. A glass of amber liquid appeared in front of me. Thomas was offering it.

"Scotch," he said. "Good for shock."

Mary with a glass of scotch in her hand sank into the remaining easy chair. "Good for everything that ails you," she said and took a gulp of her own drink.

I followed suit and felt the warmth slide down into my core. I took another sip and settled back in my chair. Gracie shuffled up to me and laid her baggy chin on my knees. I petted her. I felt the inner warmth from the scotch, the shared warmth emanating from Gracie, and I relaxed. It had been horrible. I didn't realize I was crying until a tear dropped on my hand.

"I'm sorry," I said.

"Quite understandable," Thomas said.

Mary handed me a tissue.

I composed myself but kept one hand on Gracie as I mopped my face. I sipped at my scotch and absorbed the comfort of the two sane, reliable people near me and the empathetic dog cuddling close. I was so grateful for these kind people in my life.

"What do you suppose they'll do to her?" Mary asked.

"Keep her incarcerated," Thomas said. "Get a psychiatric assessment. Charge her with attempted murder of Claire and the murder of Isobel." He enumerated his list quickly.

We were silent, contemplating Barbara's future.

"She won't be released, will she Thomas?" Mary asked.

I didn't think Thomas would know, but Mark would. I'd ask him.

"No, my dear. I doubt it very much. She's a danger to the public, and D.I. Evans will be very sure to look after Claire's interests. He will make it his business, I suspect, to keep Barbara in jail."

"Good," Mary said.

I didn't think Mark had that much influence on the justice system, but if it brought comfort to Mary, I wasn't going to argue.

We sat in another restful silence. Then Mary ventured. "About the library?"

"We will simply keep the door shut until the police are done."

"And then we'll hire Rose to do a thorough cleaning." She stated that firmly.

"Certainly," Thomas agreed. "After the police have conducted a hazards removal operation. At least that's what D.I. Evans told me would happen."

Mary studied her drink, turning the glass around in her hands.

"She was a good woman once," Mary said.

"Do you think so?" Thomas sounded doubtful.

"Well, she did a lot of good."

"That I can agreed with," he said. "But that is a different concept from being good."

Mary sipped her scotch and seemed to ponder her own words, as if they were floating in the air above the glass.

"She got the WI going. It was down to five members when she took it on."

"True," Thomas said.

"She was almost totally responsible for the new roof on the church hall."

"That as well, "Thomas said. "A woman who did good but was not in herself good. Not loving. Not kind."

"Stunted, do you think?" Mary asked.

I wondered if they talked like this in the evening when they were alone. They were shuttlecocking ideas back and forth as if they'd forgotten I was in the room.

"Mired in adolescence, I suspect," Thomas said. "Trying to create a world where she was the star. Trying to be the centre of some universe of her own making. Much like many of my students."

"Not a useful strategy. That world would get smaller and smaller, wouldn't it? In any case, it didn't work. She was always on the outside of any group. She thought she was in the centre, but really, she was on the outside. No authentic connections to people. I wonder if she felt that?" Mary mused over Barbara's psyche.

"Now she will be labelled a deviant and will have to face that designation. Once she is in jail, she will have to see herself as unacceptable to normal society. It will be tragic for her."

"More tragic for Mrs. Paulson," I reminded them and myself. "And nearly tragic for me."

There was a sudden silence as if my words had jerked them back to a murderous reality.

"Oh, my dear heavens!" Mary almost wailed. For all their concern about Barbara's values, she hadn't been an interesting, text-book case. She'd been a huge and real danger to us, particularly to me. "Claire, I'm so sorry and in my house."

"No, no. It was not your fault," I said. "What a day."

"Indeed." Thomas leaned over and patted my arm. "Would you like to stay here for the night?"

I smiled at him. What a dear. "No, thanks, Thomas. I'll go home." I gave Gracie a final pat. "And pet my own dog."

"I'll walk you home," he said.

I convinced him it wasn't necessary. I didn't live far, and with Barbara in custody, I wasn't afraid to walk home. Besides, he needed to stay with Mary. I was an independent woman, after all.

I left them to the comfort of their home, their dog and each other and walked slowly to my own house. Gulliver was ecstatic to see me. I clipped on his leash and took him for a long walk across the river, up the hill and over the Downs. The exercise felt wonderful. I would call Deirdre and tell her all about it, but not tonight. I didn't want to think about it any more tonight.

Night was falling as I unlocked the kitchen door. I paused for a moment, listening to the song thrush. It likes the evening hours and sings energetically, throwing out twitters, whistles, shrill calls and warbling notes as if having a lively conservation with itself. I fed Gulliver and dug out some ham and salad from the fridge for my supper. The scotch had long since worn off, so I poured myself a lovely Bordeaux from Saint Emilion and tumbled into bed.

TWENTY-FOUR

I SLEPT RIGHT through the night. I read somewhere that eight hours of sleep regenerates the brain—and my poor anxiety-ridden, adrenalin overloaded brain definitely needed help. Apparently, tiny cells in the brain operate like vacuum cleaners, hoovering up all the floating fragments which slow down cognition. I trust those little hoover cells had done their work last night, so I could cope with whatever the day brought. I'd slept as if I'd dropped into a deep well. If Gulliver had wanted to go out during the night, I never heard his demands. First thing in the morning, he was desperate to hit the garden. He had his breakfast. I had my breakfast and coffee. I watched my hand as I picked up the mug—no shakes, no tremors. Sleep and caffeine. That ought to reset my energy.

I left a message for Deirdre that I would call later. She was in court in any case and wouldn't be free for a few hours. It was time to put Mrs. Paulson, Barbara and the drama of yesterday behind me. I had a trip to plan. I retired to my study and worked on my upcoming tour. This would be the first for my new company British Mystery Book Tours. Five tourists. Four women from Oregon who knew each other had signed up for this tour and sent me their deposits. The outlier, the women unknown to the others, was a professor of literature. That ought to add a little erudition to the tour.

She must love mysteries since she signed up for this tour, but she might be a stickler for authentic settings. I'd have to bone up on my research. If nothing changed greatly, the tour was set. We were going to Cornwall to visit the sites of the Dorothy Martin series by Jeanne Dams, the Eleanor Trewynn series by Carola Dunn and the old favourite, the Wycliffe series by W. J. Burley. I was taking them to St. Michael's Mount which was also a site of a cozy mystery, to a smuggler's cove and to Tintagel and Port Isaac—the setting of the Doc Martin TV series. I didn't want to go to Land's End because it's ugly, ruined by concrete buildings. The Minack Theatre at Porthcurno is worth seeing, but there were no plays running at that time of year. I'd take them into nearby Porthcurno as it is beautiful and situated near Penzance. It boasted a fishermen's choir we might be able to hear. I'd check the interests they listed and made sure I included something to satisfy everyone. At least, that was my goal. I worked hard to match the interests of my tourists with the events and sights of the area we were going to visit.

Gulliver and I took a long walk in the afternoon. The weather forecast was for cooling temperatures and rain, inevitable in Hampshire at this time of year, so I wanted to enjoy the last of the sunshine. It could rain here until May.

I finally caught Deirdre between cases. I told her about Barbara.

She was speechless for a full minute. That doesn't happen often.

"Are you still there, Deirdre?"

"I'm here. I'm appalled. Is the woman crazy?"

"That's my diagnosis, but I'm not sure a psychiatrist

would agree. I'd say morally depraved, narcissistically indifferent to others, single-minded and ruthless, belligerent and aggressive."

"All right. All right," she interrupted me. "Criminally responsible?"

"I think so," I said.

"Good."

Deirdre liked to see accountability enforced. It was that passion for justice that we both possessed.

"What about you?" she asked. "Are you okay?"

"Apparently."

"Did you sleep?"

"Deeply."

"Don't be afraid to check with a physician if you need something to calm you down. That must have been a horrendous experience."

I didn't know if I was resilient or shallow, but yesterday seemed a long time ago, and my experience hadn't kept me awake, relentlessly reviewing every second of it.

"I think I'm fine."

"Take Gulliver for a walk."

"I will. He's wonderful, Deirdre. You were right about him."

"Just get out with him and walk off the blues."

Deirdre can't help but give orders. The secret of staying friends with her is to love her and ignore what doesn't suit.

"We'll probably drop over to see you," she said.

I thought she might want to reassure herself. She would have to see me to make sure I was not devastated by trauma.

"It would be good to see you anytime." I agreed to the visit.

About seven that evening Robert dropped by.

"I brought some dog treats for Gulliver." He proffered a bag. He looked a bit like a dog himself—a St. Barnard—stocky, big shoulders, reliable. Nice of him to come. I supposed the whole village had heard about Barbara by now.

"Come in. He'll love those."

Robert divested himself of his padded winter jacket, stuffed his gloves into the pockets and hung it in my closet. "Just give him one if he does something to earn it. Treats are a training tool. Have you been reading all about training?"

"I have, and it's a whole new world for me." I led the way down my hall to the kitchen. I knew he was behind me, but I couldn't hear him. For a big man, he walked very lightly.

"We've come a long way from the jerk-to-punish methods of thirty years ago," he said. "Rewards really do work better. They make a dog want to please you." He headed for a chair by the kitchen table.

I pulled down two wine glasses. "Red?" I asked.

"Sure. Just a small one. I have to do surgery tomorrow, and I can't handle much liquor."

That was another thing I liked about Robert. He was responsible without making anyone else feel irresponsible. He never suggested I shouldn't have a glass of wine and nor did he act as if limiting his wine was a moral problem—just a practical one.

I poured the wine—mine full—Robert's half-full, when the doorbell rasped its harsh announcement. Mark, and behind him, Mary and Thomas. Mary was carrying a bag from which poked the top of a wine bottle.

"Oh great. I was hoping you'd come by," I addressed that to Mark, then smiled a welcome at Thomas and Mary.

"Come in. Come in."

"Detective Inspector Evans suggested we meet at your house." Mary said gruffly. "I was going to call first, but he hustled us."

"He's like that." I hung her coat beside Robert's. The men had hung theirs up themselves and were already heading for the kitchen.

"Make yourself at home," I said to Mark's back.

He turned his head and gave me a wicked grin. "Maybe later."

I rolled my eyes.

Mary cocked her head and raised her eyebrows in inquiry.

"He's trying," I explained.

"How is he doing?" She waited for an answer.

"Pretty good." I admitted honestly.

I retrieved more glasses, and Mark poured the wine. I found some crackers and cheese and set those out.

Again, the doorbell crashed. This time it was Deirdre and Michael. I should have hung a sign "Party here". I felt a lift of spirits. I hadn't realized I was a little down until people who obviously cared about me arrived to give me their support. I did have friends.

"Welcome, you two."

"I want to know all about it," Deirdre said. She flitted into the kitchen like a robin, always busy, always alert and colourful. Michael followed her, his tall frame bulked up with sweaters, and he was a big man to start with. His brown eyes took in everyone in the room. I bet he could give you a description of us all. An intelligent man. Too quiet, I thought.

Deirdre and Michael fetched chairs from my study and the lounge and arranged them so everyone could sit and visit with one another in some comfort.

Gulliver was in heaven going from one person to another. Robert was making sure people didn't feed him crackers and cheese. Gulliver did manage to scrounge a bit from the floor, because Thomas, inevitably, spread crumbs as he gestured.

In a sudden lull in the conversation, I spoke across the room to Mark. "I have to know. Was there poison in that sherry?"

Everyone turned to Mark.

"There was yew poison in the sherry and the same poison in the spray bottle. She came prepared to kill," he said.

Robert persisted. "Yew needles are not a contact poison. You have to ingest them. She couldn't have killed Claire with the spray."

I stared at Robert. I hadn't thought of that aspect of the poison. All that ferocious hatred directed at me had made me believe I was in danger. My frantic determination to avoid that spray drove me to break Barbara's arm.

"True," Mark said.

"So, she can't be accused of attempted murder of Claire if what she was going to use wasn't lethal?" Deirdre wanted to understand the possible charges Barbara might face.

"Not for the attack with the spray bottle, no." Mark said. "But she put the poison in the sherry meant for

Claire. She will be charged with attempted homicide for that."

I thought about how she could have managed to drop the poison in the sherry. She must have put it in when I went to the file cabinet for the letters.

I shook my head. "Why would she want to kill me? I mean I know she thought I was going to find out about her thefts, but I might not have. *And* I had no way of proving she was the one who had stolen anything, even if I *had* figured out what letters were missing." I had worried that around in my head this morning.

"Yes," Robert said. "Why take the chance of murdering Claire or, for that matter, Mrs. Paulson? Barbara's thefts might never have been found out."

"Maybe she wasn't thinking clearly. She was full of hate and resentment that life was unfair," I said. "She wanted to destroy anything that stood in her way."

There was a short silence.

"Lots of people hate," Deirdre said, "just check on the Internet. But most people don't kill."

We argued about the role of hate in society and in politics. I poured more wine. At one point, Mark caught my eye and smiled. What *was* he planning?

The conversation lapsed a little, and Mary started to speak. Everyone listened.

"I think," she said, "Barbara Manning is a very self-centred woman. Always has been. Even from her early years. Isobel Paulson was a friend of my mother's. She was much younger than my mother, but they were friends in any case. Mother used to visit with her and listen to her. After Mother died, I visited with her in mother's place. It was not always pleasant, but I did it."

"You always do your duty." Thomas patted her hand.

Mary gave him an amazingly sweet smile then sat up even straighter and turned back to us.

"Isobel had difficult early years. She had been engaged to Marshall Manning, and she really loved him. Then Barbara set her sights on Marshall, his wealth and his potential for wealth and snatched him. That's how Isobel described it. 'She just snatched him.' Marshall and Barbara went away one weekend and were married. Marshall's engagement ring was still on Isobel's finger."

Gulliver lay at my feet and settled his head on his paws. He let out a huge sigh. No one laughed. We were all thinking about Mrs. Paulson and the way that tragedy might have marked her.

"That would have been a colossal betrayal," Deirdre said. She kept her eyes on Mary. I saw Michael send her a quick glance.

Mary's soft voice continued. "Isobel married Ernie Paulson, a good man, a solid man who loved her. She did her best with him, but her heart had been crushed by Marshall's desertion. She was never a happy person."

Betrayal can make a person bitter. Did I make myself unhappy because my old love Adam had not been reliable? I don't think so. Betrayal didn't *have* to make a person bitter.

"But," Thomas said. "Would you say Isobel Paulson was a vindictive person? Would she have wanted to hurt Barbara after all these years?"

"Oh yes," Mary said decisively. "I think so."

I thought about the two older women, apparently respectable, bustling with good works around town, busy with their interests in their established role in the village life, but feeling passion, frustration and hatred. I shivered.

"Barbara had a passion for fine things," I said slowly. "She had been wealthy, but her husband had gone through their money before he died." I spoke more quickly now. "Mrs. Paulson's husband left her well off. That grated on Barbara. She wanted money. She figured out how to get it from the library. Her expectation was that she could drain the collection for years. Isobel Paulson was going to interfere with that plan, so Barbara decided she would simply have to die. For Barbara, it was logical. She needed money. Mrs. Paulson was in her way. Mrs. Paulson had to die. She was just as ruthless as when she decided to marry Isobel's fiancé. She took what she wanted regardless of who got hurt."

"She had a rather simple mind," Thomas said. "Not subtle. Not cautious. She just directs her energy toward what she wants. It can be frightening." He blinked and sat back.

Mary's hand reached out and grasped his.

"That's interesting motivation," Michael said, "but how did she expect to get away with it? She left evidence at the scene of the murder, didn't she?" He sent a questioning look to Mark.

Mark nodded. "Fingerprints on the cup and on the table in the gazebo. And we found a witness who saw her go into the house from the lane."

Michael narrowed his eyes and leaned forward. "That's not enough evidence to convict her."

Mark agreed. "No. And even when we found someone who saw her picking yew twigs, that's still not enough evidence. Lucky for us she is singing like a bird."

"Really?" Deirdre said. "Didn't she have a barrister with her?

"She refused to call one," Mark said. "Too expensive."

"Penny wise, pound foolish," Deirdre almost snorted. "How did she expect to get away with murder when she left her fingerprints behind?"

Mark said. "She thought no one would suspect murder. She thought people would assume Isobel Paulson died of a heart attack—or so she says. Because Claire discovered the body and alerted the police, she also thought Claire was suspicious of her."

I was astounded. "Me?" Barbara had ideas about what was in my head, but I had been oblivious to what was going on in hers.

"She wasn't careful?" Deirdre said.

"That's right."

"It's not much of a case," Michael observed.

"No, but the case against her attempted murder of Claire is much stronger."

Deirdre sat up straight. Her eyes brightened. "What's the evidence there?"

"First, Claire's statement." He turned to me. "Which I need you to come into the station to sign."

I nodded. I could do that tomorrow.

"Then," he turned back to Deirdre. "The poison in the sherry and the spray bottle and her attack on Claire."

"That's good," Deirdre said. She meant it was "good" evidence, while still reserving her opinion of whether it was *enough* evidence.

"She poured out her story even after I cautioned her, so I heard it as well."

"That sounds much tighter," Michael said.

Deirdre nodded. "I like that bit."

Everyone stayed for another hour or so, talking about

the exigencies of evil and the possibilities of passion in this small village. They drank the wine and ate every piece of cheese I had in the house.

Deirdre and Michael had booked at the Badger's B & B and said they would be back in the morning. Mark remained when everyone had gone.

He helped me clean up the kitchen and then flicked on the fire in the lounge. I brought in some decafe coffee and put it on the low table in front of the fireplace.

Mark took my hand and pulled me down with him on the couch. I snuggled against him.

"That was pretty awful there in the library yesterday, Mark. That woman is demented."

"Fortunately, she's not—not within the meaning of the law. She can stand trial."

"I know. She's sane enough to manipulate everyone around her. Do you think she killed poor Marshall?"

"Marshall? Oh, the husband. Hard to know. That was about ten years ago. No one had any suspicions that I know of." He put his arm around my shoulders and tugged me close. I was still thinking about Barbara.

"I bet she did. Then when she wanted to get rid of Mrs. Paulson, she figured she could do it, because she'd done it before." My mind worried away at the possible crimes Barbara might have committed.

"Maybe." He sounded distracted.

I mourned the loss of those letters. "I wish I'd found the letters before Barbara did."

He pulled me closer and whispered. "On another subject.... how about I stay tonight?"

He was tempting, but my head gave instructions to ignore my heart. I felt a little off-centre, as if my stable view of life was unreliable. I hadn't assessed Barbara and the danger very well yesterday. I leaned against him. "How about you don't? Not yet."

He kissed my ear. "Too much too soon?"

"That's right." I was glad he could recognize what I was feeling.

"Your wish is my command. I'd better go."

I know one part of me would regret this. Part of me knew very well he was just what I wanted. He was in fact, almost irresistible. Later, I was sure I would be glad I'd slowed this down. Too fast, and I'd feel over-whelmed. I couldn't quite make up my mind about all of this. I was still catching up from almost dying.

Gulliver helped me out by sitting squarely in front of me, staring at me with his huge dark eyes.

"I'll see you to the door, Mark, but I have to let Gulliver out first."

"I'll wait."

Gulliver was quick, and I locked the back-garden door after he returned. Mark was leaning against the hall door jamb, watching me.

"We searched Barbara Manning's house this morning," he said.

"You did?" I was mildly interested but preoccupied by thoughts of the way Mark's muscles filled out that blue sweater.

"We found some letters."

My mind strayed for a moment then snapped to attention. "Old letters?"

"1926."

"Christie," I breathed.

"Would you like to look at them?"

"I would."

"I'll come back for you in the morning and take you

to the station. Right now, I want a proper good night."
He reached for me.

"How can I think about anything with the prospect
of looking at those missing letters?"

He hesitated. "Bad timing?"

I thought about his suggestion. The letters would
be waiting for me tomorrow. Mark was here tonight.

"I can be persuaded," I said.

* * * * *

ABOUT THE AUTHOR

EMMA DAKIN LIVES in Gibsons on the Sunshine Coast of British Columbia where she enjoys the seals, whales, mergansers, eagles and wildlife of the ocean and where she is an enthusiastic, if somewhat amateur, violinist. She has over twenty-five trade published books of mystery and adventure for teens and middle-grade children and non-fiction for teens and adults. Fiction is much more complicated and much more joyous. Her love of the British countryside and villages and her addiction to cozy mysteries now keep her immersed writing about characters who live and work in those villages. She introduces readers to the problems that disturb that idyllic setting.

Get 4 FREE REWARDS!

We'll send you 2 FREE Books plus 2 FREE Mystery Gifts.

Harlequin Intrigue books are action-packed stories that will keep you on the edge of your seat. Solve the crime and deliver justice at all costs.

FREE
Value Over
$20

YES! Please send me 2 FREE Harlequin Intrigue novels and my 2 FREE gifts (gifts are worth about $10 retail). After receiving them, if I don't wish to receive any more books, I can return the shipping statement marked "cancel." If I don't cancel, I will receive 6 brand-new novels every month and be billed just $4.99 each for the regular-print edition or $5.99 each for the larger-print edition in the U.S., or $5.74 each for the regular-print edition or $6.49 each for the larger-print edition in Canada. That's a savings of at least 12% off the cover price! It's quite a bargain! Shipping and handling is just 50¢ per book in the U.S. and $1.25 per book in Canada.* I understand that accepting the 2 free books and gifts places me under no obligation to buy anything. I can always return a shipment and cancel at any time. The free books and gifts are mine to keep no matter what I decide.

Choose one: ☐ **Harlequin Intrigue**
Regular-Print
(182/382 HDN GNXC)

☐ **Harlequin Intrigue**
Larger-Print
(199/399 HDN GNXC)

Name (please print)

Address   Apt. #

City   State/Province   Zip/Postal Code

Email: Please check this box ☐ if you would like to receive newsletters and promotional emails from Harlequin Enterprises ULC and its affiliates. You can unsubscribe anytime.

Mail to the **Harlequin Reader Service:**
IN U.S.A.: P.O. Box 1341, Buffalo, NY 14240-8531
IN CANADA: P.O. Box 603, Fort Erie, Ontario L2A 5X3

Want to try 2 free books from another series! Call 1-800-873-8635 or visit www.ReaderService.com.

*Terms and prices subject to change without notice. Prices do not include sales taxes, which will be charged (if applicable) based on your state or country of residence. Canadian residents will be charged applicable taxes. Offer not valid in Quebec. This offer is limited to one order per household. Books received may not be as shown. Not valid for current subscribers to Harlequin Intrigue books. All orders subject to approval. Credit or debit balances in a customer's account(s) may be offset by any other outstanding balance owed by or to the customer. Please allow 4 to 6 weeks for delivery. Offer available while quantities last.

Your Privacy—Your information is being collected by Harlequin Enterprises ULC, operating as Harlequin Reader Service. For a complete summary of the information we collect, how we use this information and to whom it is disclosed, please visit our privacy notice located at corporate.harlequin.com/privacy-notice. From time to time we may also exchange your personal information with reputable third parties. If you wish to opt out of this sharing of your personal information, please visit readerservice.com/consumerchoice or call 1-800-873-8635. **Notice to California Residents**—Under California law, you have specific rights to control and access your data. For more information on these rights and how to exercise them, visit corporate.harlequin.com/california-privacy.

HI21R

Get 4 **FREE REWARDS!**

We'll send you 2 FREE Books plus 2 FREE Mystery Gifts.

Harlequin Romantic Suspense books are heart-racing page-turners with unexpected plot twists and irresistible chemistry that will keep you guessing to the very end.

FREE Value Over **$20**

YES! Please send me 2 FREE Harlequin Romantic Suspense novels and my 2 FREE gifts (gifts are worth about $10 retail). After receiving them, if I don't wish to receive any more books, I can return the shipping statement marked "cancel." If I don't cancel, I will receive 4 brand-new novels every month and be billed just $4.99 per book in the U.S. or $5.74 per book in Canada. That's a savings of at least 13% off the cover price! It's quite a bargain! Shipping and handling is just 50¢ per book in the U.S. and $1.25 per book in Canada.* I understand that accepting the 2 free books and gifts places me under no obligation to buy anything. I can always return a shipment and cancel at any time. The free books and gifts are mine to keep no matter what I decide.

240/340 HDN GNMZ

Name (please print)

Address   Apt. #

City   State/Province   Zip/Postal Code

Email: Please check this box ☐ if you would like to receive newsletters and promotional emails from Harlequin Enterprises ULC and its affiliates. You can unsubscribe anytime.

Mail to the **Harlequin Reader Service:**
IN U.S.A.: P.O. Box 1341, Buffalo, NY 14240-8531
IN CANADA: P.O. Box 603, Fort Erie, Ontario L2A 5X3

Want to try 2 free books from another series? Call 1-800-873-8635 or visit www.ReaderService.com.

*Terms and prices subject to change without notice. Prices do not include sales taxes, which will be charged (if applicable) based on your state or country of residence. Canadian residents will be charged applicable taxes. Offer not valid in Quebec. This offer is limited to one order per household. Books received may not be as shown. Not valid for current subscribers to Harlequin Romantic Suspense books. All orders subject to approval. Credit or debit balances in a customer's account(s) may be offset by any other outstanding balance owed by or to the customer. Please allow 4 to 6 weeks for delivery. Offer available while quantities last.

Your Privacy—Your information is being collected by Harlequin Enterprises ULC, operating as Harlequin Reader Service. For a complete summary of the information we collect, how we use this information and to whom it is disclosed, please visit our privacy notice located at corporate.harlequin.com/privacy-notice. From time to time we may also exchange your personal information with reputable third parties. If you wish to opt out of this sharing of your personal information, please visit readerservice.com/consumerschoice or call 1-800-873-8635. **Notice to California Residents**—Under California law, you have specific rights to control and access your data. For more information on these rights and how to exercise them, visit corporate.harlequin.com/california-privacy.

HRS21R

Get 4 FREE REWARDS!

We'll send you 2 FREE Books <u>plus</u> 2 FREE Mystery Gifts.

FREE
Value Over
$20

Both the **Romance** and **Suspense** collections feature compelling novels written by many of today's bestselling authors.

YES! Please send me 2 FREE novels from the Essential Romance or Essential Suspense Collection and my 2 FREE gifts (gifts are worth about $10 retail). After receiving them, if I don't wish to receive any more books, I can return the shipping statement marked "cancel." If I don't cancel, I will receive 4 brand-new novels every month and be billed just $7.24 each in the U.S. or $7.49 each in Canada. That's a savings of up to 28% off the cover price. It's quite a bargain! Shipping and handling is just 50¢ per book in the U.S. and $1.25 per book in Canada.* I understand that accepting the 2 free books and gifts places me under no obligation to buy anything. I can always return a shipment and cancel at any time. The free books and gifts are mine to keep no matter what I decide.

Choose one: ☐ **Essential Romance**
(194/394 MDN GQ6M)

☐ **Essential Suspense**
(191/391 MDN GQ6M)

Name (please print)

Address   Apt. #

City   State/Province   Zip/Postal Code

Email: Please check this box ☐ if you would like to receive newsletters and promotional emails from Harlequin Enterprises ULC and its affiliates. You can unsubscribe anytime.

Mail to the **Harlequin Reader Service:**
IN U.S.A.: P.O. Box 1341, Buffalo, NY 14240-8531
IN CANADA: P.O. Box 603, Fort Erie, Ontario L2A 5X3

Want to try 2 free books from another series! Call 1-800-873-8635 or visit www.ReaderService.com.

*Terms and prices subject to change without notice. Prices do not include sales taxes, which will be charged (if applicable) based on your state or country of residence. Canadian residents will be charged applicable taxes. Offer not valid in Quebec. This offer is limited to one order per household. Books received may not be as shown. Not valid for current subscribers to the Essential Romance or Essential Suspense Collection. All orders subject to approval. Credit or debit balances in a customer's account(s) may be offset by any other outstanding balance owed by or to the customer. Please allow 4 to 6 weeks for delivery. Offer available while quantities last.

Your Privacy—Your information is being collected by Harlequin Enterprises ULC, operating as Harlequin Reader Service. For a complete summary of the information we collect, how we use this information and to whom it is disclosed, please visit our privacy notice located at corporate.harlequin.com/privacy-notice. From time to time we may also exchange your personal information with reputable third parties. If you wish to opt out of this sharing of your personal information, please visit readerservice.com/consumerchoice or call 1-800-873-8635. **Notice to California Residents**—Under California law, you have specific rights to control and access your data. For more information on these rights and how to exercise them, visit corporate.harlequin.com/california-privacy.

STRS21R

Get 4 FREE REWARDS!

We'll send you 2 FREE Books plus 2 FREE Mystery Gifts.

Love Inspired Suspense books showcase how courage and optimism unite in stories of faith and love in the face of danger.

FREE
Value Over
$20

YES! Please send me 2 FREE Love Inspired Suspense novels and my 2 FREE mystery gifts (gifts are worth about $10 retail). After receiving them, if I don't wish to receive any more books, I can return the shipping statement marked "cancel." If I don't cancel, I will receive 6 brand-new novels every month and be billed just $5.24 each for the regular-print edition or $5.99 each for the larger-print edition in the U.S., or $5.74 each for the regular-print edition or $6.24 each for the larger-print edition in Canada. That's a savings of at least 13% off the cover price. It's quite a bargain! Shipping and handling is just 50¢ per book in the U.S. and $1.25 per book in Canada.* I understand that accepting the 2 free books and gifts places me under no obligation to buy anything. I can always return a shipment and cancel at any time. The free books and gifts are mine to keep no matter what I decide.

Choose one: ☐ **Love Inspired Suspense Regular-Print** (153/353 IDN GNWN)   ☐ **Love Inspired Suspense Larger-Print** (107/307 IDN GNWN)

Name (please print)

Address   Apt. #

City   State/Province   Zip/Postal Code

Email: Please check this box ☐ if you would like to receive newsletters and promotional emails from Harlequin Enterprises ULC and its affiliates. You can unsubscribe anytime.

Mail to the Harlequin Reader Service:
IN U.S.A.: P.O. Box 1341, Buffalo, NY 14240-8531
IN CANADA: P.O. Box 603, Fort Erie, Ontario L2A 5X3

Want to try 2 free books from another series? Call 1-800-873-8635 or visit www.ReaderService.com.

*Terms and prices subject to change without notice. Prices do not include sales taxes, which will be charged (if applicable) based on your state or country of residence. Canadian residents will be charged applicable taxes. Offer not valid in Quebec. This offer is limited to one order per household. Books received may not be as shown. Not valid for current subscribers to Love Inspired Suspense books. All orders subject to approval. Credit or debit balances in a customer's account(s) may be offset by any other outstanding balance owed by or to the customer. Please allow 4 to 6 weeks for delivery. Offer available while quantities last.

Your Privacy—Your information is being collected by Harlequin Enterprises ULC, operating as Harlequin Reader Service. For a complete summary of the information we collect, how we use this information and to whom it is disclosed, please visit our privacy notice located at corporate.harlequin.com/privacy-notice. From time to time we may also exchange your personal information with reputable third parties. If you wish to opt out of this sharing of your personal information, please visit readerservice.com/consumerschoice or call 1-800-873-8635. **Notice to California Residents**—Under California law, you have specific rights to control and access your data. For more information on these rights and how to exercise them, visit corporate.harlequin.com/california-privacy.

LIS21R

Visit
ReaderService.com
Today!

As a valued member of the Harlequin Reader Service, you'll find these benefits and more at ReaderService.com:

- Try 2 free books from any series
- Access risk-free special offers
- View your account history & manage payments
- Browse the latest Bonus Bucks catalog

Don't miss out!

If you want to stay up-to-date on the latest at the Harlequin Reader Service and enjoy more content, make sure you've signed up for our monthly News & Notes email newsletter. Sign up online at ReaderService.com or by calling Customer Service at 1-800-873-8635.